Here Today, Gone to Maui

"Smart, funny, and as breezy as a Hawaiian night . . . I loved it!"
—Jill Smolinski, author of *The Next Thing on My List*

"The book strikes a right note in its quick, pop-culture references . . . [and] bitingly funny insights into a tourist's day in Maui." —*Honolulu Star-Bulletin*

"This fun, fast-paced story has a light romance and a titillating mystery. As the heroine makes some disappointing discoveries about her boyfriend, she also faces some realities about her own lifestyle. A nice coming-of-age story—even if the age is thirty-two." —*Romantic Times*

"Snow's novel is breezy, funny, and entertaining with authentic settings and details . . . This one stands out."
—Marylin Hudson, *Orange Coast Magazine*

"This is easily Carol Snow's best book to date—and that's saying a lot because her other books have been wonderful."
—*Curled Up with a Good Book*

Been There, Done That

"Snow's humorous, wise debut serves up romance with a bit of social commentary on the state of singledom and the benefits of maturity in a youth- and romance-obsessed society."
—*Publishers Weekly*

"[A] witty, entertaining read." —Kim Alexander, XM Satellite Radio

continued . . .

"Often hilarious, frequently poignant . . . This is a wonderful book, with well-developed characters and interesting plot twists that make it a joy to read." —*Romantic Times*

"*Been There, Done That* is a totally unique story with heartbreak, a look at what your college student is really doing, and how friendships and relationships change before our eyes. A book that will make you think, *Been There, Done That* will introduce you to a different sort of romance." —*Romance Reviews Today*

"Using humor as a delightful way to lampoon contemporary life, Carol Snow provides . . . a terrific investigative tale filled with pleasant but surprising twists." —*The Best Reviews*

"Carol Snow dares to explore some 'what ifs' of college life in a novel full of zany adventures, reflecting the wisdom of an adult revisiting the past and trying not to make the same mistakes. The author's subtle digs at ethics in journalism are right on target . . . *Been There, Done That* is insightful and fun, with a hint of mystery and romance." —*Fresh Fiction*

Getting Warmer

"With its entertaining combination of a realistically flawed heroine, sharp writing, and tart humor, *Getting Warmer* is absolutely delightful." —*Booklist*

"[Snow] cleverly combines wit and drama in a page-turning novel. Readers will be drawn to the primary characters with their effortless charm and unique ability to reinvent themselves when meeting new people. Snow's charismatic writing style is superb, making this a true winner." —*Romantic Times*

"Carol Snow does a wonderful job creating realistic, likable characters. Natalie is genuinely flawed, and readers can't help but like her for it . . . I'll be waiting on pins and needles for her next release." —*Curled Up with a Good Book*

Titles by Carol Snow

HERE TODAY, GONE TO MAUI

BEEN THERE, DONE THAT

GETTING WARMER

Teen Fiction

SNAP

SWITCH

Just Like Me, Only *Better*

CAROL SNOW

B

BERKLEY BOOKS, NEW YORK

THE BERKLEY PUBLISHING GROUP
Published by the Penguin Group
Penguin Group (USA) Inc.
375 Hudson Street, New York, New York 10014, USA
Penguin Group (Canada), 90 Eglinton Avenue East, Suite 700, Toronto, Ontario M4P 2Y3, Canada
(a division of Pearson Penguin Canada Inc.)
Penguin Books Ltd., 80 Strand, London WC2R 0RL, England
Penguin Group Ireland, 25 St. Stephen's Green, Dublin 2, Ireland (a division of Penguin Books Ltd.)
Penguin Group (Australia), 250 Camberwell Road, Camberwell, Victoria 3124, Australia
(a division of Pearson Australia Group Pty. Ltd.)
Penguin Books India Pvt. Ltd., 11 Community Centre, Panchsheel Park, New Delhi—110 017, India
Penguin Group (NZ), 67 Apollo Drive, Rosedale, North Shore, 0632, New Zealand
(a division of Pearson New Zealand Ltd.)
Penguin Books (South Africa) (Pty.) Ltd., 24 Sturdee Avenue, Rosebank, Johannesburg 2196,
South Africa

Penguin Books Ltd., Registered Offices: 80 Strand, London WC2R 0RL, England

This is a work of fiction. Names, characters, places, and incidents either are the product of the author's imagination or are used fictitiously and any resemblance to actual persons, living or dead, business establishments, events, or locales is entirely coincidental. The publisher does not have any control over and does not assume any responsibility for author or third-party websites or their content.

Copyright © 2010 by Carol Snow
Book design by Kristin del Rosario

PRINTING HISTORY
Berkley trade paperback edition / April 2010

Library of Congress Cataloging-in-Publication Data

Snow, Carol, date.
    Just like me, only better / Carol Snow.—Berkley trade paperback ed.
        p. cm.
    ISBN 978-0-425-23248-4
    1. Lookalikes—Fiction.   2. Identity (Psychology)—Fiction.   3. California—Fiction.   I. Title.
    PS3619.N66J87 2009
    813'.6—dc22   2009022373

PRINTED IN THE UNITED STATES OF AMERICA

10   9   8   7   6   5   4   3

For my brother and sisters,
Tom Snow, Kim Snow, and Susy Snow Sullivan

Just Like Me,
Only Better

Chapter One

I remember the exact moment when Haley Rush's fame reached its tipping point. I was in the produce department of Ralph's supermarket, desperately trying to concentrate on school lunches and the price of bananas, when all I could think about was my husband, Hank Czaplicki, who days earlier had announced—well, mentioned, really—that he had found his soul mate, and she wasn't me. An image of Hank kissing Darcy DaCosta, aka "North Orange County's #1 Realtor!*" flashed through my brain just as a skinny prepubescent girl with blue braces and a high ponytail appeared at my side and blurted, "Can I have your autograph?"

Speechless, I stared at her, tears making my vision the slightest bit blurry, and shook my head with confusion.

---

* In December 1996.

"*Kitty and the Katz* is my favorite show!" she squeaked.

I blinked furiously, as if trying to hit the reset button in my brain, when, suddenly, I understood. There was that girl—what was her name? That actress who everyone said looked like me. The one who could sing. She'd been in a sitcom as a teenager, and now she had her own show on one of those kids' cable networks. Bailey? Kayla? Something like that.

"I'm not who you think I am," I told the girl with the blue braces, my voice tight from the force of withheld tears.

Her shiny smile faded, just a little bit.

"I'm not her," I said, more forcefully this time.

The smile dropped, her cheeks flushed pink, and her eyes clouded with disappointment. "Sorry," she mumbled, slouching away to rejoin her mother by the bagged salads.

A few minutes later, I stood at the checkout line, clutching my cart for support, wondering what I had forgotten to buy. I'd gotten milk for Ben, bananas for Ben, Lunchables for Ben. If not for Ben, I would have crawled into bed and stayed there forever. My five-year-old son was the only thing standing between me and a complete breakdown.

When the woman at the checkout counter looked at me funny, I thought maybe tears had smudged my mascara. But no: I hadn't bothered with makeup since the day Hank walked out.

The checkout clerk pointed to the magazine display to my left. There was that actress on the cover of a glossy weekly—Haley Rush, that was her name. She was on a beach somewhere, wearing a ridiculously small white bikini, her skinny arms wrapped around the glimmering body of a sculpted young man. Above the picture, three-inch-tall block letters read, "Haley & Brady: HOT!"

Below that, Haley's self-satisfied face gazed at me from the cover of a fashion magazine. A third magazine cover showed her and the pretty boyfriend with the caption, "Haley Rush: All Grown Up and Head-Over-Heels in Love."

I looked back at the checkout woman and shrugged.

"That Brady Ellis is pretty cute," she said.

I nodded and tried, unsuccessfully, to smile.

"So . . . that's not you?" she asked.

I looked back at the magazine covers and sighed. "Only in my dreams."

Chapter Two

A year later, I was used to it: "You look just like Haley Rush."

I couldn't see it. We'd both started off with the same light brown hair, wide, pale eyes set a fraction too close together, and paint-splatter freckles, but in the past year, Haley Rush, "All Grown Up" and increasingly successful, had embraced Hollywood glamour: platinum-blond tresses, elaborate makeup, huge sunglasses, and shiny spike heels. I, on the other hand, had mastered the classic look of a depressed, divorced suburbanite: messy ponytail, baggy clothes, puffy eyes.

Not that Haley's life was perfect. According to the tabloids, she was having a terrible time choosing a gown to wear to the Grammy Awards!!! And the last time she went to Hawaii, she left buff boyfriend Brady Ellis at home!!! And when the barista at her local Coffee Bean & Tea Leaf spilled her caramel latte, she burst into tears!!! And on the way home from a nightclub recently, she ran her Escape Hybrid into a median divider!!!

Good thing she had a hit record, the highest-rated television show in the Betwixt Channel's history, and legions of adoring fans in the desirable eight-to-twelve-year-old age bracket. And, oh yeah—her net worth was estimated at fourteen million dollars. So I figured she'd be okay.

If only I could say the same thing for myself.

It was Sunday evening, and Ben was waiting for me in Darcy DaCosta's echoing, two-story foyer. Oh, sorry—in Darcy and *Hank's* foyer. California is a community property state, after all, and Darcy and Hank (if the tabloids paid any attention, they'd call them "Dank") had been married five months. Ben spent Wednesdays, Thursdays, and alternate weekends at their neo-Spanish gothic colonial mansion.

"I went swimming!" Ben crowed before I'd even walked through the tall front door (which had a caged little window that always made me think of a prison). Ben's blond hair was damp, his Ninja Turtles backpack stuffed and zipped and bouncing on his skinny frame.

He continued. "And I opened my eyes underwater and we had pizza for dinner and then I ate ice cream and I made a puddle of water on the kitchen floor but Darcy said it was okay and Darcy said that next time I come she's going to rent *Ironman* and we can watch it in the theater room and I can invite Carson!"

Just once when I picked up Ben, I'd like him to say, "I hate it here and I want to come home."

"*Ironman* is rated PG-thirteen," I said to Ben—but really to Darcy, who was standing right behind him wearing black yoga pants that looked nicer than the clothes I wore to my job as a substitute teacher.

"Oooooh! Sorry, buddy." Darcy tapped Ben's shoulder. "Guess we'll have to wait a few years for that one."

Ben gave me one of his possessed-by-the-devil looks and crossed his arms over his narrow chest. We hadn't even left Casa Darcy yet, and I was already the bad guy.

Darcy ran a hand over her short blond hair. "Didn't mean to make trouble." Maybe she meant it, maybe she didn't. It was hard to read Darcy's expressions because her Botoxed face hadn't moved since the last millennium.

Yes, Hank had left me for an older woman. Believe me, I feel bad for women whose husbands leave them for younger, fresher meat—well, I feel bad for women whose husbands leave them for *anyone*—but my situation was especially humiliating. I was about to turn twenty-nine, Hank was forty-two, and Darcy was *fifty-four.* If I couldn't keep a man in my prime, what hope was there for me later down the line?

"So Ben had dinner, then," I said.

"Pizza," Darcy said. "With carrot sticks. And one-percent milk."

"And he went . . . swimming?" Ben loved Darcy's rock pool: the cave, the waterfall, the slide, the Jacuzzi. But this was January. Southern California is warm—but not that warm.

"We told him to stay in the Jacuzzi, but . . ." She held her pointy shoulders up in defeat. "You know how kids are."

Darcy's two previous marriages had been childless.

A door shut somewhere in the bowels of the house. Sneakers squeaked on the travertine tiles, louder and louder until Hank, wearing basketball shorts and a T-shirt with the sleeves cut off, jogged into the foyer. "Hey, little man—give your dad a hug good-bye!" He dropped to his knees next to Ben and shot me a smile. "Hey, Roni."

I nodded hello and tried not to feel anything as Hank gave Ben a suffocating hug while Darcy looked on, misty-eyed. But I couldn't help it. I felt something: sadness mixed with jealousy mixed with longing.

I didn't miss Hank. Really, I didn't. I was glad to be rid of his chronic television watching, his too-loud voice, and his beer mug collection. But I missed being a family. I missed being a part of the Sunday night pizza routine.

Plus, there was something about seeing Ben with Hank. They had the same light, spiky hair (Hank's flecked with gray, I noticed for the first time), the same Slavic cheekbones and down-turned blue eyes. They shared a tendency to talk too much, to yell at the television, to laugh in their sleep.

Back at the minivan, I sighed with relief: another handoff completed amicably. I didn't worry that Darcy or Hank would be anything but sweet and gushy. They were the nicest adulterers I'd ever met. It's like they thought that if they smiled enough, maybe I'd forget that . . . Wait a minute! Didn't Hank used to be married to someone else? Like . . . me? Oh my gosh—that's right! And Darcy—wasn't she the woman who ruined my life?

No, I didn't worry about Darcy and Hank's behavior; I worried about my own. I was afraid I'd yell or cry or do something else to indicate that maybe I wasn't so happy with my newfound independence.

Ben was snapping himself into his car seat and I was opening the minivan's driver-side door when Hank came dashing out of the house. He'd lost weight in the past year, his beer belly finally beaten into submission by Darcy's personal trainer (a man, naturally; Darcy was no fool).

As Hank crossed the driveway pavers, I climbed into the driver's seat, shut the door, turned the ignition key, and put the window down. Whatever Hank had to say, he could make it fast.

"Next weekend," he said, smiling, at the window. Was he wearing cologne? With his gym clothes?

"It's my turn to have him," I said.

"Yeah, but I was wondering—could we switch? I take him next weekend and then you get him the two weekends after that? Because one of Darcy's clients gave her front-row seats to a Ducks game, and—"

"The Ducks! The Ducks! The Ducks!" Ben yelled from behind me, kicking my seat in time to his words. Sometimes I wondered if Hank and Darcy slipped Ben a double espresso before handing him off to me.

I cleared my throat. "Saturday is, um . . ."

He raised his eyebrows, eyes wide, smile quivering. Since the divorce, Hank always looked vaguely nervous around me, like he was afraid I'd cry. Or pull out a gun.

"My birthday," I finished.

His mouth dropped open. "Ohmigosh, of course! Saturday will be January . . ." He froze, trying to remember the date.

"Twenty-third," I supplied.

"I know." (Did he?) "I was just trying to figure out what today was. Never mind, then. Of course Ben should be with you."

"What about the Ducks?" Ben wailed.

"Some other time, buddy." Hank reached through the window to tap Ben's knee. "Your mom's birthday is more important."

"*I want to see the Ducks!*" He burst into tears.

Stupid Hank, stupid Darcy, stupid Ducks. And now I looked like the bad guy. Again.

"It's fine," I told Hank, my chest hurting. "Really. Ben and I can celebrate on Friday." I turned around to face my damp-faced son. "We'll go to Lomeli's for dinner—okay, Benji? And then to Baskin-Robbins for ice cream."

He nodded through his tears.

"You sure?" Hank asked.

"Sure," I forced myself to say.

"I'm sorry," he said.

I tried to smile.

Chapter Three

"What an asshole," my friend Nina said a week later, lounging on my bed with a glass of white wine as I wiggled into a form-fitting brown turtleneck dress.

"Hank feels bad."

"Don't defend him." She slid off the bed and tottered into the next room to refill her glass, taking small steps to keep from toppling over in her enormous silver heels.

"What do you think of this dress?" I asked from the doorway.

She squinted and shook her head. "Don't you have anything sluttier? You look like you're going to a PTA meeting."

Nina, who was actually the elementary school PTA treasurer, had gone all-out for my birthday dinner, in tight white jeans, a low-cut turquoise silk top, and many pounds of rhinestone jewelry. She was taking me to dinner in Los Angeles—at the Ivy, no less. Her husband, Mike, would stay home with their two kids,

Rachel and Carson. She'd invited Terri Sheffler, whose son Tyler was in the same class as Ben and Carson, to come with us. I didn't especially like Terri, but she didn't drink and had agreed to drive.

Back in the bedroom, I dug through the overstuffed closet that I shared with Ben. "Nope—nothing slutty. Maybe I'll just wear jeans."

I didn't even want to go to L.A. In fact, I had no desire to go out at all, as much as I appreciated Nina's efforts. All I wanted was to sit on my couch and wait for Ben to come home.

That morning, he'd bounded out of bed and into the living room. Ben was a noisy sleeper, so when he was with me I slept on the couch. Our quarters were tight—just two rooms and a kitchenette in a little guesthouse.

Ben grabbed my arm and shook me awake. I had a moment of happiness as I waited for him to say, "Happy Birthday, Mom!"

Instead, he'd asked, "What time am I going to Dad and Darcy's?"

Nina's voice brought me back to the present. "We should go shopping sometime," she said. "Did I show you the cute purse I got at Roadkill last week?" Roadkill was Nina's favorite store in town.

"I can't afford to go shopping."

Nina slipped off the bed and tottered over to the closet. "Where's that black sundress you wore to our barbecue last summer? Mike said it made you look hot."

Hank had never told me that any of my friends looked hot. I'd thought that meant I could trust him.

I dug out the black sundress, which looked like it belonged over a bathing suit. "I'll freeze," I said.

"You'll just have to drink more," Nina replied. "That'll keep you warm."

* * *

Two hours later, I realized that there wasn't enough alcohol in the world to get me through the evening. The fun started when Terri circled the Ivy for ten minutes, looking for parking, because she refused to pay the valet. Finally, after walking several extremely long blocks past half a dozen trendy boutiques with size 0 mannequins in the windows, we limped across the brick patio to the hostess stand.

"Inside or outside?" the pretty young woman queried.

"Whichever is better," Nina said.

"It's really a matter of personal preference."

Terri craned her head this way and that, trying to peer beyond the French doors. "Will we see any celebrities?"

"It's entirely possible."

We wound up sitting outside, near the hostess stand, because the night was warm (though not warm enough for a sundress) and we could see celebrities coming in and out—though as far as I could tell, the only people eating here were middle-aged tourists hoping to brush elbows with the glitterati. A weathered picket fence, dripping with roses, surrounded the patio. White cloths covered the tables, while red-and-white checked cushions softened the iron chairs.

As soon as we settled into our seats, Terri—who'd scored the spot closest to the propane heater—leaned her elbows on the table.

"So did you suspect anything?" she asked me. "Did you think Hank was fooling around?"

A potted African violet sat in the middle of the table, next to a flickering candle.

"No."

"Because if John ever fooled around—which he just wouldn't, he's not that kind of person—I'd definitely sense a change."

When the waiter showed up to take our drink order, I thought she'd let it drop. Instead, after requesting a Sprite, she picked up as if there had been no interruption.

"But John and I have been married for thirteen years, plus we went out for five years before that, so it's different. And plus, I just know he'd never look at another woman. Till death do us part and all that."

She plucked a piece of flatbread from the basket on the table, snapped off a piece, and chewed contentedly.

At least the service was good. Our waiter glided back with our drinks and smiled expectantly while we took our first sips. Like all of the staff, he wore a flowered tie with his button-down pink shirt. His pants were white. He wore his dark hair gelled behind his ears.

"Appetizers?" he purred, checking the other two faces before settling on mine.

"No, thanks. But I think we're ready to order dinner." I just wanted to get this over with and go home. Besides, this place was expensive, and I didn't want to waste Nina's money.

"I'll have another cosmo," Nina said, already halfway through the pink liquid in her martini glass.

"Of course." The waiter nodded at Nina and then returned his gaze to me. My ringless left hand lay on the table. I tucked it in my lap.

"The lobster ravioli appetizer," Terri said, frowning at her open menu. "Are they like regular ravioli, only with lobster?"

"Better," the waiter said.

"Fine. I'll have them. And the corn, whatever. Chowder. I haven't figured out what I want for my main course yet."

"No worries." He turned and gave me a Lifetime movie-of-the-week smile. "How do you like your martini?"

"Good." It was too strong. I'd really just wanted a glass of wine, but Nina had insisted I order something "fun."

"Another one?"

"No, thanks." I'd hardly had any of the first.

"Yes!" Nina slapped the table. "She wants one!"

"Fine," I said. It was easier than arguing.

The waiter beamed at me. "Would you like to try something different? Maybe something not on the menu? Do you want me to surprise you?"

"Sure," I said. "Surprise me."

Nina watched him walk away and then said, "He is *so* into you. I told you that dress was hot."

I rolled my eyes. "He's just looking for a good tip."

"C'mon, he's cute. Don't you think the waiter's cute, Terri?"

"A little flashy." She continued to frown at the menu. "I think I'll just get the steak."

Nina wasn't going to let it go. "I mean, he's no Ken Drucker . . ." She grinned.

I rolled my eyes. Everyone thought Ken Drucker and I were a perfect match because we had so much in common. We were both divorced. We both lived in Fullerton. We both—well, that was about it.

I had no interest in Ken Drucker. I had no interest in the waiter. When I married Hank at twenty-two, I thought my life was set. I didn't even know what interest felt like.

I slapped my menu shut and placed it on the table. "I'm just going to have a burger." I selected a piece of savory bread from the basket in the middle of the table, slathered it with butter, and was about to take a bite when—

"Caught ya!"

I froze and stared at the fit blond woman who had appeared at my side. She wore a simple white tank top, well-fitting blue jeans, and arty glass jewelry. When she saw my stunned expression, her smile grew even larger.

"Look how *white* that bread is. *Whole grains only!* You know that! As far as your body's concerned, eating a piece of this bread is like eating a great big scoop of sugar." Her voice was nasal, her accent vaguely Midwestern.

"I'm just—hungry."

"Hunger is okay!" She moved her hands as she spoke. Her glass rings shone in the candlelight. "You're listening to your body—that's good! But you wouldn't put cheap fuel in your car, would you? Same thing! You shouldn't put cheap fuel in your body."

"I put cheap fuel in my car all the time."

The blond woman laughed like that was the funniest thing anyone had ever said. I checked Nina's face. Was this some kind of prank? I wouldn't put it past her, but I would have expected something more along the lines of male strippers bearing Jell-O shots. But, no: Nina and Terri looked just as confused as I did.

"I love your hair." The blond woman reached out to touch a strand.

"Uh, thanks." Nina had convinced me to curl it and wear it down. She'd also pressed me to wear makeup and jewelry. It was all supposed to make me feel festive. Instead, it just weighed me down.

"The blond was nice for a change," the woman said. "But it was a little too Courtney Love, if you know what I'm saying. Besides, brown complements your complexion better. Have you ever considered auburn highlights?"

I shook my head in confusion—and then, finally, I got it. I would have figured things out much sooner if only the woman had been eleven years old and wearing a *Kitty and the Katz* T-shirt.

"I'm not Haley Rush."

She smiled as if I were joking and then her face froze and her eyes grew wide. "You're . . . not. Oh. My God. This is just—I've never . . . Wow."

"Do you actually know Haley Rush?" Nina asked.

"Yes! I'm her food coach—we're *extremely* close. Don't tell anyone, but Haley has a *major* weakness for Twinkies." She leaned closer to study my face. "This is just . . . astonishing. You could be twins." She held out her hand. "Sasha Reese." Her fingers were cold and bony.

"Veronica Czaplicki."

"Really?" She stared at me for a moment more. "Is it okay if I take your picture?" Without waiting for an answer, she pulled out her cell phone and aimed it at my face.

"Sure," I said, as she clicked.

"I can't wait to show this to Jay."

"Leno?" Terri asked, brightening.

Sasha gave Terri a once-over: the curled and sprayed hair, the conservative black-and-white dress, the double chin. "No."

Dinner was okay. The burger filled me up, and I got a kick out of all the diners sneaking glances my way. When he brought my second custom martini (which I disliked as much as the first, only for different reasons), the waiter actually said, "I love your work."

I said, "I love yours, too."

And he laughed and laughed and finally said, "This isn't my real work," because, you know, he's just waiting tables until he can break into "the business."

I said he just had to believe in himself, and can I have some ketchup to go with my burger?

As we ate, Terri asked if I thought that Hank had fooled around before Darcy. I shrugged and said, "Dunno," as if the thought had never crossed my mind. And then I took a really big bite of my burger so I wouldn't have to say anything more.

As Nina was finishing up her third cosmopolitan and Terri was sucking down the last bites of her fudge pecan brownie, a man dodged around the tables and stopped next to me. He wore a black T-shirt, torn blue jeans, black Vans sneakers, and an expensive-looking silver watch. His brown hair was straight and overgrown—just long enough to tuck behind his ears. His eyes were dark and sharp.

He stared at me for an uncomfortable moment. "Amazing."

Was he going to ask for an autograph? I squirmed in my seat. "I'm not Haley Rush."

He crossed his arms and continued to study me. "I know."

"Then why—"

"I'm Jay."

"I'm confused," I admitted.

He smiled, which made his eyes crinkle. "I'm Haley Rush's manager."

"Oh. Well." That explained things. Sort of. "Congratulations. I guess."

He tilted his head to one side. "Does it happen a lot—people mistaking you for Haley?"

"Sometimes."

"Constantly," Nina blurted.

Terri took a break from licking the chocolate off her fork to say, "You know, I don't really like that show, what's it called? *Kitty and the Pussies?*"

Nina howled, but I don't think Terri was trying to be funny. She continued, "It's just not believable that someone could go to medical school and tour with a rock band at the same time."

If her assessment bothered Jay, he didn't let it show.

"You even sound a little like her," he told me.

"I sing like her, too."

"Really?"

"No."

Jay's cell phone rang. Well, actually, it sang: some tinny pop sound. He held up an index finger to tell me to wait. (We hadn't gotten the bill yet; of course we'd wait.)

"See?" Nina told Terri. "You got to meet a celebrity."

"I don't think he counts," Terri said.

"What is it?" Jay said into the phone, sounding tense. He closed his eyes and shook his head. "Just tell her I'll get it on my way home." He crossed his spare arm over his chest. "Realistically? Twenty minutes. Thirty, tops."

The waiter appeared with the bill. "It was an honor to serve you," he told me. Seriously. He said that. And then he placed the bill between Terri and Nina, which I appreciated far more than all of his sucking up.

Nina opened the leatherette folder. Terri leaned over to look.

"Should we just divide by three?" Nina said.

"Well, you know, I didn't have any alcohol." Terri straightened in her chair. "So it's really fairer if we divide the food by three and then you and Veronica split the rest." I'd assumed Terri would split the cost of my meal with Nina, but, whatever. Nina could afford it.

Still on the phone, Jay hissed, *"Just tell her she has to wait."* He pushed the end-call button hard with his thumb and slipped the phone into his pocket. He smiled. "Sorry about that."

"No problem."

"So . . . Veronica, is it? That's what Sasha told me."

I nodded.

"Are you local, Veronica?"

"I live in Fullerton."

"Where?"

"Fullerton. It's in Orange County."

He wrinkled his nose, just a little.

"Just north of Anaheim," I added.

"Ahh." He wrinkled his nose a lot.

Terri held up the bill. "Okay, so I owe thirty-six dollars and you guys each owe sixty-one." Un-frickin-believable. She'd eaten more than Nina and I combined.

Nina reached for her Liz Claiborne purse. I felt bad that she was getting stuck spending so much for the two of us, but bringing Terri along had been her idea. She pulled some bills out of her wallet and dropped them in the middle of the table.

Wait a minute: three twenties and a one? That covered her, but what about me? Nina knew I couldn't afford a place like this. I caught her eye and waited for her to register the mistake. Instead, she grinned drunkenly and said, "We could go dancing. You want to go dancing?"

"I've gotta get home," Terri said, rubbing her belly. "The boys won't sleep until I've kissed them good night."

"I better use the potty, then," Nina pushed back her iron chair. It squealed against the worn bricks. "Come with me, Terri." She grinned at Jay and then at me, wiggling her eyebrows.

I scowled at her. Not interested. It's not that he wasn't cute enough; actually, with his dark hair, dark eyes, and trim build, he was just my type. (Hank hadn't been my type at all.) But if and when I ever started dating, I'd limit myself to guys with normal jobs and grown-up clothes.

Once Nina and Terri were out of sight, Jay slipped into Nina's chair. "Do you mind?" he asked (a little late).

"Of course not."

He nibbled on his thumb and studied my face. "Do you work, Veronica?"

"I'm a substitute teacher."

He nodded, considering. "So, your hours are . . . flexible."

I shrugged. "Sure."

His phone rang (sang) again. He angled away from me, but I caught every word. "I said I'd get it and I'll get it. Soon. She can wait. Twenty minutes. Well, I mean it this time. *Don't leave her alone!*"

"Problems?" I asked once he'd hung up.

"Oh, no." He chuckled. "Haley's got this addiction to Pinkberry—you know, the frozen yogurt? It's tart instead of sweet? Her assistant was just calling to see if I could pick some up for her."

"Her assistant works Saturday nights?"

"He's not working, really, he's just—hanging out. They're friends."

Our waiter came by, obviously thrilled to have an excuse to hover, and asked Jay if he wanted something to eat. Or to drink? Some bread? Water? Anything?

By the time Jay finished saying no, no, no, no, no, Terri and Nina were winding their way around tables.

Jay pulled a business card out of his pocket and pressed it into my hand. "I'd love to talk to you about a possible job opportunity," he said quietly. "Later. Away from all of these people. Just—don't tell your friends about it, okay?"

I didn't agree, just slipped the card into my pocketbook.

He popped out of the chair.

"Jay! Don't leave!" Nina said, approaching the table. "We'd love to have you join us for coffee. Or maybe a drink?"

"Thanks, but I've got to be somewhere. Nice to meet you all."

Nina's chair squealed as she pulled it back in. "They have three espresso makers but only one ladies room. That's just wrong."

Terri checked the pile of bills on the table. "Do you need any change, Veronica?"

"What? I don't think so." I unzipped my purse and pulled out the money, which was roughly what I made, after taxes, for a day of subbing. I put the bills in the middle of the table, looking at Nina one more time, to see if she'd offer to pay my half.

She didn't. Instead, she asked, "Did that guy ask for your phone number?"

I stood up, slung my pocketbook over my shoulder, and looked Nina straight in the eye. "Of course not."

Chapter Four

By Monday morning, life was back to normal. In a bad way. At eight-twenty, Ben was strapped into the minivan, his Ninja Turtles backpack on his lap. I was dressed and caffeinated, car keys jingling in my hand, standing in the doorway of what Ben and I called "The Big House." It wasn't that big, really, just a normal beige ranch house. But compared to our guest cottage, fifty feet away, it was a palace.

Both houses belonged to Deborah and Paul Mott. Their kids, Shaun and Shavonne, went to Las Palmas Elementary with Ben. I hadn't known Deborah very well before my divorce, but when she heard I was looking for a rental, she offered what I thought was a smokin' deal. For nine hundred dollars a month and "occasional" help driving her kids to school, we'd get two rooms, use of a spacious backyard, and an address that would allow Ben to remain enrolled at Las Palmas.

"I don't like to send the kids off without a good breakfast," Deborah Mott told me now, leaning against the refrigerator.

At the kitchen island, Shaun Mott, shoeless and rumpled, sat hunched over, eating Cocoa Puffs with loud, slow slurps.

"Right." I forced a smile. "It's just—I'm subbing today, fifth grade, so I'm supposed to get there early."

"Shavonne's in the bathroom, anyway." Deborah sipped coffee from her silver travel mug (which never left the house) and glanced down the hall. "So Shaun might as well finish eating."

I looked back at the driveway. Ben sat perfectly still in the minivan, eyes straight ahead. After all these months of "carpooling" with the Mott kids, he was used to being late, to going to the office for a tardy slip.

I swallowed hard and played the poor-divorced-mom card. "It looks bad if Ben gets marked tardy on his days with me. I don't like to give Hank's lawyers any ammunition."

Hank's lawyer (there was only one) didn't need or want ammunition. Hank and I had shared an overmortgaged tract house, a couple of credit cards, two cars. In the divorce, we split everything fifty-fifty only to discover that half of nothing is nothing. He gave me modest child support. Our son we shared willingly.

But Deborah took the bait. She craned her head forward, giving me an unwanted glimpse of her sun-spotted cleavage heaving above a gap in her bathrobe. "Is he making things difficult?" she asked breathlessly, fully prepared to repeat my every word to the other moms at Las Palmas Elementary.

"Not at the moment. But I have to be careful." I dropped my eyes to Deborah's Pergo floor. "So maybe you could drive Shaun and Shavonne? Just for today?"

"Oh! No!" She looked shocked. "What I mean is—look at me!"

Deborah was wearing what she wore every morning: a chunky yellow bathrobe, baggy Tweety bird pajama pants, worn blue velour slippers. Her overtreated red hair stood up at odd angles.

"You could use the drop-off lane," I said. "No one needs to know."

"*I'd* know," she said with the smugness of a person who possesses all the power in a relationship. Somewhere in the house, a toilet flushed. "There's Shavonne. See? You won't be late."

We were late. The tiny faculty lot was full, so I parked on a side street.

"You could've left us off at the school before you parked," eleven-year-old Shavonne snarled. Next year she'd be in junior high, which Deborah had already remarked was "not that far out of the way."

Ben's teacher didn't make him get a tardy slip (she'd had both Mott kids in her class and knew what I was up against), but when I went to pick up my teaching materials from the front office, Margery, the school secretary, said, "Just so you know, substitutes are required to check in at least fifteen minutes before the final bell."

"It won't happen again!" I chirped—a ridiculous statement, considering how often I was late.

Unlike so much in my life, teaching had been in the plans from the beginning. When I met Hank, I was a senior at Cal State Fullerton, just finishing up my degree. My days were spent student teaching in a second-grade classroom, my nights with Hank. It felt like the perfect life. But after graduation, instead of getting a teaching job, I got Ben. For a while, that felt like the perfect life, too. Now, all these years later, I was trying to find my way back to the classroom. Permanent positions didn't open up at Las Palmas Elementary very often; I hoped subbing would help me get a foot in the door.

When the fifth-graders went to recess, I hurried up to the teacher's lounge. Someone had brought pastries. I snagged a cheese Danish that was so sweet it made my tongue hurt.

"Good morning, Veronica. Whose class do you have today?" Gayle Fisk, the school principal, hesitated over the pastries for just a minute before plucking a bear claw. "I really shouldn't," she muttered before biting in.

"Mr. Jeffrey's," I said.

She nodded, chewing. "Lot of boys," she said after swallowing.

"They were ready for recess," I said. "All that energy. They're good kids, though."

She nodded and took another bite. My pastry was growing slippery in my hand.

"So Dr. Fisk . . ."

"Call me Gayle."

"Gayle. Any idea if . . . Any chance that . . . Do you know if there will be any positions opening up next year?"

She rubbed some sugar off her mouth and sighed. "I don't know, Veronica. It's not looking good. I'd love to offer you something permanent, but I don't think you should count on it."

I swallowed hard and nodded.

"There are plenty of other good schools in town," she said. "I'd be happy to provide a recommendation."

"I'll think about it. Thanks." I forced a smile.

Of course I'd thought about applying to other schools, but then I'd end up with a whole new set of problems. Who'd take Ben to school? Who'd watch him afterwards? If I got a job at Las

Palmas, we'd be on the same schedule. We'd have the same vacation days. It would be perfect. Unfortunately, perfection rarely worked out for me.

Nina caught up with me after school, as Ben and I were crossing the front lawn, Shaun and Shavonne trailing behind us.

"Veronica, Veronica, Veronica! Oh my GOD, you must hate me!" She was back in her normal clothes: pink T-shirt, denim jacket, khaki capris, sneakers.

"Hey," I said.

"Can Carson come over to play?" Ben asked Nina.

I said, "Not today, Ben. Shaun and Shavonne's cousins are coming over."

One afternoon shortly after we'd moved into the guest cottage, Ben and Carson were happily bounding around the bushes playing superheroes when Deborah Mott knocked on my door and said, "When we have guests over, we'd really appreciate it if you could give us privacy in the yard."

Carson, who was a head taller and thirty pounds heavier than Ben, came running up the lawn. "*Aaarrr*, matey!" It was a pirate day.

Ben held out his arm. "Stay back! Or I will zap you with my light saber!" Or maybe it was a *Star Wars* day. So maybe I'd let Ben watch a few too many DVDs. At least they inspired some imaginative play.

"She is evil," Nina said, referring to Deborah.

I widened my eyes to indicate that evil Deborah's evil children were standing right behind me.

"I can't believe I let you pay for your dinner Saturday," Nina said. "You must HATE me."

"Oh, no," I said, a bit too casually.

"I was just, you know. Really wasted."

I widened my eyes again: evil children alert!

She didn't catch it. "I felt like death yesterday. I can't even remember the last time I had a hangover." She reached into her purse and pulled out some bills. "Here. Happy birthday."

Shaun and Shavonne were right next to me now, staring at the money. I felt like a beggar. A charity case.

"Don't worry about it," I said, waving away the cash.

"Take it! It's yours! I was supposed to take you out to dinner." She tried to shove the bills into my purse.

I brushed her away. "*No*," I said. "It's fine. I'm fine."

She checked my face and then put the bills into her pocket. "So," she said. "That Jay guy really didn't take your number?"

"No."

"Too bad. He was cute."

He answered on the first ring. "What?"

"Is this . . . I'm trying to reach Jay Sharpie." According to his business card, that was his name. I'd resolved not to make any jokes about permanent markers.

"This is Jay." He sounded tense.

"This is Veronica Czaplicki. We met Saturday night. At the Ivy."

There was a long, static-filled pause, after which he burst out, "Veronica! Yes! I'm so glad you called!"

"You mentioned a job opportunity," I said.

He lowered his voice. "I'd like to tell you more about it, but not on the phone. Let's meet," he said. "Someplace where neither of us will run into anyone we know."

"I really need to know what this is about."

"I'm sorry!" His words came in a rush. "I don't mean to be so mysterious, it's just—there are privacy issues. Haley's privacy, I mean. I'll explain everything, just—not on the phone. Let me take you out to lunch. I'll meet you anywhere you like. Whatever's most convenient for you."

I was curious, I had to admit. Besides: what harm could come from meeting him in public?

"Okay," I said, finally. "Let's meet in Fullerton."

Jay made some kind of sound—a sigh or a groan. "I just . . . I don't do Orange County. How about Hermosa Beach? That's near you, isn't it?"

"No."

"I know this great little Cajun place there."

"I really need to know what kind of job we're talking about before I—"

"You win! I'll come to Orange County." You'd think he'd just agreed to pluck out an eyeball.

"Okay, then," I said. "And just so we're clear. When you ask me to lunch—does that mean you're paying?"

Chapter Five

It wasn't until I walked into the La Habra Red Robin that I realized my mistake. Jay wanted me to look like Haley Rush—and at the Ivy I had. Today, though, I was wearing one of my favorite work outfits: a knee-length khaki skirt, a navy short-sleeved sweater, ballet flats. My hair was back in its usual ponytail, my makeup limited to beige lipstick and a touch of mascara. I looked like a substitute teacher from Fullerton. There's no way I'd get this job—whatever it was.

When he saw me, Jay slid out of the booth and stood up. He clearly hadn't wasted any time getting dressed, in faded Levi's, a plain white T-shirt, and red Converse high-tops. I've known second-graders who dressed better.

"Veronica! Great to see you again. Thanks so much for taking the time to meet with me." He was looking at me a little too intently, probably second-guessing his plans, whatever they were.

"No problem." I put my Nine West purse on the bench opposite him and slid next to it. My purse was three years old, but it looked like it had only been around for two and a half.

"And thanks for choosing such a charming spot for lunch," he said. On the wall behind him, there was an enormous flag made out of red, white, and blue baseballs.

I said, "Yeah, it's comfortable—I like the booths—plus the parking's easy. I don't get out to eat much, so when I do, I like to go someplace I know will be good."

When I saw the way he raised his eyebrows, I realized his comment had been sarcastic. Oh.

He sat back down, put his elbow on the table, and leaned his chin on his hand. "You look different today."

I shrugged. "This is the real me. Sorry." Why was I apologizing? Did he even know that he needed a haircut?

A waitress in a red polo shirt came bounding over. "Welcome to Red Robin! I'm Allison!"

When I ordered my iced tea, she looked at me a little too long and finally said it: "Are you . . . ?"

"No," I said. "Sorry."

"You're used to this," Jay said once she left, his hand still supporting his chin. "People thinking you're Haley."

"Kind of." I opened my laminated menu and tried to remember whether I liked the fajitas here.

"Even though you're not dressed like her at all."

"I don't get asked as much since she changed her hair color."

"I always thought she looked better as a brunette," he said.

I shrugged. What was I supposed to say to that?

Maybe I'd have a burger. They were good here. Why else would they have a giant neon sign that read, "World's Greatest Gourmet Burger Maker"?

"Tell me about yourself, Veronica."

I put the menu down. "I'm a substitute teacher. I live in Fullerton. I look like Haley Rush."

"I knew all that already."

What in the world was this about? He already had the real Haley Rush—what use could he possibly have for me? If only my computer were working, I would have Googled Jay Sharpie. But it had frozen up three months earlier, and I couldn't afford the Geek Squad. When I was married, Hank was in charge of everything technical.

Our waitress came back with my iced tea, which she placed on a paper coaster. I ordered a chicken Caesar wrap. Jay asked whether the fish in the fish 'n' chips was fresh or frozen. The reply: "Neither. It's cooked."

Jay ordered a salad. ("Dressing on the side.")

"Are you married?" he asked.

This clearly wasn't a date, so why did he care? "Are you?"

"No."

"I'm divorced," I told him.

"For how long?"

"What is this about?"

Jay blinked rapidly. He reached into a bag on the floor, pulled out a piece of paper, and slid it across the table. "I need you to sign this."

It was a legal document. Words like *liability* and *confidentiality* leaped out at me.

I slid it back. "I don't sign anything unless my lawyers review it first." Of course, like Hank, I only had one lawyer, and she specialized in divorce.

Nonplussed, he moved the paper to one side, next to a bottle of ketchup and a plastic shaker of Red Robin seasoning. "How

long have you lived in . . . What was the name of your town
again?" he asked.

"Fullerton. It's the next town over from here, but this was
closer to the highway. Why do you want to know?"

He smiled, and his brown eyes crinkled in a way that made
him look much nicer than he probably was. "Would you rather
ask the questions?"

"Sure. How long have you been Haley Rush's manager?"

His eyes de-crinkled, and he muttered something that sounded
an awful lot like "too long" before saying, "Four years."

"So a manager . . . is that like an agent?"

He shook his head. "She has an agent, too—someone who
negotiates the business deals. I'm more involved with the day-to-
day aspects of her career: her public appearances and projects,
her licensing arrangements, her long-term artistic goals. . . ."

"Her frozen yogurt."

I expected him to smile. He didn't.

"How old are you?" he asked.

"You first."

A smile tugged at his mouth. "I'm thirty."

"You look thirty."

"Why do you sound so surprised?"

I shrugged. "I thought that in Hollywood if you looked thirty
you were actually fifty-five."

"I'm not fifty-five. And you didn't answer my question."

"Twenty-nine," I said.

"For real?"

"Yes. Though I may remain twenty-nine for the next few
years."

That was a joke (and not a terribly original one). In truth, I couldn't wait to hit thirty so I wouldn't have to listen to the other mothers saying, "I can't believe you're so *young*."

"Why did you want to meet here rather than in L.A.?" I asked.

He rolled his eyes. "In L.A. the paparazzi are everywhere. Except, it's not just the paparazzi anymore. Any guy with a camera phone can take a snapshot and sell it to the tabloids for one of those 'Stars Are Just Like Us' spreads."

"Are stars really just like the rest of us?" I asked.

He laughed and was about to say something but thought better of it.

"So what if someone took my picture in a restaurant?" I asked. "It's happened before. I just tell them that I'm not Haley Rush. It's no big deal."

He smiled. "But I don't want you telling people you're not Haley Rush."

"Why don't you just tell me what this is about?"

He shook his head and tapped his finger on the legal document.

"I won't do nude scenes," I blurted.

His eyes bugged out. "What?"

"Isn't that what you want me for? Because Haley's too big a star to take off her clothes?"

"I don't want you to be in her *movies*!" He didn't need to say it like that: as if it were so ridiculous to think that someone might pay me to take off my clothes.

He held up the paper. "All this says is that you won't tell anyone anything you learn about Haley Rush."

I took the sheet. "And what if I do?"

He folded his arms. "Then we sue you for everything you're worth. Seize all your assets. Which sounds bad, I know, but it's really standard for anyone who works with the stars—the nannies, the assistants, the hair and makeup people. It's to prevent them from selling their stories to the press. As long as you keep your nose clean, there's no danger to you whatsoever."

I brightened. "You got a pen?"

He blinked with surprise at my sudden willingness and pulled a black pen out of his pocket. I held back my Sharpie jokes.

When I handed him the signed document, he said, "That was easy."

I grinned. "I don't have any assets. So I've got nothing to lose."

He checked my signature, nodded, and put the paper in a file. Then he crossed his hands on the table in front of him, leaned forward and announced, "I want you to be Haley's double."

"But you just said—"

"Not in the movies. In real life."

"I don't follow." The movies sounded like more fun than real life.

"I will pay you to pretend to be Haley. In public. For very short, tiny, little bits of time. At least to start."

The more he said, the less this made sense. "But . . . why?"

The waitress came with the food. Jay said, "I asked for dressing on the side," and handed back the plate.

I let my Caesar wrap sit.

He cleared his throat. "Haley's fame has exploded in the last year. You can't walk past a newsstand or turn on the television without seeing her face."

"I've noticed."

"Haley wants to be available to her fans—she loves her fans, they're the ones who've made her who she is. And they want to know about her, which means she has to stay in the public eye. But at the same time—and here's the conflict—she needs the time and space to allow her creativity to flourish."

"So, she writes her own music?"

He blinked several times, in quick succession. "Haley is very involved in all aspects of her career." He licked his lips. "But the point is, Haley needs downtime. Who doesn't? Sometimes it would work better for her—better for everyone—if someone else smiled for the cameras and signed the autographs."

I tried to imagine myself smiling and signing. This was surreal.

He motioned to my food. "Don't wait for me."

I cut my Caesar wrap in half: now I was set for dinner. Did Haley bring home restaurant leftovers? Somehow, I doubted it.

I said, "Well, Haley's hardly the only starlet getting her picture in magazines."

"She's not a starlet. She's a star."

I nibbled on a fry and kept my expression neutral. The grease and salt calmed me, somehow.

"You'd just be giving people what they want," Jay said. "Casual shots of Haley looking wholesome and happy."

I reached for the ketchup. "Is Haley wholesome and happy?"

He hesitated for just a moment. "Fundamentally she is. But she's just . . . under a lot of stress."

"Where would I go on these outings?"

"For coffee, shopping, manicures—the usual stuff." It didn't sound like the usual stuff of my life, but aside from Ben, my life was pretty crappy.

"And you'd pay for all of these expenses," I clarified.

"Of course. Plus you'd be well compensated: a hundred dollars an hour."

I was so stunned that I barely even noticed the waitress delivering Jay's salad. A hundred dollars an hour to go shopping? I could get my computer fixed and buy Ben a bike. Maybe I could even save up enough money to move out of Deborah Mott's backyard.

"So, what do you say?" he asked.

I nodded, too overwhelmed to speak.

He pulled out his BlackBerry. "Let's set up a time for you to meet Haley. Tomorrow's Friday. How does two o'clock sound?"

I shook my head. "My son gets out of school at three."

He froze. "You didn't mention a son."

"You didn't ask."

"This complicates things."

"I have shared custody!" I said. (A hundred dollars an hour—!) "I'm free every other weekend, plus Wednesdays and Thursdays. And also, I'm available whenever he's in school."

"You cannot tell anybody about this job," he said. "Anybody."

"But what am I supposed to tell people?"

He poked at his salad. "Whatever you want. What is it you do, again?"

"I'm a substitute teacher."

He glared at his bowl of greens. "I think they just took off the top layer, with the most dressing, and stuck some fresh lettuce on it." He returned his attention to me. "So say you're a private tutor. To some Hollywood executive—nobody famous, just some guy with a lot of money. And his kid needs extra help, and you sent your resume into an agency in L.A. because you figured the money would be better than here."

"That's very creative," I said. (Nicer, I thought, than saying, "You're a really good liar.")

"It's a creative business," he said without irony. He put down his fork, salad still untouched, and punched the BlackBerry with his thumb. "A week from Monday work?"

"As long is it's early. Say, between ten and one. There's traffic . . ."

"Eleven o'clock." He pushed a few more buttons and then slid the gizmo into his pocket. "I'll have Haley's assistant call you with directions."

Chapter Six

I ran into Ken Drucker on Friday night as Ben and I were checking out a pile of videos and DVDs at Morningside Video.

"*Kitty and the Katz*, huh?" He stuck his hands into the pockets of his Columbia Polartec fleece and leaned over to get a better view of the cover. "My boys watch that sometimes."

"It's a girl show. Mommy picked it out," Ben said, lest he be mistaken for a pansy. "We got *Ninja Turtles*, too."

"Where are your boys?" I asked Ken to avoid talking about Haley's show.

"Just dropped them at Pamela's."

Pamela Drucker left her family the year before Hank walked out. Ken and their three boys, Brice, Powell, and Arches, had spent spring break camping in the Sierras. When they returned, Pamela was gone, claiming she needed some time alone. For Pamela, "alone" meant sharing a ten-thousand-square-foot house in Newport Beach with an "older gentleman" who owned a Hyundai dealership.

"Well, at least this gives you some time to relax," I told Ken. If the rumors were true (and they usually were), Pamela only saw her boys every couple of months for the first year; now Ken drove them to Newport Beach every other weekend.

Ken shrugged. "I figure I'll just, you know, watch a movie tonight, maybe listen to my John Denver CD's. Then tomorrow morning I'll head up to Mount San Jacinto, build a snow cave if the snow pack's heavy enough, and come back on Sunday."

"That sounds fun," I said with no conviction whatsoever.

"You like camping?" he asked.

"It's been a while," I said. "I like hiking." (That was just like walking, right?)

"Yeah?" His light eyes brightened. "Where do you like to go?"

"Um . . . in the woods?" I dropped my gaze to Ken's brown hiking boots, which he swapped for Teva sandals in the summer.

"Ha," he said without actually laughing. "Funny."

If possible, Ken was even less interested in me than I was in him.

Ben and I made a deal. He could watch *Teenage Mutant Ninja Turtles* until eight o'clock, at which point he would go to bed *with no argument whatsoever*, and I could begin my Haley Rush marathon. It wasn't the first time we'd made this kind of a bargain. I couldn't afford cable, and my television reception was so lousy that we rented or borrowed (thank you, Nina) DVDs and videos with exhausting regularity.

Unfortunately (or fortunately, depending on your perspective), both of the *Ninja Turtles* videos were defective, so we launched straight into our Haley Rush marathon. In addition to selected *Kitty and the Katz* episodes, I'd rented *Beverly Hills Bling*, a made-for-TV romantic comedy starring Haley and Brady Ellis. That one would have to wait until Ben was asleep.

I put the first *Kitty and the Katz* DVD into the machine and sat on the couch next to Ben, who snuggled against me like a puppy, his head warm underneath my chin. This was nice.

Some bubblegum music began to play, and Haley appeared on the screen in hip huggers and a halter top, a guitar slung over her shoulder.

"She looks like you, Mommy! Mommy, she looks like you!" Ben's head shot up, whacking against my chin. "Ow!"

"Sorry, Mommy—Mommy, are you okay?"

"I'm fine, Benji." My teeth hurt. "Let's just watch, okay?"

He snuggled back under my aching chin, holding his position even as he continued to yell at the screen: "That's so funny! Everyone says she looks like you, and she does! Do you think there's anyone on TV who looks like me? 'Cause it would be so funny if that kid were on a show with this lady! It would be just like you and me being on TV!"

"Yeah, funny. Benji, let's watch."

A young man joined Haley on the screen. He wore a white medical coat, a stethoscope dangling from his neck. His hair was sandy-colored and curly, his glasses thick and dark. This would be the Katz, who, according to the DVD liner, was played by an actor named Jason Price.

"Tomorrow can we go back to the video store?" Ben asked. "And get a different *Ninja Turtles* video?"

"Yes. *Shh.*"

Without meaning to, I thought: *Next week I'll be alone and I can watch in peace.* And then I thought: *No, wait—Hank had him for two weeks in a row, which means I get him for two weeks.* And then I felt really, really guilty for wishing I were alone.

I kissed Ben's blond head. "I love you, buddy."

By the time eight o'clock rolled around, I was an expert on *Kitty and the Katz*, the Betwixt Channel show that had catapulted Haley Rush to fame. Haley played Kitty Kilpatrick, a perky farm girl who moves to California to attend medical school. Her first week in Los Angeles, Kitty goes to a restaurant with some fellow students, all of whom order cheeseburgers and root beer, and, what do you know? It's karaoke night! Modest, down-to-earth Kitty wouldn't have even gone up on the stage to sing, but everyone else, with the exception of sober, eye-on-the-ball Jason Katz, takes a turn at the microphone, one performer more awful than the next, and Kitty doesn't want to seem like a poor sport.

Kitty can actually sing! (Apparently, her astonished fellow med students missed the show's opening credits.) She acts like it is nothing, only to confess later on to her new BFF, zany red-headed Liza (who is on a fast track to become a heart surgeon), that she once dreamed of a career in music, but . . .

> **KITTY (fingering empty root beer mug):** I had to choose. They say you can have it all. But you can't. I know that now. And becoming a doctor—it's just so much more important, you know? I mean, I can, like, really make a difference in people's lives.
>
> **LIZA (grabbing Kitty's wrist):** You're going to be an amazing doctor. Amazing. But that doesn't mean you have to give up music. You were

incredible up there! People couldn't take
their eyes off of you!

KITTY: It doesn't matter. I left my music behind
in Nebraska. I was in a band, but I gave it
up to come out here.

LIZA: So maybe you can find a new band!

KITTY: It's not that simple.

But, guess what? It is that simple! When Kitty and Liza
get up to leave the restaurant (not a bar—they are very clear
about that), a hardened punk girl in black leather (who in real
life would never be caught dead watching karaoke) saunters
over.

PUNK GIRL: Yo. Dorothy.

KITTY *(confused)*: My name's Kitty.

PUNK GIRL: You sure? Cuz you look like you just
blew in from Kansas on a tornado.

LIZA *(standing up and putting hands on hips)*:
That's funny. Because you look like you just
flew in on your broom with a flying monkey on
your shoulder. *[Cue laughter.]*

As luck would have it, the punk girl (whose name is Cassandra) is in a band (which isn't punk at all) and the band is looking
for a singer.

LIZA: Kitty. You have to do it. It's your dream.

KITTY: Becoming a doctor is my dream.

LIZA: Some people go their whole lives without a
single dream. You're lucky enough to have two.

But Kitty is torn, the reasons for her ambivalence expressed repeatedly by the cranky Jason Katz: "Med school is a full-time thing. Even sleeping is optional. If you can't make a total commitment, you shouldn't even be here."

Instead of telling Jason Katz to go to hell, Kitty turns her misty eyes down and forces a smile. In return, Jason taps her on the cheek and says, "Hey, I believe in you." The cheek tap is meant to convey sexual tension, but there's something about the Katz—his stiff dialogue? his smug expression? the refusal to shed the white coat, even at the restaurant?—that's just yucky.

Real sexual tension doesn't appear until season two, when leather-loving Cassandra introduces her boyfriend, Chase, to Kitty. Chase is played by the dark-haired, dark-eyed, sweet-yet-smoldering Brady Ellis.

"Yow!" I said, leaning toward the TV to get a better look.

"Mommy, I can't see."

I leaned back, my eyes still glued to the screen. "Smokin'," I murmured.

"Chase" wore soft blue jeans, a form-fitting black T-shirt, and black high-tops, a guitar slung over his shoulder. His smile revealed bright white teeth and boyish dimples. He had a shy gaze and a habit of sticking his hands in his pockets.

"Mommy, why are you breathing funny?"

(Oh, my God—I was actually panting.)

I hit the pause button. "Eight o'clock. Time for bed."

"I just want to watch to the end."

I stood up. "C'mon, buddy. We had a deal. Get your jammies on."

"I didn't get to watch *Ninja Turtles*. So I get to stay up later."

"Says who?"

He batted his pale eyelashes, put his hands together and flashed an angelic smile. "Pleeeeeease."

"Brush your teeth and get your jammies on. Then you can watch to the end. But you're going to bed the minute this is over, understand?"

Three episodes later (I am such a sucker), Ben finally went to sleep, and I slipped *Beverly Hills Bling* into the DVD player. It was a made-for-TV movie, broadcast on the Betwixt Channel, the same kids' network that produced *Kitty and the Katz.*

This time around, Haley, in the role of perky, fresh-faced Joanna Judd, has once again moved to L.A. from flyover country (Wisconsin, this time), but her ambitions have shifted. Forget medicine—Joanna Judd wants to be a star! Not because she's, like, narcissistic or anything—she's just trying to fulfill her mother's dream. Her dead mother. Who sang like an angel, her talent unappreciated out on the dairy farm. (In one flashback, we see Mama Judd singing to her cows.)

Once in L.A., Joanna needs to support herself, so she gets a job at Bling, a high-end Beverly Hills jewelry store, even though she sounds and looks like a total hick. The store owner, a fat, bald guy who's supposed to be funny but isn't, appreciates her "authenticity."

Enter Travis Trayworth (Brady Ellis) and his girlfriend, Chelsea Davenport (the actress who plays Cassandra, minus the leather and black eyeliner). Travis is a college student majoring in education. Chelsea is a viper, but Travis doesn't see that because he assumes everyone is as kind and genuine as he is. Travis's father is a benevolent Hollywood bazillionaire, which is why he can take Chelsea to Bling to pick out a diamond tennis bracelet for her birthday. (Which begs the question: what is a tennis bracelet, anyway?)

Ninety minutes later, Joanna has Travis's love *and* a recording contract. It doesn't really matter how she gets to that point (there was a very long society party sequence). I found the movie remarkably inane and predictable, and if not for Brady Ellis, I wouldn't have sat through it even once. Instead, I watched it three times, finally falling asleep on the couch sometime around two o'clock, dreaming of Hollywood.

Chapter Seven

H ello?"
"Yes, good afternoon. This is Rodrigo Gonzo, Miss Haley Rush's assistant. May I have the pleasure of speaking to Miss Veronica Zap, please?"

"This is Veronica Czaplicki."

Dead silence.

"Hello?" I said.

"Can you spell that last name, please?"

I did.

"Right. Mr. Jay Sharpie, who is Miss Haley Rush's manager, requested that I contact you regarding your meeting scheduled for this Monday with himself and Miss Rush."

"Yes," I said. "I need directions."

"May I ask where you will be coming from?"

"Fullerton."

Silence. And then: "May I ask where that is?"

"Orange County. Just north of Anaheim."

More silence. And then: "I will have to get back to you."

"Hello?"

"Yes, good afternoon Miss . . . Veronica. This is Rodrigo Gonzo again, calling regarding Monday's meeting with Miss Haley Rush and Mr. Jay Sharpie. Mr. Sharpie has asked that I arrange to meet you somewhere mutually convenient, after which I will take you to meet Miss Rush. Perhaps I could pick you up in Calabasas?"

"Calabasas is two hours away from me."

"Yes, but I need to pick you up away from L.A." He lowered his voice. "We can't let anyone see us."

"Why not just come to Orange County?"

Pause. "Mr. Sharpie mentioned your familiarity with Hermosa Beach. Perhaps that would be a mutually convenient destination?"

"Hermosa Beach is in the wrong direction."

"Pasadena?"

"It's in the other wrong direction. Look, why don't you just pick me up someplace off the highway? In Santa Fe Springs, there's a little Mexican place in a strip mall right before the I-5 on-ramp."

Pause. "I am not familiar with Santa Fe Springs."

"It's in L.A. County."

"Okay, then." He sounded nervous.

"Hello?"

"Yes, good morning, Veronica, this is Rodrigo Gonzo calling about your meeting today with Mr. Sharpie and Miss Rush."

"Right—I was just about to leave. Eleven o'clock at El Taco Loco, right? And you'll be driving a green Prius?"

"Yes. I mean no. Mr. Sharpie sends you his deepest apologies, but he is forced to reschedule due to a last-minute conflict."

"Oh."

"Tomorrow okay? Same time, same place?"

"I guess."

"Hello?"

"Yes, good morning, Miss Veronica."

"Is this about today's meeting?"

Sharp intake of breath. "Mr. Sharpie sends you his deepest apologies, but he was called out of town unexpectedly. He is sorry to inconvenience you and was hoping that we could try again on Friday."

"Try again?"

"Reschedule."

"Which is it?"

"Heh-heh. We appreciate your humor and your understanding. Eleven o'clock sound okay?"

"Good morning, Miss—"

"Rodrigo? Don't tell me you're canceling again."

"Mr. Sharpie is deeply, deeply sorry for the inconvenience, but—"

"I have a job. Another job. A real job. And this is three times that I've missed work for nothing."

"Mr. Sharpie and Miss Rush sincerely look forward to dialoguing with you at your earliest convenience."

"My earliest convenience is now. Today. You know what?
Just forget it."

What was I thinking? That I'd really get paid a hundred dollars an hour to go shopping and get my nails done? The first
rule of life: when something sounds too good to be true, it usually is.

"Hello?"

"Veronica? Jay Sharpie." So he did know how to dial his own
phone.

"Yes?"

"I'm sorry about canceling our meeting. Honestly. Sincerely
sorry. I had to fly to Rhode Island to discuss the next generation
of Haley dolls."

"Uh-huh."

"Let's try again."

"I've already missed three days of work, Jay. Trying isn't
good enough."

There was some crackling on the line. "We won't reschedule
again. You have my word."

I didn't say anything.

"Really—any time. Whatever works best for you. We'll be
there. I promise."

"Fine." I am such a wimp. "Monday morning. Ten a.m."

Pause. "Monday's out. How about Tuesday at noon?"

Chapter Eight

"Hello?"

"Yes, good morning, Veronica. This is Rodrigo Gonzo—"

"You're canceling our meeting." My voice was flat.

"What? No. Of course not!"

"Really?"

"I just wanted to confirm our meeting place. Eleven-fifteen at . . . El Taco Loco?"

"Yes! El Taco Loco—right. It's in a strip mall just off the freeway. They have really good carnitas, if you're hungry."

Dead silence. And then: "I don't generally eat lunch."

I parked outside El Taco Loco, locked my van, and went to stand in front of the smudged glass front door. The dirty air rumbled with freeway sounds.

My cell phone rang: Rodrigo. Damn it. I knew he'd cancel.
"Yes?"

"I'm here." He sounded tense.

"Where?" I scanned the lot until I saw a hand waving out of
the window of a green Prius. "Okay, I see you."

I shut my phone and crossed the cracked asphalt. I tugged
once on the handle before Rodrigo popped the lock. I slid into
the car and he locked it again.

Rodrigo Gonzo was exactly what I'd expected, only in miniature: dark hair cut short, gelled into perfect place; sunglasses
on the back (not top) of his head; buff, hairless arms; brown
eyes with thick black lashes. His blue jeans were faded, his beige
T-shirt tight. Even seated, I could see that he was at least an inch
or two shorter than me (I'm 5'4"). He weighed maybe a hundred
and ten pounds.

"You found it okay?" I said.

"You're really going to leave your car here?" he asked without answering my question.

"Sure. Why not?"

He raised his eyebrows.

I forced a laugh. "I don't think any car thieves are going to
bother with a five-year-old Dodge Caravan."

"Good point," he said with a little too much conviction.

The minivan had been Hank's doing. Ben was a year old, and
my car, a ten-year-old Camry from my parents, was giving out.
I'd been eyeing Volkswagen station wagons and Honda CR-Vs,
debating the merits of each. But when I came home from the
playground one Friday afternoon, there was an enormous red
minivan parked in front of the house.

"Who's here?" I asked Hank, who was sitting at the kitchen
table, watching TV.

"Just us."

"Then whose van is that?"

"It's yours."

I didn't ask him why he'd bought me a car without consulting me first. I didn't ask him why he hadn't traded in the Camry. The only thing I could think of was: "How'd it get here? Your car is in the driveway."

"A guy from the dealership drove the van. I thought you'd be excited. You said you never had a new car."

"I am excited."

All I could think was: why so big? Of course, now I needed the van to drive the Mott kids. Maybe Hank was just thinking ahead.

"Are we going to Haley's house?" I asked Rodrigo.

He shot me a side glance. "Didn't Jay tell you?"

"No."

"Yes."

"What?"

"Yes. We're going to Haley's house."

"Okay. And . . . where does Haley live?"

He shot me another look. His lips tightened. "I'm not authorized to tell you."

"Unless you're going to blindfold me, I'm going to figure it out," I joked.

He bit his lip, as if considering. Dear God—was he really considering a blindfold? And then I remembered Rodrigo's size: I could take this guy.

"Beverly Hills," he said finally.

"Oh. Of course." I thought about Ben and the Mott kids, who would be waiting for me after school. Beverly Hills was pretty far away. "I'll need to be back at my car by two-thirty."

"Two-thirty . . . today?"

"Um, yeah."

He pursed his lips. "That may be difficult to accommodate."

Most people associate Beverly Hills with money, stars, and glamour. Southern Californians associate it with traffic. To get there, Rodrigo drove on the I-5 freeway from horribly congested Orange County to ridiculously crowded Los Angeles. As always, the traffic stopped and started to its own inexplicable rhythms. Once we reached the city, we veered off onto the I-10 Freeway, Rodrigo's little green Prius engulfed in a canyon of loud, smelly trucks, along with a swarm of jacked-up pickup trucks, towering SUVs, and testosterone-powered sports cars. Next to us, a gray-haired man in mirrored sunglasses drove an Audi convertible with the top down, all the better to bask in the sunshine and carbon monoxide.

We picked up speed briefly before stopping dead. The dashboard clock read 12:03. I had three hours to get back to the elementary school.

When the silence became unbearable, I asked, "You from L.A.?"

"Tucson."

"What brought you out here?"

"The entertainment industry." He put on his blinker, and snuck into the next, faster lane. Traffic stopped immediately.

"Are you an actor?" I asked.

"Screenwriter."

"You wrote a screenplay? What's it about?"

His mouth tensed with indecision. I couldn't read his eyes because he had moved his sunglasses from the back of his head to his nose. Finally, he told me. "It tells the story of an artistic young man from Arizona struggling against the constraints of a conservative Mexican-American family. *My Beautiful Launderette* meets *Real Women Have Curves*."

"I haven't seen those movies," I admitted.

Even through his sunglasses I could detect disgust.

Finally, we lurched off the freeway onto surface streets, working our way past boutiques and restaurants and many, many stoplights before climbing a long, leafy hill.

Rodrigo broke the silence. "Beverly Hills is known for its many species of trees. Each street is lined with a different kind."

I said, "Really? Fullerton has that, too."

He had no response to that.

At the top of the hill, we turned on to Mulholland Drive, a windy, patchy road with a flimsy guardrail and sweeping views of the San Fernando Valley. We passed cypress trees, oleander hedges, and fortress-worthy fences. Finally, we reached a stone gatehouse shaded by ficus and magnolia trees. The gatekeeper recognized Rodrigo's car and waved us through. Immediately I saw . . . more gates. And big trees.

"How many houses are in here?" I asked Rodrigo.

"A lot." Helpful.

The gate in front of Haley's house was probably ten feet tall, dark wood supported with darker metal. Rodrigo squeezed a remote control, and the gates swung open, revealing . . .

A house. It was a big house, sure, about the same size as Darcy's (oops—*Darcy and Hank's*), but it was kind of generic: beige stucco, stack stone, clay tile roof. It was like a larger, more upscale version of the tract house Hank and I once shared.

Rodrigo parked his little car between a Mini Cooper and one of two black Cadillac Escalades. Two extremely large men in black pants and black sport shirts leaned against the more distant SUV. They wore sunglasses and clutched small walkie-talkies. Or maybe the walkie-talkies weren't small; maybe they just looked that way because the security guys' hands were so big.

I followed Rodrigo to the tall front door, which was made of some glossy, caramel-colored wood. He pushed a button next to an intercom.

"Jes?" came a tinny voice.

"It's me, Esperanza."

Static, and then: "Who?"

"Rodrigo." His mouth tightened and his lips grew white. "She knew it was me," he muttered.

There was more static and then a *click*. Rodrigo pushed open the door, and we stepped inside to . . . Frontier Land. Seriously. It looked like a lodge in Montana or Colorado—or maybe in Anaheim. There were enormous log pillars and shed antler chandeliers. Indian blankets draped the leather furniture. An enormous grizzly bear stood next to a towering stone fireplace, arms raised and teeth bared—a moment of ferocity frozen forever. Horse paintings—lots of them—decorated the knotty pine walls.

"Veronica! Welcome!" Jay, standing in front of the fireplace, wore his usual too-sloppy-for-preschool attire.

A messy blond woman, not Haley, sat on the couch.

Jay said, "Veronica Cza . . . Cza . . . Veronica, I'd like you to meet Simone LaPlante. Haley's stylist."

Simone remained seated (or *planted*—har, har) on the biggest of the leather couches. By way of greeting, she tilted up her pointy chin and raised a hand, countless gold bangles weighing down her skinny wrist, chunky rings crowding her surprisingly stubby fingers. She wore a loose gray sweater, black leggings, and slouchy suede boots.

She brushed her wild blond hair out of wide, tired-looking eyes rimmed with smudgy gray eyeliner and looked me up and down. "Size six," she declared in a monotone.

It took me a moment to realize that she was talking about me. I straightened in my brown turtleneck dress, feeling svelte and possibly even stylish—though I wished I had worn a little more jewelry.

"Yes," I said. "That's right."

Her mouth turned down. Judging by the lines on her face, her mouth turned down a lot. "Haley's a two."

"Haley's really excited about meeting you," Jay told me.

I glanced around the vast, high-ceilinged room. "Is she here?"

"She'll be down any minute," Jay said.

"I need to be back at my car by two-thirty," I said. That was two hours from now—traffic had made us late.

"Would you like something to drink? Mineral water? Pomegranate iced tea?" He turned his head and called, "Esperanza!"

"Water would be great. Thanks."

The blond woman continued to study me. I looked at her straight-on, expecting her to smile with embarrassment. She didn't.

"Esperanza!" Jay called again, louder than before. When she still didn't appear, he lowered his voice. "Rodrigo, get Veronica some water." He turned to me. "You want fizzy or flat?"

"I don't really need anything," I said.

"Bring both," he told Rodrigo, who slumped out of the room.

"She'll do," Simone announced, rising from the couch and slinging an enormous suede patchwork handbag over her shoulder. She was shorter than I would have guessed, not much bigger than a skinny eleven-year-old.

She continued, "Bone structure, features, coloring—all a good match." She looked me up and down. "But it would be better if she lost a little weight."

"I wouldn't worry about the weight thing," Jay assured me once Simone left. "Haley's actually packed on a few pounds in the last couple of months."

Rodrigo returned with two bottles of water. A stout, middle-aged Latino woman followed him bearing a wood tray. She wore bright white Reeboks, black stretch pants, and a tight, black Ralph Lauren T-shirt, the signature "RLL" emblazoned in rhinestones across her ample bosom. A knockoff Chanel clip—at least, I assumed it was a knockoff—held her burgundy hair off her face and out of Haley's food.

"Hello, Esperanza," Jay said. "You can just put the tray on the table, and we'll keep Miss Haley company while she has her . . . Is that a meal-delivery meal?"

"Is pancakes," Esperanza hissed, ignoring his instructions and heading for the staircase.

"Because Miss Sasha was supposed to talk to you about that," Jay told Esperanza's retreating back. "Miss Sasha says Miss Haley should stick to meal-delivery meals from now on."

Esperanza disappeared up the stairs without turning around.

"Haley hasn't had breakfast?" I asked Jay. It was now a quarter to one.

"It's her favorite meal," he said. "Sometimes she eats it three times a day." He cleared his throat. "Will you excuse me?" He headed up the stairs.

Rodrigo was still holding the bottles. "Here."

"Oh," I said. "Thanks." I took the plain water because fizzy stuff makes me burp. When I went to twist off the top, I realized that my hands were shaking. The silence felt unbearable.

"Have you written any more screenplays besides the one you mentioned?" I asked Rodrigo.

"I'm working on another one."

"What's it about?"

He wrenched open the mineral water. Some foam erupted out the top. He took a long drink before he finally spoke. "It's about an artistic man who moves to California from a small Arizona town only to have his dreams dashed by the corporate Hollywood machine."

I did my best to come up with a witty response. "Kind of like *A Chorus Line* meets *Erin Brockovich*?"

He wiped some fizz from the side of his mouth and narrowed his eyes. "No."

"Put it on the table, please, Esperanza." Jay's voice echoed through the high-ceilinged room. Esperanza came down the stairs first, still holding the tray. Muttering in Spanish, she placed it on an enormous wooden farm table and then stood there, hands on hips, waiting.

"You can go, Esperanza," Jay said.

Her nostrils flared. She didn't move.

The first thing I saw of Haley was her hair. It was blond, it was big, and it was sticking out in some really weird directions. She wore a purple tank top and dark plaid flannel pajama pants. Her slippers were pink and fuzzy.

"Wanna sleep," she whined.

"I make pancakes, Miss Haley!" Esperanza trilled. "Chocolate chip—*es muy delicioso!* You want whipped cream *tambien*?"

Haley shook her head.

"You want I make bacon?" Esperanza asked.

Haley nodded, and Esperanza hurried out of the room.

Jay muttered something about "meal-delivery meals" and

then put on his happy voice. "Haley, you big sleepyhead! This is Veronica, the woman I've been telling you about. Don't you think she looks like you?"

Haley didn't answer, just folded herself into a log chair upholstered in Buffalo plaid. She leaned over her plate, elbows unapologetically planted on the farmhouse table, her pale, messy hair skimming her coffee cup.

"She's not a morning person," Jay told me. (It wasn't morning.)

"What are meal-delivery meals?" I asked, just to say something.

Jay cleared his throat. "Meal-delivery meals are healthful and tasty food options delivered daily to meet optimal dietary requirements."

"They're *shit*," Haley said, finally looking my way. Kitty Kilpatrick would never say such a bad word. "Yesterday they sent me *fish*. For *breakfast*."

"Fish is commonly served for breakfast in many Asian cultures," Jay said evenly.

"I'm from Montana." Haley shoveled a forkful of pancakes into her mouth.

Okay, now I understood why Jay made me sign a legal document before I set foot in this house.

"Why don't we sit," Jay suggested, directing me to the table. "Are you hungry, Veronica? Esperanza would be happy to make you something." Sure she would.

"Thanks, I'm fine." I couldn't tell whether the sensation in my gut was anxiety or hunger.

Jay pulled out the chair at the head of the table for me, an oddly formal gesture for a guy wearing ripped jeans and red high-tops. At this level, I could see Haley's face better. On TV, she looked like a prettier version of me. In person, not so much.

A line of pimples ran along her jawline, mixing with her freckles. Last night's eyeliner formed a murky half-moon under her eyes. Her blond hair was greasy and dark at the roots. She looked neither fresh-faced nor perky.

"Wow," Jay said, looking from Haley to me and back again. "It's like seeing double."

I raised my eyebrows.

"Except for the hair color," he clarified. "So, Haley. Like I was telling you yesterday, I've talked to Veronica about doing a little work for us."

Esperanza appeared with a platter full of steaming bacon.

Haley granted her an enormous smile. "Esperanza, I love you! Can you bring me the phone?"

"*Si, senorita.*"

"We could hire Veronica on a trial basis," Jay told Haley. "Send her out a couple of times, see how it goes. How does that sound to you, Veronica?"

I nodded. "It sounds good."

Esperanza came back with the phone. Haley put down her fork and pushed in some numbers. "Josh! I can't get my TV to work! . . . The one in the bedroom—I don't know, maybe the others, too, but that's the one I wanted to watch . . . I tried that . . . Uh-huh. . . . No, Josh! Sooner! Please?" A smile flickered around her mouth, and her voice turned flirtatious. "You are the best, Joshie."

She pushed the off button and laid the phone back on the table.

Jay cleared his throat. "So what do you think, Haley?"

"About what?" She stuck another piece of bacon in her mouth and chewed with her mouth slightly open.

"About Veronica. Posing as you. So you can get a little . . . space. To gain some creative freedom."

She rolled her eyes. "Sure. Fine. Whatever."

I was twenty-five minutes late to Las Palmas Elementary. Ben was standing on the front lawn next to a pissed-off-looking Shavonne, whose bright yellow T-shirt clashed horribly with her red hair. She held her silver cell phone pressed to her ear. At the sight of me, she said, "Never mind—she's here. *Finally.*"

She snapped the phone shut. "I was talking to my mom."

She was trying to intimidate me. And she did, kind of.

"I called her," I said. "To let her know I was stuck in traffic."

Actually, I'd called to see if Deborah could pick up the children, to which she'd responded, "My understanding was that you would drive both ways today."

I kissed Ben on the top of his blond head. "Sorry I'm late, buddy."

For months after the divorce, Ben used to cry if no one was waiting outside his classroom when he got out of school. "I thought you forgot about me," he'd say—and my already-broken heart would splinter just a little more.

He'd moved beyond that fear, but he still looked shaken on the rare occasions that I was late. Right now, he glared at me.

"What?"

"I told you not to kiss me in public." That wasn't what made him mad, and we both knew it.

I tried to smile. "Where's Shaun?"

"Playground."

Mrs. Herbert, a scary third-grade teacher in a bright orange vest, got to me before I could coax Shaun down the slide. "Mrs. Czaplicki, are you responsible for Shaun?"

Some dark force was responsible for Shaun, but that wasn't what she meant. "I'm driving him," I said.

"At the beginning of the school year, all parents were required to sign a school site supervision form." Mrs. Herbert's voice was hoarse, as if she were recovering from a cold—or from a day spent yelling at her students.

"Right," I said.

She crossed her arms under her large bosom. "And that form made it very clear that the school cannot be held responsible for supervising children after three-fifteen. It is now three-thirty."

"I was stuck in traffic. I got here at three-twenty-five," I said, drowning in my inadequacies. "But I couldn't find Shaun."

"And children aren't allowed on the playground after school hours *at all* unless they are being supervised by a parent or other responsible adult."

"I know," I said. "He knows." Out of the corner of my eye, I could see Shaun sticking his tongue out at Ben.

"Parents think teachers have all the time in the world," Mrs. Herbert droned on. "That we have nothing better to do than hang out after school, but the fact is that we have our own families to go home to, plus a pile of papers to grade."

"I know," I said. "I work here, too."

"You do?"

Chapter Nine

"She loved you. *Loved* you!"

"Who is this?"

"What—? Oh, sorry, just assumed you had Caller I.D. It's Jay—Jay Sharpie. Just wanted to follow up on today's meeting and tell you how *excited* Haley is about working with you She said she felt this instant connection."

"Really? 'Cause she didn't seem all that, um . . ."

"I know. *I know!* She can come off as distant when she first meets someone. And here you are, expecting to meet Kitty Kilpatrick, and well . . . It's just been hard for her, all these people feeling like they know her. When, really, she's a very private, even shy, individual."

"What I meant was, she seemed tired."

"Oh . . . that. Right. Haley's a real burn-the-midnight-oil person. She can't help it—she's wired that way. Says that's when she does her best work. You'd be amazed at how much truly great stuff gets created at two, three o'clock in the morning. Anyway, the reason I'm calling—aside from to tell you how much Haley loved you—is to check your schedule for the rest of the week."

"I'm subbing tomorrow," I told him. One of the sixth-grade teachers had a root canal scheduled. "But Thursday's wide open."

And just like that, I was back to my real life.

"Her name is Melissa," I told Mrs. Ortega, the P.E. teacher. "She's ten." My hands shook as I poured weak coffee into a paper cup. The first bell would ring in five minutes. For once, I wished the Mott children had made me late.

"You'd think she'd get a tutor closer to home. Where'd you say she lives? Brentwood?"

"Beverly Hills. She has other tutors, too. You know, Spanish . . ." The synapses in my brain fired wildly. I really should have thought out the details more thoroughly. "Calculus."

"They've got their fifth-grader taking calculus?" another teacher called from across the room.

Ugh—how could I be so stupid?

I ripped open a packet of nondairy creamer. "Yeah, but she's struggling. They're thinking of dropping it and going back to, you know. Long division."

I hadn't planned on saying anything at all, but when I arrived at the teachers' lounge, someone said, "Hey, Veronica, where've you been?" and someone else said, "Is it true you got another job?"

So I said what Jay had told me to say—that I'd gotten a job tutoring the child of a wealthy Hollywood executive. I hadn't counted on all the questions: What's the house like? Is the kid completely spoiled? Will you get to go to any movie premieres?

"Why does she need a tutor in the middle of the day?" Mrs. Ortega pressed. "Doesn't she go to school?"

"She's homeschooled," I said. "Her father travels a lot, but he doesn't like to be apart from his family. So they go with him."

"I can't *believe* they're teaching calculus to a ten-year-old," Mrs. Ortega said. "That's just sick."

When I arrived at the El Taco Loco parking lot late Thursday morning, Rodrigo was waiting in his green Prius, the engine quietly running. I tried the door handle: locked. He popped the lock, but as soon as I'd shut myself in, he clicked it again.

"The neighborhood's not that bad," I said.

He raised his eyebrows and handed me a trucker hat and a pair of aviator sunglasses.

"Are these supposed to make me look like Haley?" I piled my hair into the cap, feeling weirdly elated by the game.

"Of course not. Haley wouldn't be caught dead wearing something like that. Simone wouldn't let her."

I felt slightly less elated.

Traffic was less hideous than it had been on Tuesday. Not that it mattered: Hank had Ben until tomorrow afternoon. I could stay as long as they needed me.

Finally, we crept through Hollywood Hills and climbed the winding streets to Haley's gated neighborhood. As we approached the stucco house, Rodrigo said, "Shit," under his breath. He turned to me. "Use your cell phone! Cell phone! Cell phone! Keep the phone on the window side! Chin down!"

"What? Who am I supposed to call?" Rodrigo and I had barely spoken since meeting up at Santa Fe Springs.

"Just do it!" His voice cracked. He plucked his own sleek phone from the console and thrust it at me.

I understood just in time. Rodrigo didn't want me to talk on the phone; he wanted me to use it to shield my face against the two photographers who lurked in the bushes outside Haley's gate. They pointed their enormous lenses at us and aimed for an instant before dropping them in disappointment.

In the driveway at last, Rodrigo, breathing heavily, brought the car to an abrupt halt. The matching black Cadillac Escalades were there, the burly—and evidently useless—security guys tossing a football near the side of the house.

I burst out laughing. "I thought you were going to drive right into the gate!"

"Good job keeping your head down," he wheezed.

"That was kind of fun," I said, still smiling. "How'd they get past the gatehouse, anyway?"

He shook his head. "I don't know. They just do. They climb over fences, or they lie. They bribe other people's housekeepers to say they're here for maintenance. This loss of privacy—it's the price you pay for fame."

I thought of my little house on the Mott's property. You didn't have to be rich and famous to sacrifice privacy. At least Haley didn't have to ask permission to sit in her backyard.

She did, however, require special assistance to turn on her music.

When we entered the living room, she was out of bed, at least, and sort of dressed, in a pink velour track suit. She was standing right next to one wall in the cavernous room, staring at a white digital control panel, a trim silver phone decorated with pink rhinestones pressed to her ear.

"It says bedroom on the top bar," she said. "But I'm not in the bedroom—I'm in the living room!"

She sighed into the phone and pushed the screen. "It's still not working, Josh!" she whined. And then: "I already hit the location button! Oh—wait. Maybe I hit the source button."

She jabbed at the touch pad some more. "It's still! Not! Working!"

My rubber-soled shoes squeaked on the wood floor. Haley turned. "Oh, wait. Rodrigo's here. He can do it."

She turned off her phone and flung it on the nearest chair. And then, lest she miss an important call or the opportunity to boss someone around, she scooped it back up and held it near her heart. "Rodrigo! All's I'm trying to do is listen to my fucking iPod, and I can't get this fucking sound system to work!" She sounded like she was going to cry.

I kept my face as neutral as possible—not that it mattered. Haley didn't even glance at me.

"It's *o-kaaaay*," he said in a soothing voice I'd never heard before. "I'll take *caaaare* of it."

Haley exhaled. "Why does everything have to be so fucking hard?" I feigned interest in a horse painting.

Grimacing with concentration, Rodrigo poked at the pad for a bit before scurrying off to another room. Almost immediately, music blared from speakers in the ceiling: bouncy bubblegum rock sung by a nasal-voiced girl.

Rodrigo strolled back in, grinning with satisfaction. "The iPod was out of the console. I found it on the floor."

Haley nodded, comprehension spreading across her familiar

features. "*Riiight*. I pulled it out because I was thinking I might go out for coffee, but . . ." She left the sentence unfinished.

She looked up at the speakers. "Can you pick something else? I'm sick of listening to myself sing."

Rodrigo went back to the touch pad and pecked at the screen until Haley's song was halted in mid- "Baby, Baby," replaced by some beat-heavy R&B.

"Where's Jay?" I asked.

Haley blinked, as if noticing me for the first time. "Are you my new food coach?"

I shook my head. "Your food coach is Sasha. I'm Veronica. Your, uh—double."

"Oh. Right. I thought you looked familiar," she said without irony. "Sasha's not my food coach anymore. I had Jay fire her."

She wandered toward the kitchen. "Jay called to say he'd be here at, like, one. So I guess you can just, like, hang or whatever."

"Okay," I said. A pile of magazines sat on an immense coffee table fashioned from snowshoes and weathered wood. I hoped to find a *People* or even an *Us Weekly* but finally settled for *Vogue*. On one of Haley's soft (*really* soft) leather couches, I flipped through the perfumed pages, which instantly confirmed my suspicions that my clothes were hopelessly out of style.

I checked my watch, annoyed by the delay, when I remembered: I was getting paid a hundred dollars an hour for this! Jay could be as late as he wanted.

When he finally came barreling in (at one-thirty), he was all apologies: Traffic! Phone calls! Putting out fires! So sorry, so sorry, so sorry, I recognize that your time is incredibly valuable, blah, blah, blah.

"No worries," I said pleasantly. (A hundred dollars an hour!)

"Have you eaten?" he asked, clapping his hands together.

"No."

"Good! Because we're going to dress you up as Haley and send you out for coffee."

My stomach fluttered. I didn't realize I'd be making my debut today. Plus, I was pretty hungry.

"Great," I said. "But how about sending me out for a sandwich?"

Jay shook his head. "Haley never eats solids in public. Though maybe she should . . ." He considered, and finally shook his head again. "Some other time. First, we have to get you dressed."

I glanced at my clothes: jeans, a long-sleeved black T-shirt, sneakers. "I wasn't sure what to wear."

"You can wear whatever you want driving over here," he said. "But when you're being Haley, you've got to wear Haley's clothes."

What had Haley worn in all of those tabloid shots I'd seen of her? I vaguely remembered some cowboy boots.

Cowboy boots were the least of it. Once I'd gotten over my astonishment at the size of Haley's closet, which was at least as big as my entire living quarters and had a door at either end, I started focusing on the individual pieces. If I hadn't known better, I would have thought I was looking at the wardrobe of a rodeo queen, not a pop star. There were cowboy hats, cowboy boots, fringed jackets, checked shirts, and white leather skirts. There were spurs and studs and spangles.

"Haley's from Montana," Jay said.

"I can see that."

"Though she's actually been in L.A. since she was nine—her mother brought her here after she won a local talent contest. Anyway. Simone should be here any minute. She was supposed to be here an hour ago. I'll call her."

He left me alone in the closet. I felt uncomfortable, like I was invading someone's personal space. Which I was.

The door on the far side of the closet swung open and Haley stepped inside.

"Sorry!" I said. "Jay just told me to . . . I'll go."

"You don't have to," she said. At first, I took that to mean that we'd get a little bonding time. But as Haley started to rifle through the racks, I realized that she was just really, really good at ignoring people. Finally, she plucked out a velour track suit— identical to the one she was wearing, only baby blue instead of pink—and retreated to her bedroom. I glimpsed an enormous log bed. What a surprise.

Once I got over the sequin shock, I started noticing Haley's other clothes: a rack of filmy sundresses, a row of exquisitely cut gowns. There was an entire wall of jeans and more pairs of shoes than I could count.

I heard Simone's spike-heeled boots clicking on the wood floors before she entered the closet. She looked at the clothes before she looked at me. Her nostrils flared. "I'd set fire to all of the Western duds, but there's so much artificial material, I'm not even sure they would burn."

I smiled. She looked at me but didn't smile back.

"Size six," she said in her flat voice. She was wearing a different gray sweater today. The sleeves looked like wings.

I cleared my throat. "Sometimes I can fit into a four."

"Vanity sizing," she announced. "You're a six."

She clicked over to a rack, still tiny even in her enormous heels. She muttered something about "Vegas cowboy crap" before pulling out a denim miniskirt with a frayed hem. She peered at the tag and thrust it at me. "You'll have to suck in your gut." She crossed the closet to the shirt wall and came back with a black tank top and a lose-knit tan sweater.

"Thanks." I waited for her to leave. She didn't.

I cleared my throat. "Is there a, um, restroom I can use?"

Simone shot her enormous eyes to the ceiling. She pointed toward the door with her beige fingernail, a hundred bracelets hanging from her skinny wrist. "Around the corner," she droned, impatient with my modesty.

Forget sucking in my gut: nothing short of surgery would make me fit into that skirt. And I don't mean liposuction—I'm talking organ removal. When I told Simone the bad news, she rapped on Haley's door once and then opened it.

"Hi, Hale—just me." She caught sight of the blue velour track suit. "Oh. My. God. *What* are you wearing?" She sighed. "Anyway, love, I'm trying to get Virginia dressed, and we're having a little trouble with the sizing."

"It's Veronica," I said to no one in particular.

Simone kept her attention focused on Haley. "Remind me, love—where do you keep your fat clothes?"

From a plastic box in the uppermost reaches of Haley's closet, Simone dug up a white miniskirt to go with the black tank top and tan sweater. The sweater was really loose around the neck—it actually slipped down one shoulder—but Simone assured me it was supposed to look that way. The slouchy calfskin boots she picked out were a half size too small and made my pinky toe hurt. I had to wear a hat, of course—something big to hide my brown hair, which Simone had already pinned up. After studying me for an uncomfortably long time, she plucked a black felt cowboy hat off of Haley's shelf and rammed it on my head. She pursed her lips in distaste. "Hideous, but it will have to do."

With Haley safely out of earshot, Simone explained the wardrobe. "I tried old Hollywood glamour with Haley, but it just wouldn't take. When I wasn't looking, she'd go right back to being Rodeo Jane."

She reached her talons up to grab a plaid cowboy shirt with silver piping and mother-of-pearl buttons and yanked it from its hanger. "This has got to go."

She scrunched the shirt into a little ball and shoved it into her handbag.

"So now we're switching gears and going for urban cowgirl," she droned. "Worn denim. Butter-soft leather. The *occasional* cowboy hat." She shuddered. "To offset the hick factor, we're accessorizing with some architectural pieces."

She plucked a pair of big, white, Jackie O sunglasses from a shelf. "Try these on."

Once she'd okayed the sunglasses, she hauled her enormous, slouchy handbag off the floor (today's choice was copper metallic with lots of rings and studs) and dug around until she found a cosmetic bag. I closed my eyes and let her pat, powder, and draw on my face.

"There." She angled me toward a full-length mirror. I opened my eyes and gasped. I looked very little like the mopey young woman in the next room but exactly like the starlet—sorry, star—who'd been gazing out from magazine covers for the past year. It was almost as if Haley Rush weren't a real person but rather an airbrushed fantasy that Simone could conjure at will.

Jay, pacing around the living room, did a double take and almost dropped his cell phone. "Call you later." He shoved his phone into a back pocket without taking his eyes off me.

"Pretty good, huh?" I said.

"Astonishing."

I laughed. "I couldn't believe it when I looked in the mirror. It really felt like Haley was looking back at me."

"Don't talk."

"Excuse me?"

"I don't mean now. I mean when you're, you know. Out. As soon as you open your mouth, you ruin the illusion."

"When we met, you said I sounded like her."

"I was just saying that."

"How am I supposed to order coffee without talking?"

"Well, obviously you have to talk a little, but keep it to a minimum. Just say what you want—a grande caramel macchiato with an extra shot of syrup. They ask if you want whipped cream, just nod. And nod again when they hand you the coffee—don't say thank you."

Now he was sounding paranoid. "You really think someone can tell I'm not Haley from two words?"

"Depends on the two words. For example, Haley never says thank you."

I assumed Rodrigo would drive me to the coffee place. Instead, Jay handed me a set of keys. "Take the Escape Hybrid." He led me through the kitchen to the garage.

The kitchen turned out to be just as disappointing as the façade: brown granite countertops, dark cabinets, commercial oven, stainless steel appliances—not a campfire, taxidermic animal, or copper pot in sight. Esperanza stood over the big sink, scrubbing a griddle.

"Pancakes again, Esperanza?" Jay asked with forced lightness. She was listening to an iPod and didn't respond.

A door at the end of the kitchen led to the garage. The first thing I noticed wasn't the demure navy blue Escape Hybrid but a great, big, jacked up, kiss-my-ass yellow pickup truck.

"Oh, my."

"Haley's Tonka toy," Jay said.

"Does she drive it much?"

"No. It's such a gas guzzler, it's bad for her image. She just likes knowing it's here. Sometimes she'll come out and sit in the driver seat without leaving the garage."

"Well, that's kind of . . . strange," I said, regretting my words immediately.

Jay walked me over to the Escape and opened the front door for me. "It's extremely strange."

Starbucks was in the Sunset Plaza, a wide, charmless, urban street of clothing stores, comedy clubs, and restaurants. After parking on a side street, I dug my cell phone out of the handbag Simone had chosen. It was soft tan leather, with a row of fringe.

I locked the car, stuck the Jackie O sunglasses in the big handbag, and opened my cell phone. About a hundred yards down the street, the security guys watched me from one of the black SUVs. Jay had instructed them to keep an eye on me but stay out of things as much as possible. We wanted the public to see that Haley Rush was unafraid to pop out for a quick errand on her own.

"Big deal in the works," I murmured into the silent phone, working my way toward the coffee shop while the SUV trailed at a comfortable distance. On the way down the hill, they had cut off a banged-up Camry that was riding a little too close on my tail.

"Lots of money," I continued. "Mm. Mm hm. . . . Maybe I'll buy a new car. Or an island. I've always wanted my own island . . ."

"Haley! Yo—Haley Rush!"

It took me a moment to realize the man on the sidewalk was talking to me. I looked up just as the flash went off. Did he really need a flash in the middle of the day?

He was middle-aged and stocky, with dark curly hair, thinning at the temples, and a three-day growth of beard. He wore baggy jeans, a black T-shirt, and running shoes. He bared his teeth in an approximation of a grin.

I waved with one pinky and smiled, my phone suddenly slippery in my sweaty hand. There. He got a shot. Would that be enough?

"And of course I'd need a private plane to get to my island," I whispered into the phone, walking faster now. "Let's put it in the contract."

I thought the Starbucks barista would say, "Oh, my God— you're Haley Rush!" Instead, in response to my whispered order, he just asked, "Would you like whipped cream with that?"

I thought the other patrons would stop what they were doing to stare at me or ask for an autograph, but they barely glanced at me before returning full attention to their MacBooks.

Haley wasn't nearly as big a star as I thought she was, at least at this coffee shop. It was kind of disappointing.

As instructed, I took my coffee to an outside table, even though it was kind of cold. The raised concrete patio overlooked the busy street. The photographer stood just below, on the sidewalk. I refused eye contact as he hauled himself up and over the railing. There were a couple of others coming over now, like ants alerted to a sugar spill.

Hands shaking, I swapped my cell phone for Haley's iPod and shoved the buds into my ears. Rap music: yuck. I scrolled through the menu, amazed that there were that many songs that I didn't want to listen to. Finally, I settled on silence, gently bobbing my head to an imaginary beat.

As a prop, Jay had given me the script from an old episode of *Kitty and the Katz*. I set it on the table.

I heard cameras clicking, one close, others from down below. The first photographer had turned off the flash, at least. I straightened in my chair and took a sip of the coffee. It was way too sweet. Was there any chance that Haley could develop a newfound affection for plain coffee with skim milk?

Another click. I tilted my chin up so he could see my face below the enormous hat. I smiled.

"Nice," he purred.

I pulled a pencil out of the big handbag and opened the script to a random page.

    LIZA: If I didn't know better, Kitty, I'd say you
       had a crush on Chase.
    KITTY: What? No! [Crosses arms over chest.]
    LIZA: [Leans forward] He is pretty cute.
    KITTY: [Looks up in mock bafflement] Is he?
       I've . . . I've . . . never noticed. [Cue
       laughter]

Click. I kept my head down. Surely he had enough shots already. I turned the page even though I hadn't finished reading. I picked up the disgusting coffee and held it to my lips.

The camera lens loomed next to my face, startling me so much that I dropped the coffee. It spilled through the latticed table right onto my white skirt and the photographer's sneakers.

"Son of a *bitch*," he said, popping up.

Behind me, I heard laughter. Two young women in tight jeans and leather jackets gave me the thumbs-up.

"You go, girl," one of them said.

"Next time, throw it in his face," the other chimed in.

I rewarded their support with a great big Haley Rush smile. I put my things back into the big handbag, dropped my empty cup into a trash can, and headed back to the Escape. The coffee-soaked paparazzi stayed behind, saying "fuck, fuck, fuck" as he blotted his shoes with little napkins. The others—there were three now—trailed me along the sidewalk. The Escalade appeared as if out of nowhere.

One of the photographers waved to the blond, neckless driver, whose name, improbably enough, was Elliott. "What else is up for Haley today, boss?"

"That's it for today, guys."

Two of them drifted away. The third trailed me like a bloodthirsty mosquito.

Elliott held out his palm. "Knock it off, or I'll cover her head the next time I see you."

The photographer spit on the sidewalk, slung his big camera over a shoulder, and strode away.

I shot Elliott a grateful smile. "Thanks."

He curled his lip a little and put up his tinted window.

Chapter Ten

I gave Jay the details of my coffee run, omitting the spilling incident.

"So, how do you . . . feel?" he asked, checking my face.

"What do you . . . mean?"

"Was it . . . okay?"

I shrugged. "Sure. Actually, it was kind of fun."

He sighed with relief. "Okay, then. You're hired. I mean, if you want to be."

"Of course I do! When do I start? I'm free tomorrow."

He shook his head. "I need to make some calls first. Schedule some appointments. Monday okay?"

I took my time getting home from Beverly Hills, stopping off at Ross to buy some desperately needed panty hose and at Ralph's supermarket to get a plastic container of freshly prepared sushi: extravagant, yes, but I had cause for celebration.

*   *   *

With my new job in the bag, I didn't really have to take a subbing assignment, but when the phone rang early Friday morning, I answered it, anyway.

"Hope I didn't wake you," Margery, the school secretary, said.

"I was up," I croaked unconvincingly.

"Right. Well. Mrs. Ortega just called in sick—something stomach-related—so we were wondering if you'd be able to take over P.E. today."

Gym class: ugh. I definitely should have let the phone ring.

I checked the clock. I had plenty of time to get ready.

"Sure, Margery. No problem."

The Motts had assigned my van a little dirt patch on the side of the driveway. I had almost made it to the street when Deborah came running out of her house, her chunky bathrobe flapping behind her like a cape.

"Veronica! So glad I caught you. Are you going to school today?"

I considered lying but was pretty sure she'd find out. I nodded, glancing at the clock on my dashboard.

"Fabulous. If you'll wait *two seconds*, I'll get the kids."

It was way more than two seconds, of course, but that wasn't the worst of it. As Shaun and Shavonne piled into the back of my van, Shaun trailing Sugar Pops, Deborah said, "Also, I was wondering—can you take Shaun to that Cub Scout thing tomorrow night?"

I shook my head in confusion. "What Cub Scout thing?"

"You know, that thing at the Brea Dam. Campfire and night hike, I think. I called Hank, but he said you had Ben this weekend."

"I do, but Hank usually does the Scout stuff." Den and pack meetings were on Thursday nights. "I'll call him."

There is no good day to sub in P.E., but this was a particularly bad one. It was unusually cold and windy, even for February. In my khaki pants, blue blouse, and cardigan, I was more warmly dressed than most of the kids (at least a quarter of the boys wore shorts year-round), but they only had to be outside for fifty-minute stretches; I was stuck out there all day.

The Las Palmas Elementary School physical education program encouraged fitness without competitiveness. As such, today was a hula hoop day: bad news for me, since it meant hauling endless armloads of hoops from the storage shed. After watching two classes of bright-eyed kids attempt (and occasionally succeed) at keeping the hoops aloft on their hips, I finally gave it a try: if nothing else, the movement might thaw my body. I'd almost (but not really) mastered it when I noticed a sixth grade boy pointing me out to his friends and laughing.

I definitely should have let the phone ring.

At lunchtime, I called Hank.

"So this Cub Scout thing tomorrow night . . ."

"Oh! Right. Did you get my e-mail?"

"My Internet's been down since November."

"Really?"

"I told you that." Several times. "Anyway, since Cub Scouts is your father-son thing, it's fine if you want to take Ben. You can just drop him off afterwards."

"Oh, wow." Hank paused—too long. "That's really nice of you to offer, Roni. It's just, Darcy and I . . . she's got this client

with a timeshare in Palm Springs. He couldn't use it this weekend, so he offered it to us."

"Palm Springs?"

"Well, Palm Desert, actually. Nice place—two bedrooms,
gourmet kitchen, golf course view. As long as we're childless for
the weekend, Darcy and I thought it would be a great opportunity to de-stress."

De-stress? Hank hadn't worked in over a year! What could
possibly be stressing him out?

"I wish you had told me about the Cub Scout thing earlier," I
said, my teeth clenched.

"It's no big deal. Actually, it should be fun—I'm sorry to have
to miss it. I'll e-mail you the specifics."

I paused for a moment to keep from screaming. "My e-mail
doesn't work."

"Oh. Ha! Right. You just told me that."

Shaun Mott, early for once, appeared at the guesthouse door
at 5:30 Saturday evening, his curly red hair puffing out from the
sides of his Cub Scout hat like a clown. Chilly air blew in around
him. "My mom told me to come over."

"We don't need to be at the park for a half hour." I had just
taken a very hot shower and had about five minutes to dry my
hair before it could be classified as Beyond Repair. "I'll come get
you when we're ready."

"My mom told me to." Shaun clomped into the little house
and plopped down on the loveseat, where he proceeded to stare,
dull-eyed, into space.

Ben, sprawled on the floor with an army of plastic superheroes, eyed Shaun's hat, shirt, and neckerchief. "Are we supposed to be in uniform?"

Shaun's lip curled into a sneer. "Uh—*yeah*."

Ben looked at me, panicked. "My uniform's at Dad's house."

"It's okay, sweetie," I said in the fake-calm voice I adopted whenever Ben freaked out because something was at the wrong house. "We'll go get it." My hair was going to look like crap.

"But Dad's not there," he whimpered.

Oops. "So, we'll get it from the housekeeper."

"She doesn't work on Saturday or Sunday." Darcy did her own dishes two days a week? Now that was shocking.

Shaun's uniform was a different color from Ben's: beige instead of blue. It had something to do with rank or age or . . . whatever.

"Hey—I bet Shaun's got an old uniform you can borrow! Don't you, Shaun?"

"My mom gives all our old uniforms to this place that collects stuff for poor kids."

In the end, Ben wore his blue Las Palmas Elementary T-shirt over another, long-sleeved shirt. Because of the temperature, he had to wear his heaviest coat (which was actually just a lined, hooded sweatshirt). "So no one will know what you've got on underneath, anyway," I chirped.

"I wish I had my hat," he said, lips quivering.

A little before six o'clock, we headed for the minivan, my hands shaking from the cold as I pulled keys from my purse. Somewhere I had gloves—I kept them in the front hall closet when I lived with Hank—but I had no idea where they were. There were so many boxes I had never unpacked.

Deborah Mott, attired in blue jeans (she'd managed to get

dressed at some point during the day), came out of the side door, two colorful cardboard cartons in her hands.

"Twenty-four Capri Suns." She heaved the cartons at me.

Oh, God. "Was I supposed to . . . bring something?"

"Didn't you get the scoutmaster's e-mail?"

I shook my head. Damned Internet.

"They assigned something to everyone. It was in the e-mail." She wrapped her arms around herself. "*Brr.* Chilly. Well, you all have fun!"

"Benji? Did Daddy mention anything about bringing something tonight?"

"No."

I tried Hank's cell phone: no answer. It was getting late, anyway; there was no time to pick anything up. Oh, well. The Cub Scout pack was huge. They wouldn't notice some little thing missing.

In the dusty parking lot, I slid my big red minivan next to Terri Sheffler's even bigger gray SUV. The vehicle was easy to identify by the license plate (FAB♥FIVE) and the row of stick figures on the back window. The stickers showed two parents, three kids, two dogs, and a cat, with a name underneath each: Terri, John, Ashlyn, Blaine, Tyler, Angel (dog #1), Laker (dog #2), and Duck (cat).

Brea Dam park was a flat, grassy expanse with picnic tables, grills, and a huge fire pit, where a bonfire now roared. The dam's gravelly wall loomed beyond us. A wooded hill rose on another side.

We hurried toward the fire, my feet already cold in backless shoes. Ben pulled his hood over his head—something he rarely did because he didn't want to mess up his spiky hair.

"You cold, buddy?"

"Don't want anyone to see that I don't have my hat."

Closer to the fire, little boys ran around in the semidarkness, while mothers fussed over a line of rectangular tables, arranging fruit and vegetable platters, store-bought cookies, and juice boxes. Fathers clustered around a couple of enormous, smoking grills, which allowed them to look manly and stay warm at the same time.

"I've got some more juice boxes," I said, handing the Capri Suns over to a woman at the tables. So what if I was kinda, sorta taking credit for Deborah Mott's contribution. She owed me.

"Terrific." The woman checked my face, tried to place me. "Your son is . . ."

"Ben Czaplicki."

"Ben! Right. Of course. He's a . . . Tiger? But I thought you were bringing . . ." She shuffled things around on the table until she uncovered a sheet of paper. She had to squint to read. "Hot dog buns. Did you switch with someone?"

"No, uh . . . I didn't know about the barbecue until yesterday. My ex-husband usually takes Ben to Scouts."

At the word *ex-husband*, her eyes popped, just the tiniest bit. "Oh! Right! So Hank is your . . . right."

"You need any help?" I asked.

She shook her head. "I'm fine."

I smiled and nodded. My face hurt from stress and cold.

"For future reference?" she said. "You can get all the information you need from our website."

I smiled some more and then slunk off to find my son. Ben was standing on a picnic table bench, arm in the air, yelling, "Ahoy, mateys!" Around him, little boys in Cub Scout caps jumped and yelped and made pirate noises.

I caught Ben's eye. "Hey, buddy. You want to find a place to sit?"

He shook his head and turned his attention back to his friends.

Some adults had arranged themselves around the bonfire in folding canvas camp chairs. I wandered over to an empty patch of dry grass and stood there, hugging myself to stay warm, gazing at the fire and only occasionally squinting at the faces around me, trying to spot someone I knew. Even Terri Sheffler would be better than nothing.

Ben had begged Carson to join Cub Scouts, but Nina refused. "It's like a Nazi cult. All those uniforms and saluting? Nuh-uh." Mostly, I think, she didn't want the 6:30 meetings to mess up her dinners twice a month.

That was okay with me. I didn't like the idea of Nina chatting with Hank and possibly deciding that he wasn't a complete and total asshole.

"Veronica? Hey!" At the sound of the male voice I turned to see John Sheffler.

"Hi, John!" I had never been so happy to see John's puffy face before. In fact, I had never been even a little bit happy to see John, who never seemed to say more than, "Hi," "Hey," and "Is that right?" At social gatherings, he favored corners, where he'd stand with his arms crossed over his striped button-down shirt—he must have had a closet full of them, all the tiniest bit tight over his belly. He'd gnaw on his bottom lip and check his big chrome watch every fifteen minutes.

Once, at a PTA fundraiser, Nina (who'd had a little too much to drink) joined John in his corner and said, "Are we keeping you from something important?"

John looked so baffled you'd think she was speaking Cherokee. Finally, he shook his head.

"You keep checking your watch," Nina explained.

"Is that right?"

"Is Terri here?" I asked him now. I'd give anything to camp next to Terri for the evening. I'd even dole out some new-and-exciting details of my divorce. Like: Hank originally claimed to have met Darcy through work, but I'd recently found out that they had hooked up at a bar. (I wouldn't tell her that it was the same bar where he'd met me. That was too painful.) Or: Hank's mother, who insisted I call her "Mom" for all the years we were married, responded to my last birthday card with a note that said, "In light of the circumstances, I don't feel that either of us should feel compelled to recognize special occasions."

As it turned out, Terri would have to wait for these juicy tidbits.

"It's just me and the boys tonight," John told me. "Ashlyn's at a friend's house, so Terri was going to take a long bath and watch a movie on television."

Oh, great. Monday I'd get to hear about how lucky Terri was to be married to John, who took the boys out on a Saturday night so she could take a candlelit bubble bath. Terri had spent a brief stint as a PartyLites home sales representative, so pretty much everything she did involved candles.

"You put your chair down yet?" he asked me.

I shook my head. "I didn't realize we were supposed to bring chairs."

I mentally thanked him for not saying, "It was in the e-mail." Instead, he said, "You can use Blaine's."

The Shefflers' blue canvas chairs were set up near the fire. I had about twenty seconds' worth of relaxation before I noticed all the eyes on me. *Hank Czaplicki's ex-wife is hitting on John Sheffler!*

Maybe it was just my imagination.

John leaned toward me. No striped shirt tonight—at least that I could see. His ski jacket was navy blue. "You having a good year this year?"

"Sure," I nodded and forced a smile. Nothing like divorce and poverty to get you off to a great start. "You?"

He nodded slowly, as if considering. "Fantastic." He held my gaze a fraction of a second too long.

Maybe it was just my imagination.

I leaned away, just the littlest bit, and looked back at the faces around me. Okay, it was true: people were looking at us. If I were married, people wouldn't think twice about seeing me chat with John. As long I was single, I was considered a threat.

"I'm starving!" I announced (even though I wasn't). "I think I'll go get something to eat."

People were already lining up at the long tables, including Ben and his fellow Tiger Scouts. I was scooping a mound of macaroni salad onto a paper plate when I heard a kid say, "Where are the hot dog rolls?"

"Yeah, where are they?" another asked.

And then: *Yeah, yeah—hot dog rolls! There are no hot dog rolls! How'm I supposed to eat a hot dog without a roll?*

When I heard an adult say, "The person who was supposed to bring them didn't read her e-mail," I wheeled around, prepared to stalk off to the bonfire with my macaroni salad. Instead, I bumped into Ken Drucker, looking very tall and outdoorsy in a dark green Columbia ski jacket, tan pants, and brown hiking boots

"Whoah!" He put a hand on my arm.

"Ken—hi! Hope I didn't get you with the macaroni."

"No, I'm fine. Is that all you're eating?"

"I'm not very hungry."

He looked toward the bonfire. "Where are you sitting?"

"Nowhere," I said. "I forgot my chair." And the hot dog rolls. And my brain.

"I've got extras in the car. I'll get you one."

So that's how I wound up spending my Saturday night in front of a fire with Ken Drucker. We talked about his recent snow camping trip and about how many times he had climbed Mount Whitney (seven). We talked about my teaching experiences at Las Palmas Elementary. We commiserated about the stresses and confusions of single parenting, and he said, "Ha!" (again, not the guffaw but the word itself) when I confessed that I was the one who'd neglected to bring the hot dog buns.

There were so many not-so-subtle looks and whispers that I blurted out, "Do you think our picture will be on the front page of the *National Enquirer* next week?" After my recent experience in Beverly Hills, I half-expected a photographer to pop out of the bushes.

"Ha!" he said.

I felt myself flush—worried for an instant that he'd take my comment the wrong way, as if I thought any of the sparks crackling in the night air were the result of chemistry between us and not the fire.

"Do you date much?" he asked. His tone of voice—purely curious and platonic—put my fears to rest.

"Nah," I said. "I don't have the time or the energy. I just want to focus on Ben, for now. How about you?"

He shook his head. "I don't feel ready yet. And I don't think the boys are ready, either. The divorce has been rough on them. Besides, I really don't meet any attractive single women."

Realizing what he'd said, he covered his face. "That came out wrong. What I mean is—"

I laughed. "It's okay."

He grinned. "I guess what I'm looking for—if I were looking, which I'm not—is someone who can share experiences with me and the boys. Someone who likes camping and mountain biking. Rock climbing, ice fishing—all the good stuff."

"That sounds . . ." I paused, trying to find the right word. "Exhausting," I finished. "And cold and wet and just generally miserable."

This time he laughed for real.

When the time came for the night hike, Ken loaned Ben a flashlight that strapped to his head. I made it halfway up the steep dirt path through the woods before tripping over my slip-on shoes.

"You go back down by the fire," Ken told me. "I'll keep an eye on Ben."

"Thanks," I said, relief gushing through me. "You're a pal."

I meant it, too.

Chapter Eleven

Monday morning, I dropped Ben and the Mott kids at school and headed for Santa Fe Springs, where I found Rodrigo waiting in the El Taco Loco parking lot.

As I buckled myself into the passenger seat of his now-familiar Prius, he handed me the sunglasses and trucker hat. He looked worn-out today, with circles under his eyes and less gel than usual in his hair.

"We're going to L.A.," he muttered, pulling out of the parking lot.

"Why?"

"Appointment."

"With . . .?"

"Hair designer."

"For . . . ?"

"Hair."

The Prius, bogged down in traffic, crawled toward the freeway entrance ramp. Rodrigo stared straight ahead, clutching the steering wheel, his lips tense and white.

"Not that it's any of my business, Rodrigo, but is something wrong?"

For a moment, I thought he hadn't heard me. Finally, he spoke. "I hate this town."

"Santa Fe Springs?"

"No—*L.A.*" He sighed with exasperation and said nothing more for the rest of the drive—unless you count a mumbled *fucking idiot* when someone in an SUV cut him off.

I liked Suck-Up Rodrigo better than Depressed Rodrigo.

The beauty parlor (I guess I shouldn't call it that) was in a green craftsman bungalow on a leafy street. The sign near the front door was so small that I almost missed it. White with a simple black typeface, it read STEFANO SALZANO, HAIR ARTISTRY. No hours of operation, no phone number: one could only assume that Stefano did not take walk-ins.

Rodrigo pulled into the driveway and parked in the back. Towering hedges surrounded a small dirt lot, so no one would see customers going in or coming out. Inside, the bungalow had wide plank floors, built-in oak cabinets, and an elaborate tile fireplace. There was a cozy seating area with velvet couches and a single styling chair upholstered in tapestry.

When we walked in, Stefano Salzano, his glossy black hair tufted like a woodpecker's crown, was standing in the middle of the room, hands clasped in front of him, a big, white, bonded-tooth smile on his shiny face. Why did his skin look so eerily smooth, almost plastic? Was it Botox? Chemical peel? Dermabrasion? I bet Haley would know.

"Veronica!" He rushed toward me. "Jay has told me every little thing about you!"

"Like what?"

He stopped short and bit his lip. "That you look like Haley? And that you, um . . . look like Haley? Okay, truth: that's all he told me." He broke into a fit of giggles, covering his mouth with a manicured hand. He had two earrings in his (slightly pointy) right ear, a loop in the lobe and a little steel ball high up in the cartilage. He wore black skinny jeans and a tight white T-shirt that showed off his sinewy, tattooed forearms.

Stefano hung my jacket and purse in a coat closet and sent me off to a spacious bathroom, which had purple walls, black-and-white checkerboard floors, a big gilt mirror, and a farmhouse sink adapted for hair washing. I swapped my cotton sweater for a black kimono that looked like silk but whose label ratted it out as polyester.

Back in the main room, Stefano offered me slippers (which I declined) and mineral water in a bright green bottle (which I accepted, even though it would make me burp). Finally, he led me to the tapestry chair. Sullen Rodrigo, meanwhile, had taken up residence on one of the velvet couches. He was so tiny, he practically disappeared among the fringed pillows.

Stefano peered over my shoulder at the mirror, patting my brown locks on the sides and ends. I examined his tattoos in the reflection. The artwork on his left arm was navy-inspired: an anchor, a sailor, a breaking wave. Cartoons ruled the right arm. Betty Boop chased Porky Pig. Tom and Jerry sipped champagne. Fred Flintstone mooned Barney.

"You ready to go blond?" Stefano asked.

"What?" I forgot about the tattoos. When he didn't react, I turned to look him straight in his shiny face.

"Jay didn't tell you?" His cupid's bow mouth twisted with amusement. "You, my dear, are going to join the ranks of Carole Lombard, Marilyn Monroe, and our own dear Haley Rush—and go platinum!"

I froze. "But—Jay said he thought Haley looked better as a brunette."

Stefano batted at the air. "Hon-bun, it doesn't matter what Jay does or doesn't like. Haley's a blonde—I do her color, BTW—and you have to match. And besides. FYI? Jay has as much style sense as my cockapoo." He giggled. "I really just wanted an excuse to say *cockapoo*."

I gulped. "Okay." It made sense, of course. To pass as Haley, I'd need Haley's hair.

Seeing my expression, Stefano gave my hair a reassuring squeeze. "*Girrrrrrl!* You are going to look *superfierce*—like a cute little man-eating sex kitten! You are going to have the men clawing at your door . . . and then you're going to come right back here and tell me all about it!"

That made me laugh. Stefano was pretentious, affected—a hairdressing and Hollywood cliché. Despite all that—or maybe because of it—I immediately adored him.

While Stefano fluttered around, Rodrigo remained on the couch, poking at his laptop and pretending not to listen. When he got up to use the bathroom, Stefano whispered, "What's the matter with Tinker Bell?"

"He's down on Hollywood, for some reason."

"Oh, please. All these people come here looking for love. Not of a man or love of a woman—but love from *everybody*. And when they're not instantly discovered, it's like, 'Why are you all so stupid that you can't see my utter fabulousness?' Probably Tinker Bell had one of his screenplays rejected. Again."

"He told you about his writing?" I whispered.

"Ugh!" Stefano ran a comb through my hair, careful not to tug. "He told me, he told my assistant, he told my *cat*—who should be around here somewhere, BTW. I hope you're not allergic."

He lowered his voice back into the murmuring range. "Anyhoo, I know some independent producers who read the script. Bear in mind, these are rich kids whose daddies set them up so they can read screenplays all day and buy independent films as a hobby. They've never actually produced anything in their lives, and even *they* said it stunk. One called it self-indulgent garbage, one said it was derivative crap, and the third called it . . . well, something that might offend those lovely shell-shaped ears."

Rodrigo came out of the bathroom and settled back among the pillows. Stefano straightened and began to whistle. He brushed a stinky white solution onto my hair and wrapped it, piece by piece, in foil. while Rodrigo tapped away on his computer.

"Writing another screenplay, Rod?" Stefano asked him.

Rodrigo kept his eyes on his laptop. "Yes."

"Well, whatever you do, don't give up your dreams. You've got too much talent to let it go to waste."

It took all my strength to keep my face neutral.

Rodrigo seemed to ignore him, but I guess he was just screening for sarcasm. "Thank you," he said at last.

When my hair was entirely encased in foil, Stefano lead me to an empty loveseat, draping it with a throw blanket so the chemicals on my head couldn't endanger the velvet. "Champagne?"

"Seriously?"

He looked up at the tin ceiling and sighed. "Well, okay. It's *technically* sparkling wine because it's from *Sonoma*, and you can't call something champagne unless it's from the Champagne region in France."

This was so much better than teaching eight-year-olds how to hula hoop.

Stefano disappeared for a moment before returning with a tall glass and a stack of reading material.

"*Variety, Vogue, Men's Health,* or *Fit Pregnancy?*"

"No *Us Weekly?* No *Star?*"

"No, no, a hundred times, no!" He shuddered. "Not since that day when Nicole came in. I'd left *People* sitting out where everyone could see it, and the cover story was all about . . . " He shuddered again, more dramatically this time.

"Tom Cruise?" I guessed.

"Other Nicole." He took a step back and studied me.

Rodrigo's cell phone rang. "Hey, honey, what's up?" Immediately, he was a different person.

". . . I don't know—a while. We're at Stefano's. Yeah—the place in Hancock Park, the little house. Jay thought the Beverly Hills salon was too risky."

"It's not a little house, it's a bungalow," Stefano said to no one in particular, fussing around with his supplies. "And it's not a salon, it's a private studio."

"It'll be a few hours," Rodrigo said into the phone, leaning forward, eyes on the ground. "But maybe we can do a late lunch? Or an early dinner . . . I don't know—Jay told me to stay . . . I just don't want him to. . . I know you do, but—Well, did you try calling Josh? What did he say? . . . God!" He sounded really annoyed. "You paid him extra to be on call! Is Jay there? Maybe he can do it."

Rodrigo squeezed his eyes shut. Finally, he said, "Baby, baby . . . it's okay! Of course I will! Of course!"

He slipped his phone into his pocket, tapped some keys on his laptop, closed it up and slid it into its black case.

"I need to pop over to Haley's for a little while," he said without looking at us.

"Troubles?" Stefano chirped.

"Nothing major. Just—that stupid AV system. She's trying to watch television, and she can get the picture but there's music coming from the speakers. And Josh is supposed to be on call twenty-four/seven, but he's in Hawaii with his girlfriend."

Stefano *tsk-tsked*. "You'd think he'd arrange for a backup."

"He *did*, but the other guy doesn't have *clearance*, and Josh should've *thought* of that."

Stefano and I didn't say anything until Rodrigo's little green car pulled out of the lot.

"The AV guy needed clearance?" I said.

Stefano giggled. "Honestly! You'd think Roddy's working for the CIA."

"Maybe he's writing a movie about spies," I suggested.

"Oh, no!" Stefano settled onto Rodrigo's vacated couch like a Persian cat. "Roddy only writes coming-out stories. One after another after another, like he's the first gay man in the universe. If he'd just get a boyfriend, it wouldn't be so bad. Instead, his life revolves around Crazy Haley."

I remembered the paper I signed. "Are we allowed to talk about this?"

"Of course! We both have *clearance*, remember? We just can't go public." He crossed his legs and put his clasped hands on his knees. "We don't have long. What do you want to know?"

My mouth dropped open. Where to begin? "Everything!"

He tapped his cheek. "Okay—the recap. You probably know most of this from the Internet."

"I don't get the Internet."

I expected the usual expressions of horror. Instead, he said,

"I've never really understood how to work it, myself. Okay. *Let's start at the very beginning . . .*" He sang to the tune from *The Sound of Music*, and then he spoke quickly.

"Haley Rush came from one of those square-shaped mountain states. Colorado or Wyoming or . . ."

"Montana," I supplied.

"Montana! Right!" He pointed at me like a game show host. "The official version of how Montana Haley became Hollywood Haley is that she was in some talent show or state fair—or maybe a talent show in a state fair—and some scouts saw her and asked her to come to California."

"And the unofficial version?" I asked.

Stefano tapped his shiny cheek. "It all started with Haley's mother. She claims she was a beauty queen once, but I've seen pictures, and—I don't *think* so. Anyhoo, she married young—you can get hitched at, like, twelve in those states. Hubby was much older, just some guy with a couple of hardware stores. Mama Rush had a couple of kids and got all fat, and hubby started running around, and it turned out he didn't have as much money as she thought he had.

"When Haley was three or five—I think it was five—her mother noticed she could carry a tune, so, voila! She turned her into her little show pony, mostly for her own ego at first, but then she started making a little money off of her. By the time Haley sang at the state fair—she was eight or nine at that point—Mama was three hundred pounds and desperate. Maybe some guy said Haley should go to Hollywood, maybe not. Most agents won't even set foot in the Valley. You think they're going to pop off to a state fair in Montana unless they've been invited to Demi and Ashton's?" He bit his lip. "Or is that Idaho?"

"Haley told you all this?"

"Ohhhh, yes. When she talks, she talks a lot. Other days she just mopes. It's like she's two different people."

"And now three," I said.

He giggled. "True. When they got to L.A., Mama and Haley lived in a crappy motel and spent their days going to auditions and modeling agencies. She has a little brother, but they left him back with Daddy. He moved out here once he turned thirteen, which worked out really well for him because it's much easier to score cocaine in L.A. than it is in Montana. And, of course, Mama and Daddy got divorced somewhere along the way, and Daddy moved to Reno to marry a cocktail waitress. Shockingly, the relationship didn't last.

"After they'd been here maybe six months, Haley got cast in a peanut butter commercial, and then there was a laundry detergent commercial. A few others, I think. Her big break came when she was a teenager and she got cast in *The Crazy Life of Riley Poole*. Remember that one? It ran for two, maybe three, seasons. Haley played the nerd."

"Is Haley still close to her mother?"

"Oh, noooo . . ." He held up a finger to signal "one minute" and disappeared into the back room, returning with a tabloid and a Diet Dr Pepper. He flipped through the magazine until he found the picture he was looking for and handed it to me.

The headline was printed in enormous letters: HALEY TO MOM: GET OUT!

There were several photos: Haley tight-lipped in big sunglasses; Haley as a young, smiling girl standing next to a large, brown-haired woman; a thin, blond, middle-aged woman getting into a car.

"This is the mother? How'd she lose all the weight?" I asked.

Stefano popped open his soda. "Stomach staple and lipo. Paid for by her salary as Haley's *manager*."

"Isn't Jay Haley's manager?"

"He is now. They met when Haley was on *Riley Poole*. Jay was some kind of production slave, and he got tight with Haley, which is kind of weird when you think that she was, like, fifteen and he was, like, twenty-five."

"Wait. So Haley and Jay were . . ."

"*Officially*, he saw her artistic potential and wanted to help her shine. Unofficially? His career was going nowhere and he saw financial potential. He's the one who convinced her to move over to the Betwixt Channel, though, so you've got to give him some credit."

"But was there ever a romance?"

"Romance! Oh, you are so quaint. She never said anything about it to me, and believe me, I've fished. What I *do* know is that Haley hasn't talked to either of her parents since she turned eighteen, and Jay hasn't exactly gone out of his way to mend the family rift."

"But what about the boyfriend?" I asked. "Brady Ellis."

Stefano licked his lips. "A tasty, tasty morsel. I keep begging Jay to let me do his hair, but I think he's afraid that I might say something inappropriate. Which I wouldn't, BTW."

"What does Jay have to do with Brady's hair?"

"Jay manages Brady, too. He's got a handful of young clients. Not like Haley—it's not a round-the-clock hand-holding dealie—but he manages the publicists, gives input on scripts, that sort of thing."

"Is Haley still going out with Brady?" If so, maybe I'd get to meet him.

"Sadly, no. Maybe they went their separate ways. Or maybe he finally figured out that she's *fucking insane*."

"What do you mean?"

Stefano tapped on his soda can. "She won't leave the house. She cries for no reason. She's on about fifteen different pills—all of them prescription, but still. She's got the emotional maturity of a two-year-old. Shall I go on?"

"Yes, please!"

He threw his head back and laughed. "Oh, I like you, Veronica Zapp!"

"Did they tell you that was my last name?"

"Isn't it?"

I shook my head. "Czaplicki." He looked baffled, of course. "Do you want me to spell it?"

"I'd rather you didn't."

"My maiden name was Foote." I'd always figured that was almost, but not quite, worse.

"Veronica Foote." He spoke the name slowly, trying it out. He took a long, long drink of his Dr Pepper and placed the can on a coaster. "You might want to just stick to Veronica. One word—like Madonna."

I'd say I didn't recognize the woman staring back from the mirror once Stefano had finally finished my hair, but that wasn't true. I recognized Haley Rush—at least, the air-brushed Haley who graced magazine covers. The blond woman in the mirror looked a hell of a lot better than the Haley Rush I'd seen skulking around in her bathrobe.

"And just a few finishing touches," Stefano said, dabbing my face with powders and shimmers and glosses. "You'll knock 'em dead at—Where are you going after this?"

"The elementary school. Oh, God. What time is it? I'd better get going." Rodrigo was back, waiting for me on the couch.

"Okay, then, lovey," Stefano said. "I'll see you back here on Friday."

"Friday?"

"For your extensions."

Oh, God.

The freeway was jammed. There was no way I'd make it in time to get the kids at school. Maybe Nina could drop off the Mott kids and take Ben back to her house till I got there.

I tried her home number: no answer. I tried her cell: same. I pulled up Deborah Mott's contact info but couldn't make myself press the button.

"I'm late," I announced into the air. That's how it felt, anyway; Rodrigo and I had spent almost an hour in the car together without exchanging a single word.

I pictured Ben standing on the front lawn, alone except for Shaun and Shavonne. I couldn't let that happen. I scrolled through the contact list on my cell phone. Oh, what the hell.

"Y'lo!"

"Hi, Hank, it's me."

"Roni! Hey. What's up?"

"I'm on my way back from L.A., and I'm stuck in traffic. There's no way I can make it to the school in time."

"You want me to get Ben?"

That was easy. My entire body relaxed with relief just as

brake lights flashed ahead of us. Rodrigo jerked the Prius to a halt. My seatbelt jerked me back.

I tried to keep my voice steady. "If you could."

"Sure, no problem," he said. "You need me to get the Mott kids, too?"

"Please," I said. "And when you drop them? If you can make sure Deborah's there. A couple of times last week she was out when we got home."

"How about I'll just hang at your place until you get home, so Big Ben won't have to go from one house to the other. He does that enough already."

"True." I felt a stab in my chest that I took for guilt until I remembered: Hank broke our family apart, not me.

"Did you get a Bluetooth?" Hank asked me.

"Huh?"

"A handless phone set. Because you're in your car, aren't you?" In California, it was illegal to talk on a cell phone while driving.

"I am," I said, shooting a glance at Rodrigo. "So I'd better go. Thanks for getting the kids."

When I got home, I fully expected to find Hank and Ben sprawled on the sofa, chomping potato chips in front of the TV. I was so grateful for Hank's help that I wouldn't have even minded.

Instead, Ben sat at the table, hunched over a worksheet, nibbling from a bowl of cut apples, while Hank fiddled with my computer.

"Mommy—your hair!"

I touched my head. "Oh. That."

Hank turned, and his eyes just about flew out of his head. "Oh, my God!"

"I, um, just thought I'd try out a new look."

"You look gorgeous," Hank said.

Heat ran through my face and down my neck. "I'm not sure it really suits me."

"Are you kidding? You're a knockout!"

Hank liked blondes: look at Darcy. If only I'd bleached my hair years ago, maybe I'd still have a family.

"Thanks for getting the kids." I was eager to change the subject.

"Anytime," he said. "I'm lucky to have such a flexible work schedule."

Officially, Hank helped Darcy with her real estate business—sprucing up homes in anticipation of a sale, lining up inspectors and appraisers, stuffing mailboxes with notepads and brochures. Unofficially, I suspected he spent most of his time doing leg crunches in front of ESPN.

He kept looking at me. "I can't get over you as a blonde."

"It's just hair," I snapped, heading for the bathroom.

When I came out, he was hugging Ben good-bye.

"Your Internet's working," he told me over Ben's shoulder.

"Really?"

"Your modem just needed to be reset. Not a big deal."

"Thanks."

"You can always call me," he said. "If something breaks or you need any kind of help or . . . whatever."

I nodded. "Thanks," I said again.

"See you Wednesday, Big Ben." Hank gave him a final squeeze. "We'll go get those rockets for the Cub Scout launch."

"Let's do it now!" Ben pleaded.

"It's not my—" Hank stopped himself before he could say "day."

He cleared his throat. "I'm really busy this afternoon. I have to do some . . . things. But Wednesday. Right after school." He held up a fist, and he and Ben tapped knuckles.

I turned the other way. This was their moment, not mine.

Chapter Twelve

When we met, I was twenty-one and Hank was thirty-five, and if that sounds like a ridiculous age gap, that's because it was. I was never one of those girls perpetually in search of a father figure. I have a perfectly nice father married to a perfectly nice mother. They still live in the house where I grew up, in a small town outside of Sacramento. And, yes, they were perfectly appalled when their college daughter announced that she was dating a man halfway between her age and theirs.

Like so many great romances, Hank's and mine began in a dark, crowded bar, late one Saturday night when I was feeling restless. In the space of the last month, I had begun my senior year at Cal State Fullerton and ended, once and for all (Really! I meant it this time!) a two-and-a-half year relationship with Shane, the boy-man I had been dating since freshman year. Shane was now a junior, even though he hadn't taken any time off. He had merely changed his major three times, from education to business to botany. Botany!

Shane was still living at home with his parents and his two teenaged sisters. His bedroom sported about thirty childhood sports trophies, an extensive video game setup, and a tropical fish tank, which he broke one day while playing basketball in the house. The shattered fish tank, for me, was the final straw. I got to his house maybe an hour after it happened, and he told me the whole story like it was so, so funny: "Kyle stopped by and he was like, 'Dude, let's go outside and shoot some hoops.' And I was all, 'Dude, can't you see I'm comfortable?' And he was all, 'Sure, fine, whatever—*catch*!'

"And he throws the ball at me, and I pass it back, but my aim was kind of off and—shit! I hit the tank and Kyle was like, 'Slam DUNK!' It was frickin' *hilarious . . .*"

He left the fish to die on the floor.

I was so upset I could barely breathe.

"They're just fish," he said, stepping around the puddle.

"I will never have children with you," I told him.

So there I was, a few weeks later, at the Verona Club, standing at a high, sticky table with a couple of girlfriends who had decided that I needed to "get lucky."

I did hope to meet someone, it's true. For years, I'd had my life mapped out: marriage at twenty-four, children at twenty-six and twenty-eight. I'd take a few years off from teaching when the kids were born, maybe go back part-time when they started school. The breakup with Shane threatened to mess it all up, but if I met someone quickly, I could get my life back on track.

But Susy, Ellen, and I were way too young for this place. We'd picked it because it was one of the few Fullerton bars where we wouldn't risk running into Shane or one of his buddies.

I walked over to the bar because it gave me something to do—and also because it was my turn to buy a round. I squeezed between sweaty, cologne-covered bodies and finally managed to catch the bartender's eye and order one Corona Light, one cosmopolitan, and a margarita (that was for me—no salt, please).

Once the drinks came, I tucked the beer bottle into my elbow and grasped a glass with each hand.

The man sitting on the stool next to me—blond, spiky hair, youngish looking (at least for the Verona Club), in a short-sleeved, button-down pale blue shirt—eyed my load and smiled. "Need a hand with those?"

He had been talking to another guy. They were drinking beer.

"Thanks, I'm fine," I said—just as someone bumped me from behind.

The glasses stayed in my hands. Their contents did not.

"I am so sorry!" I gasped.

Mouth hanging open, he stared at his drenched shirt. And then he looked at me. And laughed. "Wow. You got me good."

Next to him, his friend howled.

"I am so sorry," I said again. "Someone bumped into me."

"Don't worry about it." Still chuckling, he reached for a pile of napkins and began dabbing his shirt.

"I'll pay the dry cleaning bill," I offered.

He waved the offer away. "It can go through the wash. A little Shout, and it'll be fine."

It made a good story: When did you know Hank was The One? When I found out he knew how to do laundry.

It wasn't that simple, of course. And the laundry thing didn't strike me until later. Mostly, I was struck by his maturity, his easygoing manner, his slime-free friendliness.

"Hank," he said, holding out his hand.

"Veronica."

"I always liked her better than Betty." His blue eyes crinkled. Was he flirting or just being nice? I couldn't tell.

When his friend got up—to use the bathroom, he said, though he never came back—I took his stool. The replacement drinks were on the house. Hank had gone to high school with the bartender.

Susy and Ellen swooped in for their drinks before leaving us alone. Ellen winked at me. Susy pinched my elbow.

Hank had lived in Fullerton his whole life, he told me, save for a few "ski bum years" after college. (He'd never graduated, but he didn't tell me that then.) He had his own business, selling and installing high-end window blinds. "I tried some office jobs, but I couldn't stand being stuck behind a desk all day." He owned his own house: "Nothing big, just two bedrooms, one and a half baths. But it's got a good-sized backyard, and I like to grill."

In short: Hank was an adult. And it was dark in there, and the clientele was on the old side. I had him pegged at twenty-eight. To his credit, he had no idea just how young I was. When I told him I was completing my teacher training, he assumed I was getting some kind of postgraduate certification.

"Twenty-five," he guessed several nights later as we nibbled on tortilla chips at a Mexican restaurant. He'd done everything properly: taken my number, called me the next day, asked me out to dinner.

"Nope." I took a long sip of my strawberry margarita.

"Twenty . . . four?"

"Nope."

"Older or younger?"

I raised my eyebrows.

"Oh, God." He rested his chin on his hand and studied me. "Well, you have to be at least twenty-one because they let you into the Verona Club."

"I am at least twenty-one." I grinned.

"Are you at least twenty-two?"

I shook my head. "Sorry."

He looked horrified.

"What?" I said, feeling defensive. "Twenty-one's an adult." Unless you're Shane, of course. "How old are you?"

"Thirty-five."

I stared at him. "Wow. That's . . . that's not so . . ." Suddenly, the humor of the situation struck me. "Holy cow—you're ancient!"

We both burst into laughter: partners in the crime of inappropriate dating.

"We can see if they have a children's menu," Hank howled. "You want some chicken nuggets? And maybe crayons?"

"Yeah, well don't forget to ask for the senior discount," I cackled, tears bubbling out of my eyes.

In the end, I didn't fall in love with Hank because he knew how to do laundry. I fell in love with him because he was kind and decent, and sometimes he made me laugh. Until the day he walked out, I thought that was enough.

Chapter Thirteen

N ice work," Jay said, holding open a magazine page:
STARS—THEY'RE JUST LIKE US!

It was Friday. We were sitting side by side on wrought iron chaise longues in Haley's backyard, facing the big rectangular pool. The striped cushions were a little dusty. They made my nose tickle.

The sun hurt my eyes. I'd left my sunglasses at home, and I couldn't get the loaner pair from Rodrigo's car because he was out today, meeting with some people about his screenplay. Jay had hired a driver to pick me up at El Taco Loco. The driver didn't speak English. Even better, according to Jay, he was an illegal alien who would never risk calling attention to himself by talking to the press.

The magazine photograph showed me standing by my little table outside Starbucks, paper cup in hand, looking just like a happier Haley Rush in a cowboy hat, sunglasses, and coffee-stained white skirt. Damn, I'd looked good that day, even with the silly hat. I'd have to pay closer attention next time Simone did my makeup.

The caption read, "They spill their coffee!" And then, in case anyone didn't recognize me—I mean Haley: *West Hollywood, CA—Haley Rush loses a grip on her caramel macchiato at a Sunset Strip Starbucks.*

Oops.

"There was this photographer," I explained. "And he got right in my face and startled me."

But how could that guy have taken this picture? He'd been down on the ground, cleaning coffee off his shoes. Of course: there were two women at the other table. I'd smiled at them. One of them must have caught me with her cell phone.

"Yeah, I know. Elliott told me all about it. It's perfect." Jay tilted his face to the winter sun. He wore aviator sunglasses similar to the ones Rodrigo had loaned me.

"It was an accident," I admitted. "Actually, um . . . I wasn't sure you'd be too pleased."

He slipped down the sunglasses so I could see his eyes. They were light brown, almost gold. "Are you kidding? I couldn't be happier. There was this other coffee . . . incident. With Haley."

I did my best to keep my face neutral, but since Hank had fixed my computer on Monday, I'd spent hours combing the Internet for stories about Haley Rush. The juiciest ones detailed her romance and subsequent breakup with Brady Ellis. (I'd briefly considered using a shirtless photo of Brady as my screen saver, but then I remembered that I wasn't fourteen years old.)

According to "sources," Haley wanted a more serious commitment, while Brady, at twenty-six, felt he was too young to settle down. As he told one unnamed friend, "If we were five years older, we'd probably be engaged by now, but both of our careers are taking off, and it's hard to think about marriage." Plus, Brady was old-fashioned. He only planned to get married once, so he had to be positive he'd found the right girl.

Within days after their publicists announced that Haley and Brady were "taking a break," a photographer caught Brady eating lunch in Santa Monica with an "unidentified blonde." She wore a black baseball hat, big sunglasses, a ponytail and Lycra workout clothes. Frankly, she could have passed for Haley if not for the fact that she was out in public and not having a nervous breakdown.

A week after the photo ran, Haley ordered a caramel latte at the Coffee Bean & Tea Leaf, only to have the barista spill it on her. According to a witness, the barista was setting the cup on the counter when Haley tried to grab it out of her hand. According to the barista, Haley shouted an "epithet." (*The Smoking Gun* got a little more specific: "You fucking moron! What's your fucking problem? *Fuck!*")

Haley burst into tears and stood there howling "like a wounded animal." (It was unclear just how the "unidentified source" knew what a wounded animal sounds like, but—whatever.)

Since the coffee incident, which had happened more than two months ago, in early December, Haley had mostly stayed out of the public eye. And in her pajamas—though the tabloids didn't know that.

"The way you laughed it off," Jay said, getting back to my own coffee encounter. "Priceless. It undoes a lot of damage— shows the world that Haley is back to being Haley."

Did people's perceptions of Haley matter more than reality?

I read the caption again. "How did they know what kind of coffee I was drinking?"

He shrugged. "Everyone knows what kind of coffee Haley likes."

Jay's cell phone sang. He had downloaded yet another one of Haley's songs ("Best Friends 4Ever"). Her voice was really pretty mediocre.

"Hey, Stefano. Yeah, I know—traffic's a bitch." He squinted at my light hair. "Yeah, it looks good." He rolled his eyes. "Yes, a fabulous match. You're a genius . . . Yes, she is . . . Okay, see you in fifteen."

Stefano was coming to Haley's house because the hair extensions would take so long and also—mostly—because Haley needed to have her color done, and she refused to leave the property.

Jay said, "Stefano said you're as sweet as an Atlanta peach picked off the tree in July."

I grinned. "Stefano's a good guy."

"A peach," Jay said, smirking.

"So he'll be here in fifteen minutes?"

"If Stefano says fifteen minutes, he means forty-five. He probably hasn't even left his house yet."

"But didn't he say he was caught in traffic?"

Jay looked at me long and hard. "Do you always assume people are telling you the truth?"

"Unless they give me a reason to doubt them—well, yeah."

He closed his eyes and rested back on the chaise. "That won't last."

Stefano was an hour late. (An extra hundred dollars!) Jay had long since left, but I was still lounging on the dusty backyard chaise, so relaxed I'd almost fallen asleep. The air smelled like orange blossoms and hummed with bees.

"OMG, the traffic!" Stefano scurried across the backyard pavers. His tufted black hair had a new dash of royal blue. He'd paired blue skinny jeans with a Betty Boop T-shirt. I'd never known anyone to coordinate clothes with tattoos—but then, with the exception of a butterfly "tramp stamp" acquired by one first-grade mommy in her misguided youth, my social circle wasn't big on body art.

I stood up from the chaise and blinked into the harsh sunlight. Stefano held out his colorful arms and hugged me like a long-lost (and favorite) sister. He smelled like limes.

When he released me, he took a step back and put his hands on his hips. "Naughty girl. Where's your hat?"

"What hat?"

"The hat that is going to protect your golden hair from those nasty UVs." He *tut-tutted* and shook his head. "You been using the shampoo I gave you?"

"Mm-hm."

"And only washing every three days?"

I nodded, which seemed like less of a lie than actually saying the word *yes*. (I couldn't bear to go more than a day with dirty hair.)

Finally, he gave my face a little pat. "A little pink on the cheeks and nose. You forgot your sunblock, too, didn't you?"

"It's February . . ."

"No excuse. Your two BFFs are sunblock and artificial tanners." So that was the secret to his golden complexion. "And a hat," he added. "So, that's three BFFs. You can never have too many."

Stefano created a makeshift salon in Haley's enormous guest bathroom, which had beige travertine floors, double sinks set in a beige granite countertop, and tall cream walls that really,

really needed some artwork. Stefano hauled in a comfy padded chair ("your throne") and a hair washing basin that fit over one of the sinks.

Stefano started my extensions before Haley's color because they were going to take so much longer and also because I was, you know, awake. He had just finished combing my hair when Esperanza came in, wearing a white tank top and leopard stretch pants, a Bluetooth hugging one ear. I was all set for her to scowl and maybe start squirting disinfectant in the air. Or in my eyes. Instead, she said, "Meester Stefano! I know you in there!"

He said, "Esperanza, *mi amor*!" And then he yapped away for a while in halting Spanish.

Esperanza yapped back. Stefano said something else I couldn't understand, and she giggled. Then he kissed her on both cheeks, gave her a big hug, and complimented her maroon hair. Finally, she scampered out of the room.

"I just adore that woman!" he said.

"Huh," I said.

"Do you know that she is supporting eleven people back in El Salvador? Eleven!"

"Wow." It was hard enough supporting one person besides myself—and, really, with the custody situation, Ben only counted as half. Maybe I had judged Esperanza too harshly.

Stefano pulled out what looked like a small blond animal.

"Is that the hair? For the extensions?"

"Pretty, isn't it?"

"Is it . . . fake?"

He put a hand over his heart. "I'm going to pretend you didn't say that."

"Where does it come from, then?" I asked, not sure I wanted to know.

"Europe. Southern Spain or Italy, most likely. Asian hair is cheaper, but it just doesn't look right. Unless you're Asian, of course. It all comes in black. I colored it last night—same formula I used for Haley's extensions. Luscious, don't you think?"

"I guess."

Once Stefano put the hair and his tools on the bathroom counter, he combed my hair, twisting a section and pinning it on top of my head.

"So. Spill the dirty details. Are you having more fun as a blonde?"

I closed my eyes and concentrated on the feeling of comb against scalp. "Not really. It's kind of embarrassing. Half the people I know think I bleached my hair as some kind of revenge against my ex-husband, and the other half think I did it to impress some man." (Specifically, they thought I was after Ken.) "And I've had at least twenty people say, 'You know who you look like?'"

"Haley?" Stefano ventured.

"Mostly. Though I got two Lindsay Lohans and one Britney Spears." I opened my eyes to check his reaction.

He hooted. "Lindsay, maybe, but Britney? Not even close."

He took some hair from the counter—maybe twenty blond strands held together—and snipped the end. With his other hand, he picked up an unfamiliar appliance. It looked like a cross between a curling iron and pliers.

"That looks dangerous," I joked.

"Only if you don't know what you're doing. It's what I'll use to attach the extensions to your natural hair."

"Attach how?"

He held up the plier thing. "This is heated. The extensions

have wax on the ends. See? So I'll just put the waxy bit up against your natural hair, near the scalp, and pinch with this."

I flinched involuntarily.

"Oh, pumpkin! It won't hurt—I promise!"

"But won't it look funny?" Blond hair was bad enough. The moms at the elementary school would have a field day.

"I'll attach the strands in parallel rows under your crown. No one will see a thing. They'll just think your hair grew nine inches over the weekend."

Stefano had almost finished adding the first chunk of hair when Esperanza returned, carrying a tray. There was a pitcher and two glasses along with a plate of something fried.

"Meester Stefano, I make your favorite."

Stefano held his hand over his heart. "Jalapeño poppers?"

She nodded, beaming.

"OMG, my trainer would kill me!" He plucked a popper from the tray and slipped it into his mouth. "Yum-ME!"

Esperanza giggled with pleasure.

"Did you learn to make those in El Salvador?" I asked.

The giggles stopped. "I from Guatemala," she snarled. She put the tray on the counter—a little closer to the extensions than seemed hygienic—flashed Stefano a demure smile, glared at me, and stalked out of the room.

Esperanza might be supporting eleven people somewhere in Latin America, but she was still a bitch.

"Popper?" Stefano brought the plate over to my chair.

It was really good: a cream-cheese stuffed jalapeño, breaded and fried. "I never knew these came from Guatemala."

Stefano laughed. "Don't be silly. They come from the freezer section at Albertson's."

* * *

The first hour of extensions was downright entertaining, as Stefano told me about coming out as a gay man in upstate New York. ("If you think the NRA is a queer-free zone, you are sorely mistaken. Talk about the ultimate phallic symbol . . .")

I longed to hear more about Haley, but we both understood that it was bad form to gossip about her in her own house. Besides, our voices might travel through the vents.

"You have any good celebrity stories?" I asked him.

"Thousands," he said. "But, tragically, respect for their privacy and my career—but mostly my career—prevents me from repeating them."

By the second hour, we were both kind of worn-out. Normally, Stefano told me, he'd have an assistant helping him, but given the "confidential nature" of the assignment, he was on his own.

By the third hour, it was downright painful.

"My butt hurts," I said. My scalp wasn't feeling so great, either.

"Your butt?" Stefano shot back. "How do you think my fingers feel? And my back?"

"My neck is stiff," I whined.

"So you're saying I'm a pain in the ass *and* a pain in the neck?"

We had a good laugh.

He rubbed my shoulders. "Bear with me, pumpkin. I'm almost done."

That's when Haley chose to make her entrance. "Steeeee-ven?"

"Sugarplum!" He chucked a chunk of hair and the plier thingy on the counter. He might as well have chucked me there, too; that's how invisible I felt. He gathered Haley in his arms, actually lifting her a few inches off the ground.

"Nobody told me you were here," Haley mumbled into his shoulder. In place of a velour track suit, she wore black leggings and two layered tank tops, one pink, one mint green. It was not a good look. And I disagreed with Simone's assessment that Haley was two sizes smaller than me. One, maybe.

Stefano—or was it Steven, after all?—stroked her tangled hair, which was just a few snarls away from being classified as dreadlocks. "You were sleeping, princess. I didn't want to disturb you."

"I've been awake for, like, two hours. Esperanza brought me breakfast. And then I was just lying there. If I'd known you were here . . ."

"Don't you worry, sunshine, we'll get you going right now."

They moved toward "the throne" and stopped dead when they noticed that somebody was sitting in it. She looked vaguely familiar. Who was she again?

"Hi, Haley." I tried to smile.

"Oh," she said.

"Do you want me to, um . . ." I looked at Stefano. "Do you want to finish the extensions later?"

"If you wouldn't mind." He gave me a big, grateful smile that suddenly seemed very fake.

"No problem." *I'm being paid by the hour. That's all that matters.* "I'm getting kind of hungry, anyway. I'll just, you know. Be in the kitchen."

I was a few steps out the door when I heard Haley say, "I don't really get why she's here."

Stefano laughed—louder than he had with me. "You're one of a kind, sweet cheeks. One of a kind."

*   *   *

As I examined the contents of Haley's pantry (multigrain bread, soybean butter, sunflower seeds, herbal tea, protein powder, dried Shitake mushrooms) the urge to call Nina almost overwhelmed me. The only bad part of my new job was the effect it was having on our friendship. Since I couldn't imagine spending a lot of time with Nina without spilling the details of my shadow life, I was basically avoiding her.

The day I'd gone to school with my new blond hair, she'd done a double take in front of the boys' classroom.

"Oh. My. God. Britney Spears!" She came over, mouth and eyes wide, and touched my hair.

I looked at the ground. "It was—you know. I thought—maybe a change . . ."

"I like it!"

"Really?"

"Maybe not forever, but it's sexy. Strong. The new you. Not that there was anything wrong with the old you."

"Hank liked it."

She scowled. "Tell me you're not doing this for Hank."

"Of course not!"

"For Ken?"

"No!"

"Because I heard that the two of you were pretty chummy at the Cub Scout thing."

"Who told you that? Terri?"

She shook her head. "Holly Wert. You don't know her."

"How does she know who I am?"

She shrugged. "She knows Hank, and you're Hank's ex-wife."

"Oh." That made me uncomfortable. "Ken and I are just friends. Seriously."

"If you say so. But the blond hair's hot. I mean it."

"Thanks."

"You want to do something this weekend? I feel like I haven't talked to you in forever. I still owe you a dinner. Maybe we could check out that new Mexican place on Harbor?"

"I can't," I said quickly. "I have . . . there are things I need to get done."

"Oh." Her whole body tightened. "Maybe some other time, then."

"Sure." I forced a smile. "That sounds fun."

Haley's refrigerator offered a better selection than her pantry: baby greens, bottled peppers, barbecued chicken, smoked salmon, a drawer full of cheeses. I toasted a couple of slices of multigrain bread and made myself a chicken sandwich.

I was sitting at the counter when Jay came through the garage. He blinked at me. "Veronica," he said finally.

"Did you think I was Haley?" I put my half-eaten sandwich on the plate.

He shook his head and then tilted it to one side. "No. I was just trying to figure out why your hair looks uneven."

"Because it's not finished." I touched a long bit. "Haley came down while Stefano was working on my extensions, so it just seemed, like, well, she wanted to get her hair done, and Stefano . . ."

"Gotcha." He peered at my plate. "Esperanza make that?"

I shook my head. "She's not here. You want me to make you one?"

"No!" he said, appalled by the thought of food that hadn't been produced in a commercial kitchen or by a domestic worker. "So Haley's . . .?"

"In the guest bathroom."

He nodded and crossed the kitchen. At the door, he turned and said, "Are you doing anything tomorrow?"

For a moment, I thought he was asking me out. "No," I said, surprised to realize that I kinda, sorta liked the idea.

"Because I'd love to get you and Brady together. For breakfast or coffee—something casual."

"Brady Ellis?" Was he serious?

"Nothing romantic," he elaborated. "Just a photo op to show that Haley's over him. That they're friends."

"Brady Ellis," I repeated.

"Yeah. You know—Haley's boyfriend. Ex-boyfriend. Whatever. He's my client, too, and I'm pretty sure he'd be happy to help Haley out. I just need to talk to him first, get him up to speed."

"Breakfast with Brady Ellis," I said, as if the words could make it real.

"Or maybe just coffee. That okay with you?"

I grinned. "Anything to help Haley."

It didn't even occur to me to wonder how Haley would feel about my "date" with Brady until she caught me going through her closet.

"Oh, sorry," I said. "I hope you don't mind that I'm, uh—I like your hair."

It really looked good: long and gold and sleek.

She rolled her eyes up toward her layers and shrugged. "Yeah,

Steven's awesome." It wasn't modesty she conveyed so much as recognition that the hair wasn't really hers.

"So, I guess he's ready for me then?" I asked.

"He said to tell you to give him fifteen. Esperanza just got back. I think she's making him something to eat."

"Okay. Thanks." I started to back out of the closet.

"Did you need something to wear?"

"Well, yeah. Just . . . Jay wants me to go out tomorrow. So I need something casual. But cute. I mean, so *you* look cute in case anyone takes pictures."

She bit her lip and squinted at the mass of clothing.

"It's with Brady," I blurted. "Just breakfast or coffee—something really platonic." My cheeks burned. Haley's face was a complete blank.

I turned my attention back to the overstuffed racks. "Most of these probably won't fit me," I said. "But maybe if you've got some more of your fat clothes?"

That got a reaction. "Simone is such a bitch. Here." She pulled a simple denim sheath off a hanger.

The fit wasn't perfect (my butt was bigger than Haley's), but it was close enough, and Haley dug out a pair of pink cowboy boots that I fell in love with immediately. They hardly hurt at all, at least as long as I didn't try to walk in them. She let me dig through her drawer of costume jewelry. I picked out a silver lariat necklace, dangling earrings, and a chunky pink bracelet.

Haley offered a final touch. "Take Pookie." Pookie was a fuzzy pink koala backpack.

"You think?" I said, reluctantly reaching out.

"Oh, definitely. It's totally me—just sort of fun and goofy, not all boring and grown-up."

"Right," I said. "Sure." Even the girls in Ben's first grade class would think Pookie too juvenile, but what did they know.

Stefano (Steven? I wanted to ask but didn't dare) took about an hour to finish up my extensions, and then he gave me the rundown on their care. I could wash and style them like my regular hair, as long as I was careful. In a few months, they'd have to be readjusted for hair growth. Would I still be pretending to be Haley in a few months? Well—why not?

Stefano acted the same as always: glib, giggling, and adoring. But for me, things had changed. After hearing him gossip about Haley and then seeing the way he fawned over her, I couldn't help but wonder what he really thought.

Was that how Haley felt about everyone?

Chapter Fourteen

When I climbed into Rodrigo's little car Saturday morning, he said, "It's early—you want me to find you a Starbucks?"

"Thanks, but I had coffee at home."

He moved his sunglasses from the back of his head to the front and pulled into traffic. "That's so excellent that you get to meet Brady."

"Yeah, it is. Though I'm kind of, um—" I stopped myself before I could say "freaked out."

Rodrigo caught my blush. "There's nothing to be nervous about. Brady's a genuine person. It's too bad he and Haley couldn't make the relationship work."

"Why'd they break up?" I asked.

He shook his head. "She won't talk about it. I'd actually be really curious to hear his side of the story. Love your hair, by the way. I'm not sure I told you yesterday."

I touched my head. "It feels weird—all these little clumps where the extensions are attached. I got my comb stuck in one this morning."

"Ouch." He turned the radio to an R&B station and hummed along.

Had Rodrigo been stealing some of Haley's happy pills?

I adjusted my trucker hat and slipped on the aviator shades. They'd gotten scratched since the last time I'd worn them, making everything out of my left eye the slightest bit warped.

And then I remembered. "How did your meeting go yesterday? Weren't you talking to somebody about your script?"

He sighed with pleasure. "It was phenomenal. Finally, someone gets me."

"That's wonderful!" It just went to show: if you work hard and you hold on to your dreams, anything can happen.

Eyes on the road, Rodrigo said, "You know, I haven't told anyone this, but I was thinking of just quitting the whole Hollywood scene and going home. That's how bad everyone had made me feel about myself."

"Well, thank goodness you didn't! Does this mean someone bought one of your screenplays?"

He tilted his head this way and that. "We haven't signed anything yet. Which does cause me some anxiety. But they really, really liked the second screenplay. They just want me to modify it a little bit, kind of play up some of the minor characters."

"I'm happy for you," I said.

He looked away from the road three times to check my face for sincerity. "Thanks," he said finally.

As long as we were such good friends, I asked him about

something that had been puzzling me. "Why does Jay dress like such a slob?"

"It's his way of showing people that he's too important to bother with a little thing like personal grooming. Usually it's the writers who dress that way—I never will—but Jay identifies with the creatives."

"Is he really that important?" I asked.

Rodrigo snorted. "Jay's only important for as long as he has Haley."

I thought I'd have a good hour to get dressed at Haley's house before heading out for my hot date—oops, I mean "brief platonic encounter"—but when I walked in the front door, Jay looked up from his laptop and said, "The spray people just called. They should be here in five minutes."

"The spray people?"

"Yeah. So you should probably get changed. There's a bikini waiting for you in the guest bathroom."

I blinked with confusion. "Aren't I going to meet Brady this morning?"

"Yeah, later—that's why we have to get you sprayed now. I pushed breakfast back to noon, by the way. So I guess it's lunch. That should give you time to dry."

Finally I understood. "Are we talking about a spray tan?"

He poked at the keys on his laptop. "What else would we be talking about?"

"But Haley's kind of . . . pale." On her early magazine covers, her skin was always a smooth and even brown, but I'd never seen her looking anything other than sallow.

"I know." Jay hit a final key on the computer as if marking

the end of a crescendo and stood up. "And Simone says that's got to change, especially if Haley's going to insist on wearing pastels. And that means you have to match. We've never used this tanning crew before—hope they're okay. I've got the usual company coming to do Haley later."

"Why not use the same company for both of us?"

His phone rang (sang). He pulled it out of his pocket and frowned at the display.

"Because it would be hard to explain why Haley Rush was pale in the afternoon when she'd been sprayed in the morning. I'll call them back." He hit a button on his phone and stuck it back in his pocket.

"But what if she comes downstairs while I'm getting tanned?"

He snorted. "Sure. That's going to happen." It was nine o'clock in the morning.

"Anything special I need to know?" I asked.

He considered. "Just smile politely—a little shy, a little warm, but not too warm—and don't say anything."

I raised one eyebrow. "What? You don't want me launching into a discussion of the importance of tanning to society?"

His eyes popped open. "Whoah!"

"What?"

"That thing you just did with your eyebrow—raising it. There was a director that wanted Haley to do that for a movie, and she just couldn't make it work. She spent hours in front of the mirror. It's just weird to see you do it."

I flushed with pride. Haley could sing, act, and dance better than I could. And as Simone would never tire of reminding me, she was thinner. But I was the eyebrow-raising champion of the world. Go me.

Jay said, "Just make sure you don't do that around the

paparazzi. Or around the spray-tanning people. Or in public. Or . . . anywhere."

I raised my eyebrow again, higher this time. "I'll try to remember."

It's hard to say which part of the spray tanning was most unpleasant. To start off, there was the bikini issue. I was expecting to find one of Haley's castoffs in the bathroom, but no: the suit still had its Target tags attached. Unfortunately, the tag said, "Size 2." After feeling flattered for about a tenth of a second ("Someone thought I was a 2!"), I had to admit that, one: the suit had been bought for Haley and, two: it was going to be way too revealing in an entirely non-sexy way.

The suit was all white and just the tiniest bit see-through. It rode up so far and was cut so low, it bordered on obscene. There've been gynecologist appointments where I've felt less exposed. Plus, it was still February—not bikini season at all—and let's just say I have some issues with unwanted body hair.

The spray tan people set up a curtained station on a concrete patch in Haley's backyard, off by the pool equipment. Swathed in an oversized beige towel, I scurried out the bathroom, through the house and across the pavers. At least Jay stayed in the house: that was one thing to be thankful for. The thought of exposing my soft flesh to Jay was too mortifying to contemplate. Rodrigo, stationed with his laptop on one of the pool chaises, was a little too close for comfort, but I didn't care as much what he thought about me. Not that I cared so much about Jay's opinion, just—you know.

There were two "tanning therapists." One was male, the other female, and both were extremely buff and incredibly—surprise!—tan. They wore form-fitting black pants and white

T-shirts that said EVERGLOW. Their teeth were bright white, bordering on fluorescent. They both had light eyes, his hazel, hers green, which looked almost spooky against their dark skin. The tan boy was called Matthew. I couldn't quite catch the tan girl's name, but it sounded kind of like Couch.

Matthew said, "It's an honor to meet you, Miss Rush."

Couch said, "Hey, girlfriend, we gotta get you some *color*."

I blessed them with a half-smile and looked at the ground.

"If you could just remove your towel, Miss Rush."

I nodded but continued clutching the terry until the very last moment, when I was surrounded on three sides by black vinyl curtains. I took the towel off and chucked it beyond the tanning station, onto the concrete, taking care not to meet Matthew's or Couch's eyes.

Couch stepped into the semi-enclosure and wrapped my big blond hair with something like Saran Wrap. Or maybe it was Saran Wrap. Then she stepped back and studied me (which was mortifying). "Straps, girlfriend."

"Huh?"

"We don't want you havin' no tan lines." She reached around my neck and undid my bathing suit tie.

I managed to catch the top just in time.

"Now turn around," she instructed, after which she tied my top straps below my arms. It almost (*almost*) would have been better to go topless and just admit that everyone could see everything, anyway.

Matthew was in charge of the application. With a hose and nozzle attached to a bottle of dark liquid, he reminded me of the Terminix guy who sprays the Motts' yard for bugs every three months.

"Just spread your legs a little there . . ." God, that sounded obscene.

He started with my shoulders and worked his way down. I must have looked tense because he said, "Nothing to worry about. We've got moisturizers in the tanning solution, some alcohol and plant extracts. All natural—there's even walnut extract for a more natural brown."

I thought: *natural if you're a tree.*

Next to me, the pool pump, which was on a timer, switched on, emitting a loud whirring noise. I tensed.

"Relaaaax," Couch said from just outside the curtain.

Shut uuuuuup, I thought.

I liked Matthew better. "What makes your skin change color is DHA. That's a natural sugar." He spoke loudly to be heard over the pool equipment. His voice had a singsong quality, as if he had memorized this "here's what we're doing" speech. Which he probably had.

He said, "The DHA reacts with the proteins on your outermost layer of skin. It's that reaction that causes the color change. The DHA works with your natural pigments. So, it's all natural. You can put your arms down now."

I did.

Matthew examined my arms with a puzzled expression. "You did exfoliate this morning, didn't you?"

Huh? I shook my head. I'm not sure I've ever exfoliated in my entire life. I certainly hadn't done it this morning.

Matthew froze. "This is not—maybe—didn't you read—you were supposed to—I guess someone didn't tell you—" So much for the singsong tones.

"The tan might be blotchy," he said.

Clearly, that required some kind of response. "Ugh," I grunted.

"No, it looks good!" Couch piped up from the outer confines of the stall. "Just from looking, I would have guessed you had exfoliated!" She was a terrible liar.

The spraying felt okay, like a slightly damp tickle. The only pain was psychological. Matthew did my shoulders and back, arms, torso, and face (I held my breath). And then it was on to the nether regions.

"In the future?" he said to my hip. "You should probably shave or wax twenty-four hours before your treatment."

Oh, my God. Could I be any more humiliated?

Actually, yes.

"What's really cool about the tanning?" Couch said. "Well, it makes you look all, like, healthy, but you already knew that. But it also minimizes any imperfections. Like blemishes. And, you know. Cellulite."

For once, I was earning my money.

When Matthew was finally, finally done, I lunged for the towel, but he stopped me. "No! You'll ruin your tan!" Remembering his place on the food chain, he added, "Miss Rush."

I must have looked puzzled (or panicked), because he said, "You have done this before, haven't you?"

Until recently, Haley had been known for her perma-tan. I nodded.

"Okay, so um . . . It'll take eight hours for the tan to fully develop. Don't shower until then."

I eyed my brown body with confusion. How much darker was I going to get?

"That's just the guide color," Matthew said, pointing to my (blotchy) brown arm, which, come to think of it, looked more spray-painted than tan. "It'll wash off. The real color needs time to react with your pigment."

Wait a minute. I was going to meet Brady Ellis with the completely fake tan that precedes the kind-of-fake tan?

"Make sure you wear loose clothing today," Matthew said. "But you know that already, right?"

I nodded and tried to control my agitated blinking. Rodrigo was still camped on the pool chaise. Jay was outside now, too, sitting at the big round table, working on his laptop. The table was on the way to the door; there was no way to get inside without passing him.

I ducked back into the curtained enclosure so Jay couldn't see my mouth move. "Do you have a robe?" I whispered.

"What?"

"A robe. Something loose. Just to get me to the house."

"No. Sorry." Matthew looked genuinely sorry.

"You don't need a robe, girlfriend!" Couch piped in. "You look hot!"

"How'd it go?" Jay took off his sunglasses for a better look. It's not like he leered or anything, but the gesture still made me feel naked—which I practically was.

I skittered around to the far side of the table and stood behind a chair. "It was okay. Fine. Good. I should probably get dressed."

"Maybe it's just the light . . ." he said finally. "But the color . . ."

I glanced at my arm. "The tan takes eight hours to fully develop. This is just the temporary color. It'll wash off. But for now it does look a little . . . fake."

"Oh," he said. "Shit."

I can't explain why that made me feel better, but for some reason it did.

"I'm not usually around when Haley gets sprayed," he admitted. "And she doesn't go out much, so it's not usually an issue."

"They didn't say anything when you scheduled?" I asked.

"Rodrigo made the call last night. He always schedules Haley's tans."

Rodrigo was still stationed on a lounge chair next to the pool, hunched over his laptop. I said, "He knew about my date with Brady."

Jay raised his eyebrows.

"I mean, my appointment." I cleared my throat. "I'm surprised he didn't realize the timing would be a problem." Maybe he was so excited about his career news that he hadn't thought about timing problems. Or maybe . . .

"Rodrigo's a prick," Jay muttered.

That seemed unnecessarily harsh.

I edged away from the table. "Okay, then. I'll go change. What should I do with the suit?" It was now more brown than white.

"Just throw it in the trash."

So that explained the tags: Haley would never wear a cheap bathing suit unless it was disposable.

"I didn't think Haley would wear Target clothes," I said.

"She wants to." Jay slipped his sunglasses back on. "She tries to. Or, she used to, anyway. She'd put on a disguise—a wig and sunglasses and a sweat suit or something—and sneak off to a strip mall in Encino. Then, when she wasn't looking, Simone would go into her closet and haul everything away."

"That's terrible!" I put my hands on the table and leaned

forward, my emotions so intense I forgot that I was practically naked.

Jay slipped his sunglasses down on his nose and peered over the rim at my breasts. "Nice."

I straightened and crossed my arms over my chest. "Yeah—if you like orange boobs."

Brady got to Fred Segal first. When I arrived at the blocky, ivy-covered building, wearing the denim dress and shaking in Haley's pink cowboy boots, he was sitting at a shady outdoor table, reading the newspaper and drinking from a tall glass. I stopped in the parking lot, a few paces away, and stole a moment to study him.

His hair was dark brown, almost black, a mass of perfectly messy waves that bordered on ringlets. His skin had a hint of gold just uneven enough to be real. His nose was straight, his lips full, his cheeks clean-shaven. His shoulders were so square they were almost pointy. His forearms, darker brown than his face, were roped with muscle and the tiniest hint of veins.

The hostess stand was outside, under a giant magnolia tree. I didn't even have to say anything: the girl recognized me immediately.

"Right this way." She led me across the brick patio to Brady. Diners glanced up, pausing just long enough to register me as Someone Worth Noticing before going back to their meals.

As I approached the table, Brady looked up from his paper and smiled. My entire body went warm. I'd seen his dimples on TV, of course (that's what the pause button is for), but that was different. Right now, those dimples (the one on the right slightly deeper than the left), his eyes (a bottomless almost-black), and that smile (there are no words . . .) were all directed at me, Veronica Czaplicki!

Well, okay—at me, Haley Rush. But still. I could only hope that no one caught my expression, because there was no way I was looking "over" Brady Ellis.

He put the paper on the table and stood up, staring so intently I dropped my gaze to his muscled-but-not-bulky calves and his brown leather flip-flops.

Brady was shorter than I expected, maybe five foot seven. That meant he was three inches taller than me—perfect dancing (or kissing) height.

Ahem.

"Hey, Hale!" he said. "You look great. I mean that. Thanks for coming."

I looked up at him and froze. Hadn't Jay told him that I wasn't really Haley?

When he saw my expression, he gave me a brotherly hug that lasted maybe three hours less than I would have liked. "Nice to meet you," he whispered in my ear.

I exhaled.

Of course. No wonder he'd been so convincing: he was an actor. Duh. I knew that. I was just a little distracted. I was just . . . *Oh, my God, was this man hot, or what!!* No wonder Haley was so miserable. It was bad enough having Hank walk out. How would it feel to lose beautiful Brady Ellis?

Brady pulled out my chrome-and-wicker chair. It wasn't until I sat down that I realized just how wobbly my legs were.

"Thanks," I said.

"You're welcome." He went back to his seat, which wasn't directly across from me—more like two o'clock to my ten o'clock, both of us slightly angled out to the parking lot, just enough to allow photographers a good shot.

"It's good to see you," he said, his straight, dark, perfectly groomed eyebrows raising just a little bit with humor.

"It's good to see you, too." My heart was beating so fast I could barely sit still.

"Coffee?" A pretty waitress appeared at my side. She had dark bangs falling in her eyes, a butterfly tattoo on her shoulder, and a butterfly ring on her thumb. She wore jeans and a lacy white tank top. In short: she was about five thousand times cooler than I.

"I, um . . ." Damn. What was I supposed to order?

"You probably want a latte," Brady offered.

I nodded, memory kicking in. "With low-fat milk and three shots of caramel syrup," I mumbled.

"I'm really sorry." She sounded really sorry. "But we don't have caramel syrup. Do you like mocha? Or vanilla, maybe?"

Panicked, I looked at Brady. Didn't he know everything about Haley? Apparently not.

"Vanilla," I said. "Please." Oops. I wasn't supposed to say please.

"Are you ready to order?" the waitress asked.

I kept my face pointed down so my voice wasn't too distinct. "Baby spinach salad with egg and lemon." Jay had picked that out from the restaurant's website.

"Can I get a menu?" Brady asked.

Oh, crap. How was I supposed to know what they had when I hadn't even seen the menu yet? No matter: the waitress just said, "Sure," and went away.

I was still wearing Haley's furry pink backpack. I slid it off my arms. Above me, Christmas lights twinkled on a latticed patio cover.

"Pookie!"

I held up the pink koala. "You've met?"

"Oh, yeah." He laughed. "I hate that thing."

Score one for Haley. I stuck the backpack on the brick floor, by my feet.

I leaned over the table to whisper. "The waitress seemed pretty unfazed. Didn't she recognize us?"

"Oh, I'm sure she did. They get a lot of celebs here—they're used to it. Smile."

"Huh?"

Too late: the click came from the parking lot, slightly behind me and to my right. The photographer, a stubble-cheeked Mediterranean-looking guy in basketball shorts, took a few steps forward to get a better shot of my face. I smiled. *Click.*

"One more," Brady told the man. "I was squinting."

Click.

"Got it," the guy said. "Thanks, man."

"Later," Brady said.

"You know him?" I asked when the man had gone.

"Oh, sure," Brady said. "His name's Franco. I called him—told him we'd be here. I called a couple others, too. They should be here soon. Here's the thing about the paps. You treat them right, they'll treat you right. So, you're going out somewhere, you're looking good—you call them up and say this is where I'll be. They get their shots, you get your publicity."

"But what if you don't want your picture taken?"

"You got a good relationship with them, they'll leave you alone if you're out in gym shorts and a baseball hat or whatever."

It's not like his clothes, gray cargo shorts and black T-shirt, were so much dressier than sweats, but they were cut so well, they probably cost more than my nicest dress. Then again, with a body like that, it didn't really matter what he wore.

I twirled a strand of fake blond hair, the situation's fantasy quality making me unusually bold. "I bet you look pretty good in gym shorts,"

A slow smile spread across his face. "I bet you would, too."

The waitress ruined what was turning out to be the best moment of my life by coming back then with two menus and my coffee. Brady ordered a beefsteak sandwich. The waitress said, "*Excellent* choice," in a tone that suggested that a less savvy customer might order something less excellent. The spinach salad, perhaps?

When she left, I took a big gulp of coffee, almost gagging when my sweet-detecting taste buds sent a distress signal to my brain. "This is revolting."

Brady grinned. "Haley usually puts a couple of spoonfuls of sugar in on top of that."

A random waiter appeared at my elbow. "Is something wrong? Would you like something else? I can get you something else."

I shook my head. He scurried away.

Brady leaned forward, chin on hands, and studied me. I mirrored his position. He had a small freckle under his right eye. His eyes weren't black, after all, just an incredibly dark, rich brown. His lashes were as thick and curly as his hair.

In the parking lot, a camera lens glinted in the sunshine.

"Nope," He said finally, leaning back in his chair.

"Nope what?"

He leaned forward so I could hear his almost-whisper. "You don't look like her."

My mouth dropped open. "Do so!"

"Maybe a little," he conceded.

I leaned forward so he could hear me whisper. "Don't go saying that to Jay, or I could be out of a job."

He touched my cheek. I froze, fearful that any movement might make him take his hand away. He took it away anyhow but kept looking into my face. I've never been hypnotized, but I'd guess this is what it feels like.

Finally, he leaned back into his chair, bit his lip, and looked up, thinking. "This is going to sound obnoxious," he said at last. "But people have always noticed my looks. Even when I was a kid, I was just really . . ."

He looked to me to finish the sentence. I tilted my head to one side and kept my mouth shut.

"Not ugly." He rolled his eyes with self-deprecation.

"Really?" I raised one eyebrow and then immediately pulled it down when I remembered Jay's warning.

"Hard to believe, I know." There were those dimples again.

"So I guess," he continued, "well, it's not like I don't notice if someone's attractive. I mean, Haley—the minute I saw her I was like, *wow*."

And he didn't think I looked like her? Damn.

"But the thing is, I'm so used to people judging me by my looks. Some people like me because of them. Other people don't like me because of them. Because of that, I think I get beyond the exterior faster than other people."

"Gotcha." Sort of.

He continued, "So on the outside, yeah, you and Haley could be twins. But I saw beyond her outside a long time ago. It's inner beauty that counts for me, you know?" He squinted and leaned forward. "I could swear your skin has gotten darker just in the time we've been sitting here."

"Oh, God." I held out an airbrushed arm. "Does the tan look fake? Because it is."

He threw back his head and howled with laughter.

"What?" I demanded. "You're a Hollywood actor. Surely you've seen a fake tan before."

"All the time. Only no one ever admits it. They're always like, 'I was up in Malibu for the weekend.' Or, 'I spent a lot of time outdoors when I was in Cannes.' It's just, I don't know, cool that you'd be so honest about it."

"Well, you know, I have a lot of inner beauty."

"I'm sensing that. You've got a lot of outer beauty, too."

The waitress brought our food. I couldn't eat a bite.

Chapter Fifteen

Monday morning, I was late for my subbing assignment in Mrs. Largent's first-grade class (Shaun Mott couldn't find one of his sneakers, which turned out to be under the couch, approximately sixteen inches from his other sneaker), but when I saw Nina standing outside the door, arms crossed, it was clear I'd be even later.

The first-graders were lined up outside Mrs. Largent's door. I directed them into the classroom and told them to spend five minutes on their independent reading. They filed in serenely and pulled books from their desks. Mrs. Largent had trained them well.

I turned my attention back to Nina, forced a smile and thought, *Please don't say anything about my hair.* I'd pulled it back to minimize the impact of the extensions, but it still seemed a little, well, trashy. Besides that, it looked like I had just spent a week on a beach in the Bahamas. As promised, the tan had finally come in. It looked good and only a little bit fake (a real tan wouldn't be so even), but I still felt self-conscious. When Jay had told me he wouldn't be needing me to do any double work for the entire week, I tried really, really hard to wash the brown off my skin. It had faded, but not enough.

So far, it had all been for nothing, at least from a press standpoint. As of Sunday night, my relentless Google searches had turned up no shots of Brady and me.

But Nina didn't say anything about my appearance. Instead, she cleared her throat, tilted her chin up, and said, "Terri asked me to ask you if Ben is coming to Tyler's birthday party this weekend."

"Tyler's—what?"

"His birthday party. The invitation said to RSVP no later than last week, but Terri said she hasn't heard from you." Why was Nina looking at me like this?

"I never got an invitation."

"Everyone else got theirs."

"Well, I didn't." And then I understood: "I bet she sent it to my old address."

Her face relaxed with forgiveness. "You're probably right. Can he make it?"

"Saturday? I guess so. What time?"

"Noon. It's kind of a drop-off party, but adults can stay if they want. John's going to do hamburgers and hot dogs, and Terri's got this big treasure hunt planned in the backyard. It's a pirate theme. She got a refrigerator box, and she's turned it into a ship. Last night she stayed up till one o'clock making telescopes out of paper towel rolls."

"Cute." I tried to sound sincere, but Nina caught a whiff of sarcasm.

"Oh, please. Who has that kind of time? I told Terri that when a woman starts making pirate ships and telescopes, it's time to either get a job or have an affair." Now she was sounding more normal.

"Tell Terri I'm really sorry—I mean, I'll tell her myself, just if you see her first."

"So, you're going to stay for the party, right? It feels like I haven't talked to you in ages. Besides, I want to hear about your new job and your trip to, uh . . ." She tapped my arm and smirked. "Bali?"

"Bali is so last year," I joked. "I got this tan in another, less populated South Sea island."

She snickered and kept smiling until I got back to the subject of Tyler's birthday. "The party sounds fun, but I have some stuff I need to do on Saturday," I said. "So I think I'll just drop Ben off."

Her face shut down. "Oh. Right. Well, happy teaching."

"Sure. Thanks."

Although Ben was in first grade, he had a different teacher, and I had never been inside Mrs. Largent's classroom. The little chairs were arranged in tables of five or six. Butterfly paintings hung from a cord strung across the room. The walls were covered with students' labored printing and yet more artwork.

If I could teach any grade, I'd pick first. The kids are so cute and still excited about learning. Plus, they're funny. They say exactly what they think.

Like a little girl wearing a *Kitty and the Katz* T-shirt: "Mrs. Czaplicki, you look just like Haley Rush! Do you know who Haley Rush is? She's on my favorite show!"

"I do know who she is," I replied. "Other people have told me I look like her, too!"

Or, from a little boy with squeaky sneakers: "Why are your legs lighter than your face?"

"My—what?"

In an effort to counteract my hair and tan, I had outdone myself in putting together a boring outfit: a white blouse and a knee-length khaki skirt.

"Not your whole legs," he said. "Just the bottom part."

Twenty faces turned to stare. All weekend, I'd been watching the progress of my face and my blotchy arms. Since Haley's denim dress didn't qualify as loose, I'd thought it would rub the color off my torso, but that tan had held up surprisingly well. Not that it mattered; no one was going to see my bare tummy, anyway.

I hadn't gotten a really good look at my legs. My little house was kind of dim, and on Sunday I'd worn long pants. But now, under the fluorescent lights, I bent down, and—oh, no. Each leg had a line below the knee that demarcated the light and dark zones. Damn pink cowboy boots.

I cleared my throat and pasted a stern expression on my face. "It is not nice to stare at other people. It is not nice to point out ways in which other people are different."

Twenty little mouths gasped. Twenty little faces folded in shame. Forty little eyes shot away from my legs.

I love first-graders.

Mrs. Largent (who was out for "elective surgery"—though no one seemed to know what that meant) had left a detailed lesson plan. The kids spent twenty minutes using pinto beans (uncooked) to practice addition. We talked about their observations for ten minutes, and then they spent fifteen minutes writing equations on paper. I loved the way they held their pencils, so awkward and yet so reverent. I loved the way they stuck out their tongues in fierce concentration as they attacked double-digit numbers.

Sometimes when Ben was with Hank, I would leaf through old photo albums. When Ben was tiny, I had an ill-advised romance with scrapbooking, which meant that I'd sacrificed a lot of photo space for fancy-edged papers, glossy stickers, and the inane ramblings of a sleep-deprived mother. ("Benji used to cry when I put him in the bath, but now it's his favorite time of day! *Splish-splash, splish-splash!* Don't forget your duckie, sweetheart!")

When I'd page through the albums, I'd ignore all that silliness and just focus on Ben's face from a year or two ago, before his toddler softness had begun to melt away. And then, inevitably, I'd cry: not because I wouldn't see him for a day or two (though that didn't help) but because the simple passage of time meant I was losing my little boy, and there was nothing I could do about it.

Maybe that, really, is what I loved about teaching little kids. You helped them and loved them and watched them grow, but when they left you, a new crop came in to take their place. Time stood still. Innocence endured.

At ten-thirty I took the kids out to the blacktop for physical education. Mrs. Ortega was ready with piles of blue plastic jump ropes.

"Hey there, Mrs. Czaplicki!" she said a little too loudly. (Mrs. Ortega said everything a little too loudly.) Around us, kids began jumping rope, the sound like whips on pavement.

"Did you see that picture on the Internet this morning?" Mrs. Ortega's voice boomed.

"Uh, no." The Internet was a big place. She was going to have to be a little more specific.

"That Haley what's-her-face. You know the one I mean? From that kids' show? There was a picture of her at a café with some guy. When I saw it, I was like—what's Mrs. Czaplicki's picture doing on the Internet?" She laughed (loudly).

I said, "I'll have to check it out."

She bent over and squinted. "For a minute, I thought your legs had lines on them. But it must just be the shadow from your skirt."

"Must be." I smiled pleasantly. And then I practically sprinted back to the classroom.

I'd kept my cell phone turned off all morning. There was a message from Jay: "Don't know if you saw the press this morning. Call me."

Did he sound happy? Annoyed? Or just neutral?

"Hi, Jay." I sat at Mrs. Largent's desk and fiddled with a yellow pencil.

"Veronica."

"Hi." The pencil point jabbed my finger.

"Have you seen your picture today?"

"Um. No." I put the pencil down.

"It's online. Your publicist—I mean, Haley's publicist—said *Us Weekly* is planning to run it in its next issue."

"I guess that's . . . good?"

He was quiet for so long I thought we'd lost the connection. Finally he spoke. "Do you want to know the picture caption?"

"Of course." I picked up a pink eraser and squeezed it tight.

" 'Is the Romance Back On?' " he read.

148 Carol Snow

"I guess that's not the angle you were going for," I said. And then, in my defense: "We were just talking."

"While gazing longingly into each other's eyes."

I stopped squeezing the eraser. "Excuse me?"

"That's what it says. *'Pop princess Haley Rush and supposedly former flame Brady Ellis grabbed a bite at Fred Segal Melrose while gazing longingly into each other's eyes.'*"

"You can't go out to lunch with someone without making eye contact."

"You're both leaning over the table so far, it almost looks like you're making nose contact."

"Oh." I was screwed.

"Plus there's a shot of you hugging hello or good-bye. You've got that stuffed dog on your back."

"It's a koala."

He sighed. "Haley's publicist was thrilled."

"She was?" I perked up.

"Of course, she thought it was really Haley in the picture. She's going to release a statement from Haley saying that she loves Brady deeply as a friend but at this time their relationship remains platonic."

"Did Haley really say that?"

"What do you think? Anyway, like I told you, Haley's got some recording sessions scheduled this week, so we need you to lay low."

"What do you mean?" I'd already been seen by at least a hundred people that morning, maybe more.

"Stay out of L.A."

"Oh! I can do that."

"And keep next week open. Maybe we'll send you out for Pinkberry. Or maybe . . ."

"What?"

"It might not be a bad idea to set you up with Brady again. For coffee or shopping or something."

"I'll keep my week open!" I said helpfully.

There was another message on my phone. It was from Hank.

"Hey, Roni. I was just going through a pile of mail on my desk and there's this birthday party invitation that got forwarded from our old address. For Ben. It's coming up—Saturday, I think—at the what's-its, the Shefflers. It's already past the RSVP date, so you might want to call what's-her-name, Terri, and tell her if you can make it.

"Sorry I didn't tell you earlier. But I'm sure it will all work out."

Chapter Sixteen

Hank was always sure that everything would work out,
which, unfortunately, wasn't the same as making sure that
everything worked out.

Nowadays, he said, "It will all work out" when he forgot to
send in Ben's permission slips or pass on phone messages. When
we were married, he said it when his business was too slow to
cover our monthly bills. But most memorably, "It will all work
out" was what he said when I told him I was pregnant.

It was early February. A Sunday. We had been dating for four
months.

It had been raining for days; television news reports featured
mud slides and car wrecks. Water seeped in around the edges
of Hank's drafty little two-bedroom house. The backyard, all
lawn, looked like a swamp.

The television was turned to CNN. Hank was sitting on a

backless brown stool at the kitchen counter, reading the sports section of the *Orange County Register* and slurping coffee out of a Disneyland mug. Disneyland was only five miles from his house, so close we could hear the fireworks at night as we lay in Hank's lumpy queen-sized bed. Hank went to bed at nine o'clock each night, so when I spent the night, I did, too.

We had never been to Disneyland together. A few years later, when Ben was two, my parents gave us annual passes for Christmas, and we'd hit the theme park every Sunday for two months until we both admitted we hated the place. But I didn't know that then.

All I knew was that the pregnancy stick I'd bought at Long's Drugs had two lines instead of one, and that second line meant that my life was about to change forever.

Hank's kitchen was dark but functional: a long orange Formica counter, dark brown cabinets that reached to the ceiling, a brown stove, a brown refrigerator, a big yellow sink with a window that looked out to the bare backyard. There was no room for a dishwasher, but the kitchen—in fact, the whole house— was such a step up from my shared college apartment that it felt like a palace.

There are things I hadn't told Hank. That I had lost my taste for coffee weeks earlier. That my breasts were tender. That my abdomen ached with what felt like menstrual cramps, but that never yielded any blood.

I had never told him I loved him. But I did. Didn't I?

Pulse racing, I crossed the tan linoleum to the counter. Hank glanced up from his paper, gave me a fond smile, and rubbed my arm once before reaching for his coffee cup.

The pregnancy stick was still in my hand. I considered placing it on the counter in front of him. That would be dramatic.

But since it was covered in my urine, it would be gross, too. I kept it in my hand.

"I have something to tell you."

He looked up from his paper and smiled neutrally. He didn't look concerned or worried—as if nothing I could say could affect him all that much. Since the night at the bar, Hank and I had spent a lot of time together—at least four nights a week—but the relationship continued to have an easy-breezy feel. We had passed the two big holidays, Thanksgiving and Christmas, without either of us suggesting that we spend them together.

When Hank saw that I was tense and borderline teary, he tilted his head to one side, furrowed his brow, and encircled my waist. "Something wrong?"

"I'm pregnant," I blurted. I held up the stick in case he needed proof, but he barely even looked at it. Instead, he stared at me, as if checking my expression for any indication that I might be joking.

When he didn't say anything, I felt compelled to fill the silence. "I don't know how it happened. I know they say that no protection is a hundred percent reliable, but we were so careful. This is just—this is so not in the plans."

I would graduate in a few months. After that, I would teach for a couple of years, get married, and teach for a couple more. Then, and only then, was I supposed to have a baby.

I needed Hank to know that I hadn't gotten pregnant on purpose. That I wasn't trying to trap him.

"I don't know what to do." In a rush, the tears came. He jumped up from the stool, the wooden legs shrieking against the floor. He took me in his arms and held me tight.

"*Shh*," he whispered into my ear. "*Shh*."

"I just don't know what to do," I sobbed again.

"It's okay," he murmured. "It will all work out."

I didn't have the vaguest idea what he meant by that, but for some reason it made me feel better.

And it did work out—at least in the short term. Hank didn't propose marriage so much as suggest it. And I didn't accept so much as agree.

We were married in Hank's backyard on March seventeenth. After a rainy winter, the ground was still soggy, but at least the skies were clear. A For Sale sign hung in front of the house. We'd already put in an offer—well, Hank had, anyway—on a brand-new twenty-one-hundred-square-foot, three-bedroom model across town.

We commissioned a cut-rate caterer to provide hors d'oeuvres and cake. Thinking it was a St. Patrick's Day party, the caterer brought a green cake decorated with candy shamrocks. I was upset for maybe thirty seconds before I realized how appropriate it was: nothing quite works out the way you plan it. I wished I'd told Susy and Ellen, my maids of honor, to wear green instead of "whatever you want." They wore black.

My parents, trying their hardest to look pleased, came down from northern California. Hank's sister and her husband flew in from Colorado, and his mother drove in from Redlands. His father had died years earlier.

Hank's brother-in-law was the only relative who really seemed to enjoy himself. He got drunk on green beer (one of my friends brought the dye) and said, "I always said, the only way Hank was ever gonna get hitched was if he got some girl in trouble!"

Otherwise, ours was just your basic, low-budget, backyard wedding. Music played from a boom box, but no one danced.

Friends took photographs, and some remembered to give me copies. One of Hank's friends from high school—a big, bald guy with a goatee whom everyone called Jacko (even though his name was Daryl)—flirted outrageously with pretty Susy. Out of earshot, she howled with laughter and said, "Ew, he's old!"

Later, when everyone was gone, Hank carried me over the threshold—otherwise known as "the back door."

"Gettin' a little heavy there, missy."

"It's all baby weight," I responded, a running joke throughout the pregnancy. (If my weight gain had indeed been all baby, Ben would have weighed forty pounds at birth.)

"And that's missus to you," I added.

He grinned. "I'll try to remember that." He set me down gently.

"I wish you could have had the marriage of your dreams," he said—a Freudian slip for the ages. "I mean, the wedding."

"I loved my wedding. It was perfect."

"You're right. It was."

All at once, I was filled with happiness. Hank was kind and gentle, playful and good-looking. He had a steady job. He had bought me a house. In the fall, when we had our new baby, we would truly be a family. Things were happening faster than I might have liked, but in the end I was getting everything I had ever wanted out of life. Hank was right: it had all worked out, after all.

Six years later, Hank would marry Darcy at the Ritz Carlton in Dana Point. There would be exotic flowers, a string quartet, and gallons of champagne. Ben, dressed in a tiny blue suit, would be the ring bearer.

But I didn't know that then.

Chapter Seventeen

"Sorry Brady couldn't be here instead of me," Jay said later that week, handing me a little cardboard cup filled with Pinkberry frozen yogurt. He'd gotten me Haley's favorite: original flavor, topped with pineapple.

"You mean, you asked him?" Too late, I realized he'd been joking and that my quick, desperate response made me look like an idiot.

"Ha-ha, funny," I added, oh-so-cleverly.

We put our yogurts on a retro-cool white plastic table away from everyone else and sat in matching green Lucite chairs. Around us, the walls glowed orange. Someone in line did a double take; otherwise, people ignored us.

Jay pulled out his phone and pushed a couple of buttons. "We're here, but we're alone." He swept the room and the entrance with his eyes. "So call them *again*."

The call over, he placed his phone on the table, right next to his yogurt. "Damn Rodrigo."

"What?"

"A couple of paps were supposed to be waiting when we got here." He shook his head. "Oh, well. Maybe someone will catch us with a cell phone camera."

I was wearing the white miniskirt again (the dry cleaners had removed the coffee stain), along with an artfully faded green tank top (chosen to stand out against the orange walls), big sunglasses, and tan cowboy boots. Simone had proclaimed that cowboy boots would be Haley's signature item, which was unfortunate since all ten pairs pinched my toes.

"Do you have Pinkberry where you live?" Jay asked.

"Yes," I said. "We have cable TV and running water, too."

"Testy."

"Just trying to channel you-know-who," I said, though we both knew I was still annoyed about the Brady comment. "Why does she like this stuff, anyway? It's expensive and it tastes bad." With my precious little spoon, I added a speck of pineapple to a speck of tart yogurt.

Jay scooped up a bit of green tea yogurt (no topping) with his own teeny tiny spoon. "Partly, I think she just enjoys sending people out to get things for her. But also, she's got a major sweet tooth, and it's one of the few desserts low enough in calories for her to have."

"But it's not even sweet."

"She adds sugar."

"Why not just let her have ice cream? Or even normal frozen yogurt? Would it be so terrible if she gained five or ten pounds?"

"Yes."

I curled my lip in disgust.

"Try not to gaze at me with too much adoration," Jay said dryly. "We wouldn't want to give people the wrong idea."

No mention of our outing turned up in the press, and Jay didn't call again until the next Friday.

"Do you have your son this weekend?" he asked.

"No, he's with my ex-husband."

"Do you have any plans?"

"My landlord is having a Pampered Chef party tomorrow afternoon, and I told her I'd go."

"A—what? Never mind. How'd you like to have a sleepover with Haley tonight?"

"Excuse me?"

"A sleepover. Slumber party? Whatever you girls call it. It would be a good opportunity for you and Haley to bond. You can watch movies, do each other's hair. You know—girl stuff."

"Um . . . okay." This was weird. But it was work, and work was good. "Will anyone else be there?"

"No. Rodrigo normally stays over Friday and Saturday nights—Esperanza's there during the week—but he has a conflict. A meeting. Something." He dropped all attempt at lightness. "He didn't tell me what it was, and I don't really give a shit. I was supposed to meet him here at three to go over some issues, and he called me fifteen minutes ago and said he wasn't going to make it. Like it was no big deal. And I have a previous commitment—he fucking *knows* I have a previous commitment—and it's already two o'clock and . . . "

"You want me to babysit!" Now I got it.

"No!" he said. "Just, Haley gets lonely and—"

"She needs a babysitter."

He was silent for a moment. I wished I could take my words back; I didn't want to jeopardize my job.

"Please don't use that term in front of her."

An hour later, "my" driver—the one with questionable immigration status—showed up at a park down the street from the Motts' house. I didn't want to leave my van in the strip mall parking lot overnight; nor did I want Deborah Mott to see me climbing into a Town Car. We endured two hours in traffic before finally reaching the Gates of Haley.

Haley opened the door. She was in her pajamas already—or maybe she had never gotten dressed. Her pants were pale blue with white clouds, and her baggy white T-shirt said, I ONLY LOOK INNOCENT. Her wild blond hair was pulled back in a messy ponytail, and a smudge of something white ran across her cheek.

"Hey." She lifted up a big bottle of red Gatorade as if making a toast and took a swig that left a red mustache above her lip.

"Hi," I said.

"Esperanza and I have been making muffins."

"That's nice." So far, we were bonding beautifully.

I left my overnight bag by the front door and followed her into the kitchen. Esperanza stood over the sink, washing a glass bowl. The air smelled full and sweet. Esperanza looked up from her work and gave me the friendliest, warmest smile. I beamed back— she liked me, after all!—and said, "Something smells delicious!"

Too late, I realized the smile had been intended for Haley. Esperanza scowled at me and went back to her work.

I opened the big refrigerator. I was really thirsty, and there was no way I'd ask Esperanza to get me anything.

"What are you looking for?" Haley asked, scratching her nose and leaving yet another flour mark.

"Something to drink. Water's fine." I took a green bottle and shut the door.

"There's orange soda in the pantry. Ginger ale, too, I think."

"Really?" I'd missed them the other day. Ginger ale sounded really good right now. I started to walk toward the large closet.

"Not that pantry," Haley said. "The good one." She pointed to a tall cabinet next to the refrigerator.

The good pantry did indeed have orange soda and ginger ale. Also: grape soda, Dr Pepper, Yoo-hoo (Yoo-hoo!), Bugles, Ruffles, Cheetos (regular and hot), Twinkies, Chips Ahoy, Double Stuf Oreos, Ring-Dings, Cap'n Crunch, Reese's Puffs, Pop-Tarts, and a giant plastic canister of red Twizzlers. My blood sugar spiked just looking at it all.

I pulled out a can of ginger ale.

"I buy those M&M's you ask for, Miss Haley," Esperanza said. "You see them?"

"Yeah. I think I'll have some." Haley rifled through the cabinet and pulled out a big brown bag, which she ripped open before even closing the door.

She caught my eye. "I'm not, like, bulimic or anything."

"I didn't think that!" Of course I did.

"I just like knowing it's here. In case I want it." She reached into the bag, took out a big handful, and shoved the candies into her mouth.

"Sure." I nodded. In an attempt to sound convincing, I added, "I always keep some treats on hand for my son. Cookies or chips or something. Of course, I'm the one who usually ends up eating it all."

She swallowed, her hand frozen in midair, ready to plunge back into the bag at any moment. "You have a son?"

I nodded. "Ben. He's six."

"Can I see a picture?"

"Um, sure."

My purse was by the front door, next to my overnight bag. I pulled Ben's first-grade portrait out of my wallet. It wasn't a great shot: his smile looked more like a grimace, and his usually spiky hair was flat on one side. Still, the image made me smile and ache at the same time. Ben would be eating dinner at Casa Darcy right around now, or maybe they'd all gone out to the Claim Jumper, Ben's favorite restaurant. Every time Ben told me about the places he went with Hank and Darcy—the baseball games, the theme parks, the restaurants—I felt envious: if only I could do those things with him, too. But I felt grateful, too, because Ben wouldn't be cheated out of the experiences that his classmates took for granted and that I couldn't afford.

"Here he is." Back in the kitchen, I put the photo on the counter because Haley's hands still had flour on them. "He's got this whole fake-smile thing going on right now. I hope it's just a phase."

She leaned over the image and stared at it for longer than I would have expected. "He doesn't look like me," she said, finally.

I blinked at her. "Um . . ."

"I mean, like you," she said. "I just thought that maybe . . ."

"Oh, right. Of course. He looks like his father."

"You're married?"

"Divorced."

She nodded as if that were the expected answer and studied the picture some more. "I want to have a whole bunch of kids someday. When I grow up."

Was she joking? No: her expression was sincere and wistful. Haley had been in show business since she was nine—younger than Shaun Mott. Instead of growing up too fast, maybe she had never grown up at all.

Later, after Esperanza had left and Haley had eaten two chocolate chip muffins and half the bag of M&M's, she sat on a stool and stuck a bare foot on the counter. Not surprisingly, considering how her boots pinched, her feet were narrower and more sharply angled than my slightly squared models.

"You want to paint our toes?" she chirped.

"Um, sure." This really was a slumber party.

She left her empty Gatorade bottle on the counter and pulled another half-empty one (blue, this time) from the fridge. I scored another room-temperature ginger ale.

Upstairs, on her knotty pine dresser, she had the polishes already laid out: pink, red, black, peach, silver, blue, green—you name it, she had it.

I reached for a muted rose that looked like every nail polish I had ever bought.

She snatched it from my hand. "Too boring!"

I was taken aback for just an instant before I realized that she was right. I chose a deep, blood red.

"Better," she said. "This one'll help you get in touch with your inner whore."

I forced a laugh. "I don't think I have an inner whore."

"Of course you do. Everyone does. Let's see. Jay? That's easy. He whores himself for money. Rodrigo whores himself for success—or he tries to, anyway. For Esperanza, it's all about steady work. Simone's a total whore. She'll do anything as long as she can control people. And Brady whores himself for everything."

I decided to let that one pass.

"And how about you?" I asked.

Her face turned sad. She took a long drink of her blue Gatorade and wiped her mouth with the back of her hand.

"I keep trying to whore myself for love," she said finally. "But it doesn't seem to be working."

We climbed onto the log bed and took turns doing each other's toes while listening to rap and R&B from a portable Bose iPod player; she'd given up on the sound system.

"This is fun!" she said, lounging against a mass of throw pillows (and a few stuffed animals) as I painted her pinky toe.

"It is!" I fake-agreed. It would have been fun if I'd been thirteen. Or if Haley's mood swings weren't quite so disturbing. Or if I were drinking wine instead of soda.

She began to sing along to the music, her voice low and mournful.

"You sing really well," I said, sounding more surprised than I'd intended.

"That's not what the critics say."

"You can't listen to them." (Note to self: Google "Haley Rush music reviews.")

She stared at the ceiling. "The last time I did a concert—this was like a year, a year and a half ago—this total dick wrote, 'Probably half of the preteens in the audience can sing as well as, if not better than, Miss Rush.'"

"That's just stupid." Pinky toe finished, she shifted her weight and presented the other foot. She pulled a lavender unicorn from among the pillows and held it to her chest.

"I was so psyched when they told me I was going to cut a CD. I never really cared about acting, you know? But my whole life I dreamed of being a singer. But then they made me sing these fucking songs I didn't even fucking like. And they were way too high and fast for my voice, and . . ."

She chucked the unicorn across the room. My hand slipped; cotton candy pink polish smeared over her toe, but she didn't seem to notice.

"They were right, the critics. The *fuckers*. My voice did sound whiny and thin." She forced a smile. "Usually it's good to be called thin."

"Maybe next time you can do the kind of music you like." I painted her toes quickly, sloppily.

"Do you want to hear a song I wrote?" Toes unfinished, she scrambled off the bed and retrieved an acoustic guitar from a stand in the corner. Back on the bed, she adjusted her body around the instrument and began to play.

The tune was a little bland. The lyrics (*When you look at me / You see what you want to see / Why can't you let me be / The me I need to be*) were not the most original. But Haley's music had a simple, mournful, heartfelt vibe entirely missing from her pop tunes.

When her final chords lingered in the air, I asked, "Will that be on your next CD?"

"Nope." She slid off the bed and placed the guitar back on its stand.

"Why not? It's really good."

"Because it will not appeal to my fucking *demographic*." She downed the rest of her Gatorade in one angry gulp.

"How do you know? They might love it."

"That's what I said!" Oh, God—was she going to cry?

"But it's your CD. Don't you get to decide?"

"It's not my CD." Her voice was flat now. "It'll have my name and my picture on it, but it's not mine. But the money's good, and that's all that matters, right? Do you have any more pictures of your son?"

"What?" The sudden change in subject confused me. "Not on me, no."

"Oh." Her face darkened: she was thinking about her career again.

"There are some pictures of Ben online, if you want to see them. His Cub Scout troop has a website. Do you have a computer?"

She retrieved a big Mac laptop and booted it up. The Cub Scout website's photo section included a shot of Ben taken during the night hike at the Brea Dam. He was standing next to Ken, both of their faces slightly bleached by the flash, the background black.

"Is that his dad?" Haley asked.

"No, his dad wasn't there, so my friend Ken took him on the hike."

"Is he your boyfriend?"

"Ken? Oh, no. People keep thinking there's something between us because we're both divorced, but we're just too different. He's really outdoorsy, and I'm really . . . indoorsy."

"He's cute." She leaned closer, looking a little too interested for my comfort.

"Yeah, I guess. But we just don't have anything in common, plus he's got primary custody of his three boys, so he doesn't have much time." Single parenthood was a major turnoff for every guy I'd met; presumably it would work the same magic on Haley.

Or not.

"Boys?" Her voice turned dreamy. "I love little boys. They're so cute and funny and cuddly. What are their names?"

I cleared my throat. "Brice, Powell, and Arches."

"Oh, my God—those names are fucking awesome." She put a hand on either side of the screen, as if it could bring her closer to Ken.

She said, "If I ever have a son, I'm going to name him Caden. I used to think Aidan, but I like Caden better. And if I have a girl I'll name her Britney. Because I think it's important to have a strong role model."

"You wanna watch a movie?" I asked, desperate to change the subject.

It worked. Haley shut down the computer and happily led me downstairs.

I had missed Haley's screening room on my earlier visits. It was at the end of a long hallway, past the guest room. And it was really, really cool, with three rows of red velour armchairs (with built-in cup holders), vintage movie posters (some of them signed), and a TV screen twice the size of Darcy's biggest set. Red velvet drapes on either side of the screen made the room feel like a miniature old-time theater, as did the glass concession stand and old-fashioned popcorn-maker.

"Twizzlers? Dots? Milk Duds? Reese's?" Haley, perky again, stood behind the counter. "The popcorn machine's busted."

I accepted a box of Twizzlers, along with a can of Diet Coke from a mini fridge next to the broken popcorn maker.

"I wanted a soda machine," she told me, popping open a Mountain Dew, the radioactive yellow liquid spraying her I JUST LOOK INNOCENT T-shirt. "But they said I couldn't have one because there's no water line in here. Sucks."

"Does," I agreed.

"I'm gonna get ice from the kitchen. You want some?"

"No, thanks."

"How about a straw? I've got the bendy kind."

"This is fine. Really."

I half-hoped (okay, whole-hoped) that Haley would choose one of her own movies so I could see beautiful (and non-whore-like—she just said that because she'd been hurt) Brady Ellis on the big screen. Instead, we watched Jennifer Garner in *13 Going on 30* because some website said it was the ultimate slumber party movie. I had to keep reminding myself that Haley was twenty-two and not twelve.

What had Brady ever seen in her? What in the world did they talk about?

By the time the movie was over, I'd polished off the entire package of Twizzlers and was feeling mildly ill. Haley kept an icy cup of Mountain Dew in one hand and a succession of candy bars in the other.

"I wish I could meet a guy like that," Haley sighed, as the credits rolled.

"You can probably meet that very guy," I said referring to the movie's romantic lead. "He probably lives in L.A. Of course, he could be married."

"I'm not talking about the *actor*," she said. "I'm so sick of actors. They're so fake and full of themselves. What I mean is, I wish I could meet a real guy. Somebody normal who's not into designer clothes and facials and all that shit."

I took a small bottle of water from the mini fridge and tried to keep my voice casual. "Brady seemed pretty normal." (For a superhuman sex god.)

"Oh, Brady. He's just. You know. Whatever."

"Right." (You are useless, Haley. Useless!)

I fished a little more: "But I guess the two of you just didn't quite . . . I mean, it wasn't exactly . . ."

She looked at me with the kind of blankness that can't be faked.

"It didn't work out between you." When she still didn't respond, I moved on to more immediate concerns. "We should probably have dinner."

"This is dinner." Haley put her drink in her chair's cup holder and ripped open a package of Reese's (her fourth or fifth—I'd lost count). "What do you want to watch next? I was thinking either *Legally Blonde* or *27 Dresses*."

"Either sounds good, but I really need some food."

She held out the orange package. "Have a Reese's. They have peanut butter."

"Do you have anything more substantial?"

"Sub . . . I don't know what that means."

"Like—real food? I could make a sandwich, maybe."

"No bread. Jay threw it all away. Without asking me. Because Simone said I was getting fat. Jay can be a real dick sometimes. And Simone is always a dick. She has cool accessories, though." She shoved the rest of the peanut butter cup in her mouth and continued to talk with her mouth full. "Esperanza bought all this stuff this afternoon. I love Esperanza."

"Well, maybe I'll just go see what you have. I just need some real food."

Her face lit up with excitement. "Let's go get some Pinkberry!" She started laughing, which tipped over into hysteria. "We can go out somewhere! I really want to!"

"But we can't," I said. "At least, not together."

"Why not?"

I pointed to her face and back to mine. "People might notice a slight resemblance."

She smiled. "I don't give a fuck. I need my Pinkberry. It's like, cleansing—all those micro thingies eat up all the bad stuff. Like, they cancel it out. And, you know, I've had a lot of junk food today."

"Oh," I said. "My." *Think, think, think.* "Oh, wow—look at the time. It's too late! They'll be closed." It was probably true, too, thank God.

Her face twisted with disappointment, but she recovered fairly quickly. "Let's go for a ride, then!"

"I don't know if—"

"Yes, yes, yes, yes, yes!" She grabbed my hands and jumped up and down. "We'll take the truck up the hill and look at the stars! No one will see us! It'll be fun! Fun, fun, fun!"

"Maybe we should check with Jay." Maybe Jay had a tranquilizer gun.

She stopped jumping. Her smile fell. She squeezed my hands until they hurt and looked me in the eyes. "Jay doesn't pay you. I do."

The night was cold. I shivered in my denim jacket. Haley hadn't changed out of her pajamas. Instead, she just slipped into a pair of worn Ugg boots, threw on a pink velour hoodie, and grabbed the keys.

Mulholland Drive was dark, and Haley drove too fast. The big yellow truck lurched through the potholes and around the sharp curves. Beyond the edge of the road, city lights twinkled far, far below us.

At a turnout, she pulled over. The truck's headlights illuminated a sign: NO PARKING AFTER 9 P.M. It was after ten o'clock, but there was no gate, no one to make us leave. She turned off the ignition and turned up the radio, fiddling around until she found a country station.

She hopped out of the truck, leaving the keys in the ignition and the door open, the *ding-ding-ding* just audible over the music. I followed her to the guardrail, hoping to God we wouldn't be out here long enough for the car battery to run down. In front of us, a dark, brush-covered ravine plunged down to the wide, flat, sparkling valley floor.

"You like country music?" I asked. We hadn't said much on the drive.

"No." She slurped some Mountain Dew from her travel cup. "But when I was little, my dad used to take me and my brother camping. We'd pile into his truck and drive out to the middle of nowhere. If it was dark, he'd leave the car running for a little while, with the headlights shining on our campsite and country music blasting on the radio."

She tilted her face up to the night sky, which wasn't black so much as murky gray, the stars a pale reflection of the city lights below. "When I come here, I can almost believe I'm back in Montana. I mean, as long as I don't look down."

"Aren't you cold?" I said. Her velour hoodie was no warmer than my jacket.

"I like being cold. I'm from Montana."

"We should probably be heading back."

Something rustled in the bushes below us. She peered over the railing. "Do you think it's a fox?"

"Maybe. Or a rat or a snake." When she didn't say anything, I added, "The battery's going to run down if we're not careful."

"It's fine."

"I'm going to wait in the truck."

As I turned to go, she stepped over the guardrail and began scrambling down the ravine.

"What are you doing!"

"It's too bright up there," she called. "I want it to feel dark. And woodsy. Where do you think the fox was? I want to find it."

"It might not be a fox."

"Maybe I can find a clearing. Maybe we can camp here. Wouldn't that be fun? To spend the night?"

"It's not safe," I said. "And we're not even supposed to park here after nine o'clock."

"Do you always do what people tell you to do?" Her voice was getting fainter.

Now I was angry. I climbed back into the truck and shut off the radio, plunging us into a silence that made the night seem even more ominous. Stupid Haley. She didn't even care if we ran down the battery.

I grabbed the door handle, prepared to shut myself in until Haley came to her senses, only to realize that such a thing might never happen. My mother instincts kicked in. I couldn't just leave her out there.

Back outside, I slammed the door shut and went back to the railing. My gut clenched when I didn't see her. Finally I made out her dark shape, lying in a clearing.

I thought she was asleep until she raised her arms over her head and stretched like a cat. She pulled herself up in one smooth motion, climbed back up the hill, and stepped over the guardrail. She paused to brush leaves and grass off of her cloud-patterned pajama pants.

At the truck door, she turned around, "You coming?"

Chapter Eighteen

Saturday morning, I was exhausted, still drained from an evening spent trying to keep Haley from going over the edge, both literally and figuratively. I was deciding whether to go back to sleep or get out of bed when someone knocked on the guest room door.

I pushed myself up against the pillows. "Yeah?"

Jay poked his head through the door. "Coffee?"

"Oh! Hi." I tried to smooth down my masses of hair.

He had two paper cups. "Simone's going to be here at eleven-thirty, and she usually sets up her racks in this room."

I rubbed my eyes. "What time is it?"

There were no clocks in the guest room, just a queen-sized log bed, a bent willow Adirondack chair, and a bunch of wildlife photographs (two bears, an eagle, and a fish).

"Almost eleven."

"Wow. Really? I never sleep this late."

I adjusted the covers around my lap. My night clothes were nothing exciting: a pale blue T-shirt and drawstring pants. Suddenly, I wished I were wearing a strappy nightgown or maybe some silk pajamas. Some Hollywood vanity must have rubbed off on me.

It had yet to rub off on Jay. Today he wore faded black jeans, black high-top sneakers, and what looked suspiciously like a white undershirt.

He said, "Simone will have one of her assistants with her, but she's already signed a nondisclosure agreement, so it's okay if she sees you." He held out the cups. "Skinny latte or plain black coffee?"

"Which do you want?" I asked.

"Doesn't matter."

"You must have a preference."

"Either's fine."

I raised one eyebrow.

He grinned. "I told you to stop doing that." He looked younger than usual today—something about the way his hair was falling in his face. Plus, he'd shaved. If I didn't know him, I would have pegged him at about twenty-three.

"I'll have the latte," I said. "But only if you really don't care."

"Of course I care. I'd rather have the plain coffee."

Since there was no night table, Jay handed me the cup. It was extremely warm, even through the corrugated cardboard cuff. When I pulled off the plastic top, steam rushed up to kiss my face.

I blew gently, and the froth trembled. "No supersized caramel macho whatever?"

"It's already been delivered and ignored."

Haley got her coffee first. Of course she did.

He snorted. "Though what she really needs is a Bloody Mary." He sipped his coffee. "Ow, this is hot."

I stared at him. "What do you mean—a Bloody Mary?"

He sighed. "Haley got smashed last night. And now she's hungover. Which is really bad timing since Simone is only available till one, which means that Haley has got to get her ass out of bed."

I shook my head. "That's not possible. I was with her all night."

"And how did she seem to you?"

"Kind of . . . bipolar. Normal one minute and then just totally insane. I thought it was because of her medications or even that it was just her personality. I didn't think there was any booze allowed in the house. I didn't smell anything."

"Vodka," he said.

The big bottle of Gatorade. The Mountain Dew in the travel cup. Of course.

"I'm sorry."

He sighed. "It happens. Unfortunately, it happens a lot. There wasn't much you could have done, even if you'd known."

"But where did she get it?"

"Rodrigo, Esperanza—who knows? She could be getting it from the pool boy or the gardener. Pretty much anyone."

I thought back to when I was her age and well-acquainted with every bar in Fullerton. "She is over twenty-one," I said. "As long as she's not driving . . ." I remembered our ride into the hills and shuddered.

"Haley can't drink," he said flatly.

"Because she can't control it?"

"Because another *Kitty* movie is set to begin filming in June. But the insurance company has made it perfectly clear: unless

Haley stays sober, they're pulling out. With no insurance, there's no movie, and no TV show, either. Which means there's no CD, there's no T-shirts and lunch boxes and dolls. There's no money."

That seemed pretty extreme. "Just because of that thing that happened in Starbucks? And the, um, incident with the Escape?"

He pulled the top off his coffee and blew. He checked my face. "*Kitty and the Katz* stopped shooting two months early because of Haley's behavior. It was . . . erratic. To say the least. It wasn't just because of the alcohol, but that certainly didn't help. Some days she'd be so hungover that she couldn't remember her lines. Other times, she'd get in her yellow truck and disappear for two, three days at a time. The first time it happened—" He stopped.

"What?"

"I thought something had happened to her. An accident or—something."

"Did you file a missing persons report?"

He shook his head. "The press would have had a field day. Her career would be over."

"But what if something had actually happened? What if she was hurt?"

"We all looked for her—Rodrigo, her agent, her publicist, me. Finally, she drove home, took a shower, and slept for three days. We told the producers she had the flu. They were not pleased."

As if to close the conversation, he took a big gulp of his coffee. "Ow!" He touched his mouth.

"Careful," I said. "You wouldn't want to get burned."

At least I wouldn't have to face Simone looking like a slob. Deborah wanted everyone to dress up for her Pampered Chef thing ("attire: dressy," the invitation had read), so after a quick shower I slipped on the outfit I usually wore to weddings: a periwinkle blue linen sheath, white jacket, and white sandals. It was simple, classic, pretty. What could Simone possibly say?

This: "Holy fucking shit."

She was in the guest room, sorting through a rack of glittery gowns.

Standing in the guest bathroom doorway, I tried not to flinch. "I'm not trying to look like Haley. I have a party."

Simone's assistant, an emaciated girl in skin-tight jeans and spike-heel boots, stopped lining up shoes to examine me. After looking me up and down and up again, she wrinkled her nose ever-so-slightly and went back to the shoes.

"What kind of party?" Simone demanded in her trademark monotone.

"A garden party." Well, it was going to be outside, anyway. Deborah knew I couldn't afford to buy any kitchenware, but she needed a minimum number of guests to get her free gifts.

"You cannot wear that," Simone said simply.

I forced myself to stand up straight. Minutes ago, I had felt pretty. Simone had ruined everything.

"What, exactly, is wrong with my outfit?"

"One." Her index finger had an enormous amber ring on it. "The dress is polyester."

"It looks like linen," I said.

"It looks like polyester that's meant to look like linen but doesn't. Two." Her middle finger held a stack of thin gold wires. "The jacket is too casual for that dress, the cut is too boxy for your body type, and it hits you at the widest part of your hips."

"And it's not lined," the emaciated assistant added, glancing up from her shoes.

"Three." There was a gem of indeterminate origin on Simone's ring finger. "We're in March, not July."

"It's Southern California."

"It doesn't matter."

I swallowed hard. What was I supposed to wear? My black sundress that I used as a bathing suit cover-up? My brown turtleneck dress that everyone had seen me in a million times before?

"Thank you for your opinion," I said primly, fighting back tears. Maybe if I left soon, I could stop off at Ross or T.J. Maxx.

Simone snapped her fingers. "Get the Princess Grace."

The assistant scurried out of the room.

Shocked, I stared at Simone. She looked at the ceiling. "Don't get excited. It's not a *real* Princess Grace," she droned. "It's a vintage reproduction of a dress Princess Grace wore on her honeymoon. If it were real, I couldn't possibly let you wear it. And, of course, it wouldn't fit you. Grace was tiny. We haven't taken it in for Haley yet, so it might work."

She went back to poking through the dresses. I stalked across the room, my white sandals digging into my feet, and stuffed my pajamas into the duffle bag.

The assistant, who had trouble walking in spike heels, tottered back in with a dress encased in plastic. When she hung the dress at the end of the wheeled rack, Simone plucked at the plastic with her talonlike nails until she revealed the treasure underneath.

The dress was a shimmery silk, champagne with just the slightest hint of pink. The neck fell in graceful folds; otherwise, the line was simple and fitted. It looked like it would end just above my knee.

"It's gorgeous," I murmured.

"Try it on."

I checked her face to make sure she meant it.

In the guest bathroom, I couldn't get out of my boxy unlined jacket or my fake-linen sheath fast enough. I left them folded on the counter and stepped into the Princess Grace(ish) dress, the silk caressing my bare legs. Once I'd managed the slightly sticky side zipper, I took a deep breath and looked in the full-length mirror. The dress fit perfectly, accentuating my narrow waist while falling gently over my hips and ending just above the knees. I didn't look like myself or like Haley. I looked like someone better, richer, more elegant.

Shoulders back, chin held high, I strode into the guest room.

Simone gestured at my sandals. "Those shoes are disgusting." She made a lousy fairy godmother.

"They're all I have. And Haley's won't fit."

She snapped her fingers at the assistant. "Accessories trunk." She peered at my feet. "Size eight shoes."

I looked at my feet. "They used to be a seven and a half, but they got bigger when I was pregnant and never went back."

Simone rifled through the dresses on the rack and ignored me.

In the end, Simone paired the dress with silver pumps, a pearl choker, a purple rhinestone cocktail ring and dangly pearl-and-rhinestone earrings. She pulled and yanked at my real and borrowed hair, and then she twisted and pinned it into a retro-glamour hairdo.

"Thanks," I said—the word woefully inadequate.

She kind of shrugged with her eyebrows. "I had nothing better to do. Just make sure you give everything back to Jay when you're done. And tell him to get the dress dry-cleaned."

Jay poked his head in the room. "Haley will be down in three, five—maybe ten minutes."

Simone pursed her mouth. "I'm leaving at one whether she's here or not."

Jay tried to smile. "Maybe you could just leave the clothes and she could look through them at her leisure—you know, see what she likes best, and then tomorrow or maybe Monday you could—"

"No."

"Right." Jay's eyes flicked over to me and widened. "Wow."

I blushed. "It's a fake Grace Kelly."

"Vintage reproduction," Simone clarified before making an odd guttural sound.

"You look nice," he said in what I hoped was a major understatement.

"Just like Grace Kelly, right?" I joked.

He considered. "Maybe Grace Kelly with freckles."

Simone snapped her fingers at the assistant. "Do her makeup. Heavy on the foundation."

"I like the freckles," Jay said, crossing his arms and leaning against the door. He was pretty cute, I had to admit (especially when he was saying nice things about me).

Simone looked at the ceiling and made her guttural sound again. "You are unqualified to have any opinion about beauty or style," she told Jay.

Jay went back upstairs to check on Haley, and I sat on the edge of the bed while the assistant brushed and patted and drew on my face.

"What are these dresses for, anyway?" I asked. "Does Haley have an awards show or a premiere or something?"

"Private party," the assistant said.

My eyes popped open. Haley would actually brave a party? I just managed to avoid being blinded by an eye pencil. "Sorry," the assistant murmured.

At that, the Golden Girl herself stumbled into the room. She

looked like hell: dirty hair, pimples, under-eye circles. She was
still wearing her jammie pants and the I ONLY LOOK INNOCENT
T-shirt, which now had a fruit-punch-red stain on the front. I
vaguely remembered her spilling some Gatorade (and vodka, I
now realized), the night before.

Simone didn't comment on her appearance, remarking instead,
"Haley, love, I'm sorry to drag you out of bed like this. I've got
a rather difficult client scheduled at one-thirty, and I wanted to
make sure we had something here that would work for you."

Haley rubbed her face with her hand. "Whatever."

Simone pulled a midnight blue minidress off the rack. It had
long sleeves with round cutouts on the shoulders and back. "This
is from Stella's latest collection. It's hard to see in this light, but
this dress has dark blue metallic threads throughout. It would
really pop under the lights."

"'Kay." Haley turned as if to go back to bed. Jay put his hand
on her shoulder and guided her back into the room.

"Here's another one." Simone presented a strapless silver
dress. "Simple but hot. We could add some wow with dramatic
accessories."

"Whatever. Just pick one."

"Now, love." Simone tried to catch her eye, but Haley wasn't
playing. "These pieces aren't loaners. Before you make an invest-
ment, you need to make sure you've made the right choice."

"Wait, wait, wait." The money talk caught Jay's attention.
"This is a two-hour gig. Can't she just borrow something like all
the other times?"

Simone gathered her words. "You've got to remember that a
private party doesn't have the same kind of exposure as, say, the
Grammys." There was an uncomfortable silence. Finally, Simone
added, "Or even some of the lesser award shows or a Hollywood

premiere. It's not very likely we'll see a good shot of Haley in this dress in print anywhere, which means the designers don't get their free publicity."

"But she's gotten loaners for private parties before," Jay said.

"Yes, but the last one . . . actually, the last two . . ." Simone nibbled on her pointy nail. She started again. "When designers lend pieces out, they assume that the clothing will be returned in the same condition."

In other words: you can't get Gatorade stains out of silk.

"Oh," Jay said.

"Right," Simone responded.

The assistant said, "Close your eyes," after which she did something really unpleasant to my eyelids.

Fifteen minutes later, I was in the tan-and-brown kitchen with Rodrigo. We sat at the island and downed bottled water. The soda had mysteriously disappeared from Haley's pantry, along with all of the junk food.

Rodrigo had come bursting into the guest room, apologizing for his lateness. When he saw me, he had gushed appropriately and even managed to whisper, "I've seen that dress on Haley, and don't tell, but it looks better on you."

Rodrigo was definitely growing on me.

"So what did Haley end up wearing to the Grammys?" I asked now.

He checked the doorway before leaning close to my ear. "Nothing!"

"She went naked?"

He covered his mouth to suppress his laughter. "No! She had a gown all set to go—something on loan, of course, I think it was a Zac Posen—but when the limo came she refused to get in. Jay was furious. It's not like she was up for an award, but it's the most important face-time of the year. Simone was ticked, too, since she'd arranged for the gown and jewels and all kinds of freebies."

"Too bad I wasn't around. I would have loved to go." I was only half joking. If I felt this good in one of Haley's backup dresses, what would it be like to wear a designer gown?

"Did you have a good meeting last night?" I asked him.

His face lit up. "It was stupendous. Thanks for asking. You're the only person around here who seems to understand how much this means to me. Jay thinks my entire life should revolve around Haley—and I love that girl, don't get me wrong, she's like a sister to me. It's just . . ."

"You have to put yourself first sometimes."

"Exactly!" He squeezed my forearm. "How was she last night, anyway?"

"Drunk!" I whispered. "And I didn't even know she was drinking because she hid the stuff in her Gatorade and Mountain Dew. She drove me up to an overlook and started climbing down the ravine. It was really scary."

"Oh, my God. Did she seem suicidal?"

"Oh, no—nothing like that. Just unbalanced."

"Did she say if anything was upsetting her?" His concern was genuine. How sad that Haley's maid and assistant were the only two people who seemed to have her best interest at heart.

"She talked about her music—about how the record producers make her sing songs she doesn't like."

"It's got to be more than that," he said, shaking his head. "She doesn't talk about it much, but I know her whole family situation bothers her."

"She talked about her dad a little."

"Oh, yeah? What did she say?"

"That he used to take the kids camping when they were young. He'd pile them into his pickup truck and play country music."

The footsteps outside the kitchen stopped us. We picked up our water bottles in unison and drank.

It was Jay. "Hey, Rodrigo. Simone's about to leave, and Haley wants your opinion on a dress."

"Anything for Haley." I couldn't tell whether or not he was being sarcastic. He gave me a conspiratorial smile before hurrying away.

I slid off my stool and smoothed the silk dress around my hips. "I should probably get going. Is Rodrigo going to drive me, or did you call the car service?"

"Neither," he said. "I'm headed that way anyhow, so I'll drop you off."

"You're headed toward Fullerton? What—Are you going back to the Red Robin for another salad?"

He grinned. "Actually, one of my clients is performing at the Improv in Brea. He's just the opener, but it's a nice break." He plucked at his T-shirt. "I guess I should put on something nicer."

"You think?" I raised one eyebrow.

He raised one eyebrow right back at me, and I suddenly felt all smiley and flushed and fluttery and—holy crap! Had I developed a crush on Jay in the last five minutes?

"I'll need to stop by my apartment to get clothes," he said. "Do you want to wait here, or . . ."

"I'll come with you."

* * *

Jay's house wasn't at all what I expected. Not that I'd given it a lot of thought, of course, but I would have pegged him as a black-leather-couch, stained-shag-carpet, dirty-dishes-everywhere kind of guy. And I would have guessed he lived in a soulless high-rise with lots of glass and maybe a workout room.

Instead, his duplex, on a leafy street off of Melrose, was two-story, white stucco with arched windows and a red roof. Banana palms and flowering bushes crowded the tiny front yard. A wooden gate led to a small, shady courtyard with two iron chairs and a shared table. The air hung heavy with the smell of orange blossoms.

"What would you call this style? French? Spanish?" I asked as Jay turned his key in the front door.

"It's called a Romance house." When he saw my expression, he laughed. "It is! A bunch of these were built in L.A. right before the Depression. Architects didn't take them seriously because they were so quirky and Hollywood. But I like it."

Jay lived upstairs. We held on to an iron railing and climbed the rich wood steps. The first room I saw was a small den rounded like a turret. Tall, skinny windows had been left open to let in the sweet winter breeze. Farther down the hall and through French doors, the living room had an arched picture window that overlooked the street. Another set of French doors led to the dining room.

Everywhere I looked, framed photographs mounted in wide white mats covered vanilla-colored walls. There were black-and-white shots of train tracks and lonely roads, full-color shots of oceans and forests. There were candid shots of people: a man on the beach, buried up to his neck in sand; a child touching one finger to a turtle; an old woman peeking out from under the umbrella. The colors were rich, the shadows sharp, the angles precise.

"You collect photographs?" I asked.

"No—just take them."

"Really? You're talented," I said. "You could sell these."

"Nah, it's just a hobby."

He led me into the kitchen, which had a black-and-white checkerboard floor and simple white cabinets. A small deck lay beyond.

"You want something to eat? Drink?"

At Haley's house, I'd scored a piece of smelt bread with soy butter, but my body didn't register that as lunch. "What do you have?"

He put a hand on the white refrigerator and then stopped. "Um . . . nothing?" He looked vaguely embarrassed. "I don't eat at home much."

"But you're secretly a gourmet chef, right?" I teased.

"I'm a pro with a can opener and the microwave. Does that count?"

"No. But you get points for honesty." I ran my hand along the white counter. Suddenly, I had a vision of working in this kitchen: chopping vegetables for a salad or stirring a homemade soup on the range. I wondered what his dishes looked like and what it would be like to share a candlelit dinner at the dining room table.

He opened the refrigerator and peered inside. "I've got water, Diet Coke, Caffeine Free Diet Coke, orange juice, and wine and beer. And if you're hungry, I've got an opened can of refried beans, but I have a feeling they've gone bad."

"Tempting," I said. "But wine sounds great."

When he went to change his clothes, I returned to the living room, where brown leather couches (not as soft as Haley's but nice) formed an L around a big square coffee table. Against one wall, shelves held books on film and photography, paperback mysteries, and highbrow hardbacks. On a side table next to one of the couches, snapshots showed an older couple sitting together on a patio bench; two tiny kids—a boy and a girl—on Santa's lap; and the same boy, a bit older, about Ben's age, ankle-deep in the ocean.

I heard his footsteps in the hallway. "Are these family pictures?" I turned around, and—whoah!

"You look, you look . . ." I stopped myself before I could say "handsome," "hot," or any other potentially embarrassing adjective.

"Like a talent manager?" he suggested, straightening his tie.

"I dunno. Maybe. You look nice." I tried to keep my tone light.

He'd traded his jeans, T-shirt, and high-top sneakers for a well-cut gray suit, crisp white shirt, and a black tie. Suits always made Hank look vaguely uncomfortable, plus they never fit him right: straining around the buttons, too long in the sleeves. But Jay looked completely at ease, as if he got dressed up every day.

He tugged at a lapel. "Simone got me a great price on this suit, back when she liked me."

"She doesn't like you anymore?"

He considered. "She doesn't like the situation. Too many people know she dresses Haley, and Haley looks like crap half the time. So it reflects badly on Simone. She keeps threatening to quit, but the money's too good. Anyway—yes. Family pictures." He strode across the light wood floors until he was standing so close to me I could feel his body heat and smell his mint toothpaste.

He pointed to a picture. "These are my parents before my dad passed away. My mother lives with my sister's family now." He picked up the Santa picture. "And these are Milo and Sophie. My sister's kids."

"Where do they live?"

"Long Island." He gazed at the picture, his expression just the tiniest bit sad.

"Do you see them much?"

"A couple times a year. Not enough." He put the photograph back on the shelf and checked his silver watch, which for once went with the rest of his clothes. "What time do you have to be at your party?"

"Not for a couple of hours."

"In that case, you want to sit out on the deck?"

He poured himself a half glass of wine and pulled a box of Wheat Thins from the pantry. Outside, there was a little wrought-iron café table and two chairs. Below us, the backyard was green and lush. A brown bird hopped around on the grass.

"So, did you ever want to be a professional photographer?" I asked.

He shook his head. "Filmmaker. I went to NYU."

"But then you came out here and had your dreams squashed?"

"Nah. Long before I graduated, I realized I didn't have what it takes. But I liked being around creative people, and the film industry sounded cool, so I came out here not really knowing what I wanted to do. I figured I'd find a niche in the entertainment business, and I have."

The wine was better than the stuff I usually drank: smooth with a hint of vanilla.

"How many clients do you have besides Haley?"

"Eight." He offered me the Wheat Thins box. I plucked out

a slightly stale cracker. "That's all I can handle right now since Haley takes up so much of my time."

"Are they all actors?"

He shook his head. "I've got a standup comic—that's the guy I'm going to see tonight—and a performance artist. The rest are actors, mostly young, though a couple have been in the business a long time."

"Anyone I've heard of?"

"Aside from Haley and Brady, no. At least not yet. But it's an incredibly talented bunch. Amazing. And I just feel bad that . . ." He stopped abruptly and sighed.

"What?"

"They deserve more attention than I've been able to give them."

That's when he kissed me, without hesitation or embarrassment, like it was the most natural thing in the world. I put my arms around his neck and kissed him right back. We pulled back just enough to look into each other's eyes.

He stiffened.

"What?" I said.

He loosened his arms and smiled with faint embarrassment. "For an instant, I just . . . You look so much like Haley . . ."

I pulled back as if I'd been bitten. Of course Jay didn't like me for myself. Everything was about Haley, even this.

I forced a laugh.

I stood up and smoothed the silk dress. "Thanks for the wine. It went straight to my head."

His face strained with embarrassment. "I didn't mean to—"

I cut him off. "It's fine. Really. It was a nice kiss, and it didn't mean a thing. The last thing I need right now is anything that . . . means anything."

I smiled my best Hollywood smile. "We should really get going."

When the Mini Cooper pulled up in front of the Motts' house, Deborah was outside, hanging a polyester flower wreath on her front door, in preparation for the Pampered Chef party.

"Veronica? Is that you?" When Deborah realized I was with a man, she hurried down the front steps, almost tripping over her high heels.

I scrambled out of the car and shut the door. Surely Jay would get the message and peel away before Deborah got to us. Or not.

The passenger window slid down. Jay held my eyes. "Thanks for staying over last night."

Brilliant, Jay. Good timing.

"Oh, hello!" Deborah bent down to peer through the car window. She was all dressed for the party: black dress pants a size too small, a magenta satin blouse, and way too much makeup. Once she'd gotten a good look at Jay, she smiled at me. "I was wondering where you were last night. I saw your van in the driveway, and I knocked on your door, but . . ."

What had she wanted me for? Chauffeur duty? Babysitting?

"I was out," I said.

"I see that." She leaned even closer to Jay, her head practically through the window. "Have we met?"

"I don't . . . think so." He studied her face as if trying to place her.

"I'm Deborah Mott. Veronica's friend."

"Jay Sharpie."

"Sharpie? Like the pen?" Nice, Deborah. Really sensitive.

He didn't even flinch. "Just like the pen."

"And you know Veronica . . ." Deborah paused to let him fill in the blank.

"Yes, I do," he answered.

"Well, good night," I said, eager to end this encounter.

"I'll call you," Jay told me. Was he being oblivious or mischievous?

I gave him a tight smile and a little wave. He put up the window and drove away—but not before giving me a long look that was clearly supposed to mean something. But what? Sorry I kissed you? Sorry you're not Haley?

I began walking up the driveway, overnight bag in hand. "So, I'll see you in about an hour," I told Deborah.

She bounded after me. "He's *cute*, Veronica! How did you meet him?"

"Just, you know. Around." I kept walking.

"I've noticed a change in you lately. You seem . . . different. In a good way. And I don't just mean your hair color." She grabbed my arm, made me stop. "Wait a minute. Hasn't it gotten longer?"

"Extensions," I said. "I got them a couple of weeks ago."

"Is it serious?"

"The extensions?"

"No, the *relationship*. With *Jay*."

"No! It's not even—it's nothing."

"But you spent the night. That's not nothing. Maybe it'll turn into something more, you know. *Permanent*."

"See you in a little while, Deborah."

"Permanent, get it? Like a Sharpie?"

"Got it, Deborah. See you in a bit."

Chapter Nineteen

When Jay called, a week and a half later, on a Thursday, it wasn't to discuss our kiss. But that was okay. I was over it. Really.

"Haley's supposed to attend a film premiere this afternoon—this animated thing with talking sheep. But she won't get out of bed. Brady's already tipped off the paparazzi. So if she doesn't show up . . ."

"Word might leak out."

"Right."

"She was going with Brady?"

"Not really. They were going to arrive separately and then hang out together once they got there."

"Maybe that's why she doesn't want to go," I suggested. "Because she was afraid it would be awkward." Much like this phone conversation.

"Mmm," he said. "So—are you free?"

"To go to a film premiere with Brady?" I suddenly realized where this conversation was headed. Oh! My! God!

"Not with him." His voice was tight. "You'll arrive in separate cars. But the thing is, there may be some other people there from the Betwixt Channel, so you really, really have to keep a low profile."

"But I can talk to Brady?"

He sighed. "Yes. You can talk to Brady. We'll stay on either side of you and tell people that you're fighting laryngitis and need to save your voice for an upcoming recording session."

"Clever."

"Not really, but it will have to do."

The last time I'd ridden in a limousine was my senior prom. This was better. For one thing, I wasn't wearing a pink satin gown with spaghetti straps (though I felt pretty hot in it at the time). Instead, Simone—who didn't even react when I told her that the Grace Kelly-ish dress (which I'd returned) had been a big hit at the garden party—dressed me in a western-cut, white-denim mini dress and the adorable (if slightly painful) pink cowboy boots. Since the premiere was during the day, she felt we could get away with huge white sunglasses and a straw cowboy hat. She hated the hat, which nudged the outfit into "costume territory," but the bigger the accessories, the less the possibility that someone might notice that I wasn't actually Haley Rush.

My monster hair, worn loose, helped on that front. It shielded so much of my face, I could be almost any young star at all.

Inside the car, two rows of seats faced each other. I sat on one

side, Jay on the other. In honor of the film premiere, he wore a
T-shirt with no stains and jeans without holes.

He pulled out his phone. With a tiny pointer, he poked at the
keypad and squinted at the screen.

"Damn," he said finally.

"What?"

"One of my clients had an audition yesterday—guest spot on
NCIS. I thought he had a good shot, but . . ." He shook his head.

"Maybe next time," I said.

"He's thirty-eight. There may not be a next time."

A soundproof privacy screen sealed us off from the driver.
There was satellite radio, a television, and a video game console.
Ben would have loved this car.

An ice chest held sparkling water and plastic cups. "No champagne?" I said. A little bubbly might have calmed my jitters.

"Haley doesn't drink."

During the ride to the theater, which was out in Brentwood,
near UCLA, Jay, all business, gave me the rundown. Along the
red carpet, there would be photographers, entertainment reporters, and cameramen. I would stop and smile. I would pivot
around to give the photographers a straight-on shot. And then
I would hurry past the entertainment reporters into the theater.
In still shots, I could easily pass for Haley; video was harder to
master, and YouTube was to be avoided at all costs.

When we got into the theater lobby, Brady would be waiting for us, but I was not to look overly excited. He would give
me a friendly hug. I could hug him back, but without too much
enthusiasm.

Mmm-hmm. Good luck with that.

"When we get inside, you and Brady will go into a corner,"
he said. "You'll want to look deep in conversation—well, not too

deep since you are supposedly trying not to waste your voice—
but still platonic. I'll hang nearby so no one interrupts. There
could be photographers, so watch your facial expressions."

"What do you mean?"

"No adoring gazes," he muttered.

His phone buzzed. He checked the screen, said, "Shit," and
turned it on.

"Hey, Jeff . . . yeah, I just got the e-mail. Sorry, dude, but it's a
no-go. I know . . . I know. Sucks, man, but don't give up—you've
got real talent . . . Right . . . I know . . . okay, later."

He sighed and slipped the phone back into his pocket. "Where
was I? Oh, right. As soon as they open the theater doors, we're
in. You'll sit between Brady and me. When the media's gone,
maybe forty-five minutes or an hour into the screening, we'll slip
out a side door."

"Why not stay until the end?" I asked.

"It's a movie about talking sheep," Jay said, as if that was
enough of an explanation.

He twisted open a bottle of Perrier and handed it to me. "Did
you practice the autograph?"

I set my Perrier in a cup holder (you'd think a car this fancy
would have a table) and pulled a pad and pen out of my simple denim clutch. (Simone thought the big fringed pocketbook,
paired with my cowboy attire, would make people "question
your taste level.")

In big, bubbly script, I wrote "Haley Rush," followed by a
heart.

Jay studied the paper. "That'll do."

The street outside the theater was jammed with limousines in
all shapes and colors: dark green Hummers, navy SUVS, black
stretches like ours.

Jay slid open the privacy screen. "Main line," he told the driver.

The driver edged his way close to the red carpet. A young man wove among the cars to reach us. He had thick black glasses and floppy hair in desperate need of a trim.

Jay pushed a button, and the tinted window slid down.

"Haley Rush," Jay said.

Behind his big glasses, the young man squinted. He looked at the brown clipboard in his hand and flipped through some pages. "Who set you up?"

"She got added late," Jay said.

The young man looked back at the red carpet, as if trying to decide whether or not I was worthy of walking it.

"It's *Haley Rush*," Jay emphasized. "From *Kitty and the Katz*. You know—the number one rated show on the Betwixt Channel?"

The young man studied me again, more intently this time, appraising my big hair, my exposed legs and arms, the buttons left open below my neck.

"Okay," he said finally, waving the limo toward an open patch of road.

The driver jumped out and jogged around the car to the back door. Jay climbed out first. The driver held out his hand to help me. I took it, careful not to make eye contact, careful not to thank him.

Jay put his arm around my shoulders and guided me toward the carpet, where two skinny blond women in tiny, shiny dresses were posing for photographers. On the concrete to one side of the carpet, a short line of people, most of them either well-dressed or good-looking or both, stood behind a velvet rope, waiting their turn.

A ponytailed young woman, clipboard in hand, saw me standing on the sidewalk, waiting for instructions. She nodded once and unhooked the rope, allowing Jay and me to jump to the head of the line.

"Give it a few minutes," she said, glancing back at the shiny-dress women, who were half-pretending to be engaged in deep conversation with a couple of the photographers. "You'll be next." If she was excited to be talking to Haley Rush, she didn't let it show.

Behind me, a very tall, very pretty woman in a low-cut tight black dress and silver spike heels sighed with disappointment at getting bumped. Her date, a middle-aged paunchy bald guy in a polo shirt, put his arm around her waist and rubbed one bony hip. "Won't be long."

"We can wait," I said without thinking. How many times had I warned Ben of the evils of cutting in line?

Jay squeezed my arm and forced a laugh. "Kidding," he told the woman with the clipboard.

Nonplussed, she rehooked the rope in front of us.

I met Jay's eyes. I wanted to tell him I was sorry for the outburst, but opening my mouth again would only make things worse. He blinked rapidly, as if questioning the wisdom of bringing me along.

Not that anyone was paying any attention to me; there was too much else going on. A giant sheep balloon, like the kind you'd see in the Macy's Thanksgiving Day parade, floated above the theater. On the other side of the red carpet, children in cotton clothing stroked gawky white lambs while their hovering parents clutched hand sanitizer. Even from here I could smell hay and animal sweat.

It was hard to see what was happening on the red carpet

itself. Behind the lines of photographers, people—normal people in gym shorts and khakis and Old Navy jeans—peered around shoulders and photo equipment, hoping for a glimpse of a celebrity.

Suddenly, a sound like chanting monks filled the air. *Haley Rush Haley Rush Haley Rush Haley Rush* . . . The photographers were passing along the news of the next big arrival: me.

I caught Jay's eye. He nodded.

"You're up," the girl with the clipboard said, unhooking the velvet rope.

"Haley!"

"Haley!"

"Hey, Haley—over here!"

I was glad to have sunglasses to protect me from the flashing cameras and the hot, towering lights that lined the carpet. Jay kept his hand on my back. "Smile," he murmured, his breath hot on my ear.

I smiled. And I waved. When I moved too fast, Jay squeezed my arm. I stopped and turned to allow everyone a straight-on shot.

"Haven't seen you out here for a while, Haley," one photographer said.

Jay answered for me. "She's been holed up, working on her next album pretty much nonstop. She's got to save her voice today—fighting laryngitis. No questions, guys."

A little red-haired girl held out a paper and pen. I wrote *Haley Rush* and drew a big, fat heart. I wrote the name again on the back of a grocery list and a third time on someone's arm.

"Mind if they get some photos of Haley alone?" yet another assistant asked Jay. He released my arm and melted away, like a puppeteer behind a curtain.

The camera flashes, coming from all directions, made me feel like I was living in slow motion and filled me with a warm, happy glow. So this is what it felt like to be adored. In all my life, I had never felt so beautiful.

And just like that: it was over. The monk chant returned, different this time. Instead of *Haley Rush Haley Rush Haley Rush*, it was *Reese Reese Reese Reese*: no need for a last name.

Reese Witherspoon, looking ravishing and not costume-y at all in a simple dress and cardigan, strolled onto the red carpet, holding hands and swinging arms with two picture-perfect children.

Jay retook my arm. When we passed the entertainment reporters with their microphones and camera crews, Jay didn't have to make any excuses for why I wasn't talking. They were too busy trying to score an interview with a bigger star. Moments later, when we traded the California sunshine for the theater lobby's fluorescent lights, the fans and photographers had forgotten all about us.

Inside, it was more like a cocktail party and less like a parade. Clusters of people stood around smiling and chatting, holding plastic cups of wine and soda. Their laughter was too loud, too fake. All around the lobby, in the open, in the corners, even in the middle of conversational clusters, people talked into trim cell phones or poked at their tiny keypads.

Here and there, I recognized some faces: young actors and actresses from television shows that Ben liked to watch (and that were available on DVD). Otherwise, there seemed to be two entirely different crowds. There were the carefully groomed J. Crew wearers. And then there were the messy hair, faded T-shirt, artistic eyewear fans. One thing they had in common: an entourage of pretty, young, blank-faced women in revealing clothing.

Brady was not there.

Jay swore under his breath and pulled out his phone.

Two pretty young things, one male, one female, spotted me from across the room. They waved. I waved back.

"You were supposed to be early!" Jay snapped into the phone.

A very toned man in black pants and a tight white shirt offered a tray of little cheesy things.

"Porcini mushroom and sheep's milk quesadillas," the server said, offering me a white cocktail napkin patterned with sheep.

The quesadillas smelled wonderful, but before I could grab one, Jay held up his hand. "No, thanks." The server moved on.

I scowled at Jay. He ignored me.

He ended his phone call by saying, "Just hurry up."

"I'm hungry," I told him. Besides, I was curious to taste sheep's milk cheese. Was that like goat cheese?

"So am I." He slid the phone into his pocket and crossed his arms over his chest. "But do you see anyone else here eating?"

He was right. Plenty of people held plastic cups, but although there were at least four people passing trays, no one but children seemed to be taking any food.

"That's just stupid," I said.

"There's plenty about this industry that's stupid," he said. "You can't think about it too much."

"Were you talking to Brady?" I think I get points for not asking the instant he hung up.

Jay nodded. "He's stuck in the red carpet line. He didn't want to be the first one here, so now he's late." He shook his head with irritation.

"Why didn't they put him to the front of the line like us?"

"Brady's C list. Maybe C-plus on a good day."

"That's rude," I said.

"It's just the way things work. Maybe he'll make it up to the B list, maybe he'll fall to the D. But for now he's a solid C. You've got to understand: this is a business. And the actors are products. The smart ones understand that."

"And the not-so-smart ones?" I didn't have to say Haley's name.

"It's just a phase," he said. "She'll be fine."

Someone touched my arm. "Haley?" It was another clipboard person—a young Asian woman with bleached blond hair. She wore a sleeveless black blouse, black jeans, big hoop earrings, and chunky shoes.

I smiled.

Jay touched my back. "Haley can't speak," he blurted. "I mean, she *can*, of course—it's not a Helen Keller situation." He forced a laugh. "But she's saving her voice for a recording session."

"I understand completely." The clipboard woman turned to me and lowered her voice, as if in deference. "I adore your voice, Haley—so full of emotion."

I smiled and adjusted my hat.

"Anyway. We've got Kim Rueben and Rafael Suarez over there." She pointed across the room to the two good-looking people who had waved at me earlier. "We'd love to get a *Crazy Life of Riley Poole* reunion photo."

Thank God I wasn't allowed to speak. I had no response for that one. *The Crazy Life of Riley Poole* was not available on DVD, which meant I had never seen it. I had no idea who Kim and Rafael were or how well Haley knew them.

"Ummmmm," Jay said, cleverly drawing out the sound to buy himself an extra two seconds. "Do we have time?" He feigned interest in a gigantic sheep poster. "There's been so much buzz

surrounding *Baaad Boys*—we don't want to miss a single instant
of the film."

"Don't worry—we're good." She turned and waved us
behind her.

Jay held me back far enough so he could whisper in my ear.
"We're looking at a hug situation. Maybe even a kiss—cheek,
not lips. Here's the deal. You worked together when you were
teenagers. Neither of them act anymore. Kim went to UCLA film
school. Now she's directing documentaries or short films or one
of those other things that doesn't make any money. Rafael left
entirely—last I heard, he was at Harvard Business School. Years
ago, the *Riley* producers tried to make it look like the two of you
were sweethearts, but everyone knew he was gay."

He strode ahead of me. "Raffie! Kimmer! I haven't seen you
since the *Vanity Fair* party!"

Rafael, olive-skinned and handsome, with sharp brown eyes
and a strong jaw, got a handshake and a half-hug. Kim, tall and
willowy, with curly brown hair and an easy smile, received an
extended squeeze and a kiss on the cheek.

Kimmer turned to me. "You look beautiful, Haley. I mean,
your hair and your skin . . ."

"Did you get taller?" Rafael interrupted. We stood at eye level.

"It's the shoes," Jay said, pointing to the pink cowboy boots
(which had almost completely cut off the blood supply to my
feet). "Haley's dying to catch up with the two of you, but I've
forbidden her to talk. She's got a big recording session coming
up, and she's fighting laryngitis."

Kim smirked at Jay's posturing, which made me like her
immediately. I hugged them both (forgetting the kiss, but oh,
well), and then the Asian woman with the bleached blond hair
herded us over to a platform.

The photo station was much smaller than the red carpet—just a few steps up to a plywood rectangle. Four photographers waited with heavy cameras as the Asian woman positioned Kim, Rafael, and me in front of a backdrop decorated with repeating Nokia logos.

"Can we get you without the sunglasses, Haley?" one of the photographers asked.

I reached up to the glasses—what choice did I have?—just as Jay yelled, "Wait!"

I froze.

He scrambled over to the edge of the platform and motioned the photographer to lean down.

"Eye infection," Jay murmured. "Nothing contagious, just—you know. Not pretty."

The photographer shrugged with defeat, and then he and the others lifted their lenses.

"This way!"

"Now over here!"

"Great smiles, beautiful!"

When the photographers had gotten enough shots of the three of us, the clipboard woman bounded up the steps and gently pulled Kim away. "Now let's get one of just Haley and Raffie. You know—for old-time's sake."

Rafael stood behind me, his hands around my waist as if we were posing for a prom picture. He spoke under his breath, his tone utterly deadpan. "I can't wait to get you alone and ravish you, you dirty girl—just like when we were young."

Remembering what Jay had said about Rafael's sexual orientation, I burst out laughing. The photographers caught the moment. It was a great shot, even with the sunglasses. It would bring a good price.

As soon as the pictures were done, Jay pulled me away. "There are some people here that I need Haley to meet. But Raf, Kimmer—it was great to see you both. Let's do dinner sometime soon."

Rafael shrugged. Something shut down in Kim's eyes.

Jay spent the next ten minutes avoiding conversations with an agent, an investor, and a songwriter. Brady, along with a small crowd of pretty young things, finally came in just as the clipboard hordes began herding us into the theater.

In a swarm of perfect people, Brady stood out. His hair had been trimmed since I'd last seen him, and his face was freshly shaven, soft and smooth.

He wore leather pants and a plain white T-shirt. Until that moment, I couldn't have imagined a straight guy looking anything but ridiculous in leather pants, but Brady was the exception. When he put his hands in his front pockets, the outlines of his pectorals showed through the T-shirt.

Thank God I couldn't talk. If I'd managed to say anything at all, it was sure to be moronic.

Brady spoke to Jay first. "The E! Entertainment woman— must be new, I've never seen her before—almost interviewed me. She had the microphone in my face and everything, but then she shoved me aside for this nine-year-old because she thought he was the voice of youngest sheep. But it turns out he wasn't."

"Maybe if you'd gotten here on time, you would have gotten an interview," Jay said, his jaw tense.

Brady noticed me. "Hey, Ver—Haley." A smile spread across his face. His eyes crinkled and his dimples deepened and my knees just about buckled under my weight.

"Hey," I said.

"Don't talk," Jay commanded.

"No one can hear her." Brady reminded him.

"But they can see her mouth moving, and I've just spent the past half hour telling everyone she can't talk because she's saving her voice." Tension made his lips white around the edges. Actually, Jay was looking rather white all over. Maybe he needed to call the EverGlow people.

Brady tucked his hair behind one ear. He looked me up and down. "You look really . . . really . . ."

"Western?" I suggested.

Jay glared at me. I covered my mouth in mock shame.

"Yes," Brady said. "Very western. And also very pretty."

I felt myself flush.

"Though you'd look prettier if you took the sunglasses off. Isn't it hard to see in here?"

"Her eyes are a brighter blue than Haley's," Jay whispered. Around us, people were filing into the theater. Jay chewed his lip with concentration. "You can take them off when we get inside."

"Gee, thanks."

"Don't talk."

All around us, people gushed:

"*. . . one of those rare stories that's accessible to both adults and children . . .*"

"*. . . so much for us all to learn . . .*"

"*. . . world-famous for his work in animal voice-overs . . .*"

I followed Jay into the second-to-last row. Once I settled onto the comfy seat, I finally took off my sunglasses.

Brady leaned forward to see my face. "Much better."

"Thanks," I mouthed.

We locked eyes. I forgot to breathe. Brady dropped his gaze and smiled shyly.

He plucked at his trousers. "Are the leather pants too S-and-M?"

Fighting a giggle, I shook my head.

"Seriously?"

"Yes!" I whispered. "I like them."

He sighed. "I just hired a stylist and she told me to wear them. And, you know, it's embarrassing enough that I've even *got* a stylist, and now she's got me looking all Village People. She said it'll make people notice me, and I'm all—that may not be a good thing." He ran a hand over the leather. "It's crazy soft, though, I've gotta admit. Feel it."

Did he just say—? Fingers trembling, I reached over and stroked a spot just above his knee as dirty, dirty thoughts swam through my mind.

In the aisle, the film's director, producer, and voice-over cast filed in to the theater. Everyone started to clap, which unfortunately meant I had to take my hand off Brady's leg. A couple of people tried to get a standing ovation going, but it didn't take.

The theater had a shallow stage with a microphone on one side. Once the cast had settled into the first few rows, a skinny guy with salt-and-pepper hair bounded up the stairs and stood in front of the enormous blank screen. He wore khakis, a pale blue polo shirt and white sneakers. Anyone who dared wear such boring clothes had to be very, very important.

The applause started up again, along with the standing-ovation attempt, but it still didn't take.

The thin man held up both hands. The applause stopped almost immediately, and the crowd craned forward.

"Executive producer," Jay murmured in my ear. I'd almost forgotten he was there.

Hands in pockets, the man spoke into the microphone. "Five

years ago, someone came to me with a screenplay and said, 'This is a movie that has to be made. And you're the man who has to make it.'"

He paused so we could all take that in.

"And so I asked him, 'What's it about? The civil rights movement? War? Genocide?' And he said 'no.'"

Here he paused even longer, which seemed kind of silly since we all knew what he was about to say.

"And that's when he told me it was a movie about sheep." He grinned.

Obediently, people in the audience threw back their heads and laughed. A few clapped.

His face grew serious, impassioned. "And on the surface, yes—*Baaad Boys* is a movie about sheep. And if you ask young children why they liked it, they will say it's because it's so funny, or they like the music, or they like animals. But what they learn from this movie—what we all learn from this movie—is that *it is okay to be different*."

Brady leaned so close to my ear, I could feel his body heat. "Friend of mine saw this movie at a private screening last week."

"Any good?"

"He said it was worse than *Air Bud*."

Ben actually liked *Air Bud*, but I didn't say that. It didn't seem like the right time or place to tell Brady that I had a child.

Finally the producer got off the stage and the movie began. It was about a herd of well-groomed sheep that follows the sheepherder without question until they all stumble across a blue sheep living in a cave. Separated from its parents at birth as the result of a mountain lion attack, the blue sheep was raised by birds who have since flown away. No word on why the sheep turned blue.

The blue sheep joins the herd. Before you know it, the other sheep start using berries to dye their fleece. No one wants to be shorn. One sheep (now purple) sprouts dreadlocks. The sheep-herder turns mean.

Brady's friend was right: it was much worse than *Air Bud*. But I didn't care because I was sitting next to Brady Ellis, who would occasionally lean over, lightly touch my bare arm, and whisper in my ear: "Jay should give you hazard pay for this." Or, "Check it out—the kid three rows in front of us is playing with his Nintendo."

"That's baaaad," I whispered.

"Very baaaad."

"*Shh!*" Jay said in my other ear.

Brady fought a smile. "Baaad girl," he mouthed.

Less than an hour into the movie, as the early exit traffic increased, Jay pointed his thumb toward the door. I slipped my sunglasses back on and groped my way toward daylight.

In the lobby, Jay called the driver, and Brady lingered. He reached out like he was going to take my hand. Instead, he brushed the backs of my fingers with the backs of his. A current ran up my arm and through my body, all the way to my toes.

He smiled shyly and then dropped his eyes to the ground. "I'd like to see you again."

"You would?"

"Why do you sound so surprised?" He touched my cheek. I was grateful for my big sunglasses, which allowed me to gawk at him with undisguised lust.

"Well, let's see. How about—because you're a big star and I'm just this random girl." I couldn't remember the last time I'd thought of myself as a girl rather than a woman. It was kind of nice.

He slipped his hands in the front pockets of his soft, soft pants. "Not much of a star. I'm totally B list."

"Well, you're going to be a huge success," I said. "I can tell. So, um—yes. I'd love to see you again. But . . . do you mean as myself or as Haley?"

He laughed. "That's a funny question. I want you to be yourself. I don't care who you look like. You can dress up like Cinderella for all I care."

"I don't know about Cinderella. I've always been more partial to Snow White."

He grinned. "If you're Snow White, I'll be Happy."

I fake-winced and then started to giggle. "That was bad."

He pulled out his cell phone. "Can I have your number?"

Jay came over just as Brady finished inputting all of my information. "The driver's bringing the car around front."

Brady held my eyes. "Later, Ver—I mean Haley." His smile let me know the slip had been intentional.

I expected Jay to chide him, but he was already involved in another phone call.

Later, in the limo, I pulled out a tiny mirror to check my makeup and fuss with my hair. "That went well."

Jay raised one eyebrow.

"Anytime you want me to do something like this . . ." I said. "It doesn't have to be a film premiere. Brady and I could go to the beach, maybe, or just out to dinner."

"This isn't a dating service," he said, offending me on more levels than I knew I possessed.

I pulled off the cowboy hat and fluffed my pale hair. "I'm just trying to do my job."

Chapter Twenty

Friday morning, all alone, I made a big pot of coffee and settled myself in front of the computer, where I did an images search on "Haley Rush." Sure enough, there I was in my cowboy hat and sunglasses, standing on the red carpet, hand on hip, posing for photographers. It was hard to believe that was me. I looked so happy, so confident. I looked like a movie star. I looked like someone Brady Ellis might want to date.

Would he really call?

My photo showed up on a celebrity gossip site called *Get This!* The caption was uninspired: "Haley Rush attending the *Baaad Boys* premiere in Brentwood." Underneath, there were viewer comments—lots of them! How cool was that?

What is up with the cowboy hat and boots? She looks like she is going trick-or-treating.

Well! That was rude. But it's not like I picked out the clothes. Simone should feel bad, not me.

Those sunglasses look stupid. Way to big. Her eyes were probally blood shot, she was probally trying to hide them.

My eyes were not bloodshot, thank you very much! They are just a brighter, prettier blue than Haley's. So there!

She has sellulight on her thighs. Gross.

I have . . . what ? Ohmigod! Cellulite? I do not! It's the lighting! It's the angle! It's . . . okay, maybe that dress is a little too short to be flattering, but—

She looks like she is preggnent.

I am not preggnent! Or pregnant! How could these people be so mean?

I closed out the site, shut my eyes, and tried to calm my breathing. Once I was back to normal, I clicked right back to the picture and read every comment. A couple of people chided the meanest commentators to cut me some slack, but most took delight in trashing my hair, my hat, my body—even my pretty pink cowboy boots.

I had pored over Haley's photos before, but I had never read the comments. Now I went back to the image search and clicked on some of the more familiar shots.

People were kind at the beginning of Haley's rising popularity, but they had grown increasingly cruel. Her eyes were too close together, her fashion sense was off, her posture was bad. They called Pookie, the fuzzy pink backpack, "childish," "stupid," "retarded," "lame," and "like something she ripped off from one of the tone-deaf kids who thought she was a good singer."

Haley had encouraged me to take Pookie on my lunch date (oops—platonic encounter) with Brady. She knew there would be pictures. Was she thumbing her nose at the photographers? At the public? Or at me?

When my phone rang Sunday morning, I hoped it was Brady. Three days had passed without a word. But no: it was just Jay. "Do you have any idea where Haley might have gone?"

"She's missing?"

"Rodrigo popped out to get her some Pinkberry last night," Jay told me, his voice tense. "And when he came back she was gone."

"What about her car?"

"She took the truck."

Haley, the truck, and Mulholland Drive were a frightening combination. But surely someone would have noticed if a bright yellow truck had driven off the edge.

"Have you called the police?"

"No. I'm sure she's fine. And like you pointed out, she's an adult. She can do what she wants." He was a lousy actor. "Just— call me if you hear anything."

I refused to worry about Haley.

I closed out the computer and got down to the business of a normal life, vacuuming and dusting, cleaning the shower and scrubbing the toilet (which was getting pretty disgusting). And then I headed to my favorite Target, the one in Amerige Heights.

I had just finished loading my cereal and was headed for women's clothing when I ran into Nina.

"Hey!" I wanted to give her a big hug, sneak off to Starbucks, and tell her all of my secrets. But I couldn't, of course.

"Hello." She did not appear to be in a mood to hear my secrets, anyway.

"Where are the kids?"

"Home." She crossed her arms.

"Oh. Ben's at Hank's this weekend."

She looked around the store. "Ken here?"

"Ken Drucker? No. Why?"

"I heard you were with him this morning."

"I was home this morning. I cleaned the toilet." My back tightened with irritation. Nina was mad at me because she thought I was going out with Ken and hadn't told her? How do these rumors start?

"Well, that's weird." She couldn't decide whether or not to believe me. "Because Terri just called me. She went to Yogurt-land after church. She swears she saw you there with Ken. She said you smiled at her and everything."

Oh. My. God.

Nina saw my expression. "So you were there?"

"I gotta go!"

"But what about the stuff in your cart?"

"Later! I just, I just—I'll see you later."

Ken's ranch-style house, painted two shades of green, was smaller than the Motts'. It had a flat, neat lawn in front and big, leafy trees on either side. Haley's big yellow truck was parked in the concrete driveway.

When no one answered the doorbell, I turned to leave, only to see Ken and Haley, pink-cheeked and holding hands, walking up the driveway, a chocolate Lab at Ken's side. Ken wore cargo shorts and a black shirt, both made of some high-tech moisture-wicking material. Haley wore her usual velour sweats (mint green today), which for some reason looked plusher in

Fullerton than they had in Beverly Hills. Her messy hair was pulled back. She wore a baseball cap that said MAMMOTH MOUNTAIN. It had to be Ken's.

"Veronica—hi!" Ken said. "I was just showing Haley some of the trails." She refused to meet my eyes.

"I heard you went for yogurt this morning," I said. The dog trotted over, sniffed my crotch, and returned to Ken.

Ken said, "Haley told me she liked Pinkberry, and I told her, Haley, you've got to try Yogurtland! She likes it even better. Don't you, babe?" He leaned down to check her expression: sweet, wide-eyed bliss. Of course, she was an actress. She probably had an entire catalog of facial expressions.

"I didn't realize you two had even met," I said.

"Really? I thought you two told each other everything." He dropped Haley's hand and put his arm around her shoulders.

"Not everything," Haley said in a little baby voice.

Oh, God. Had they had sex? Was I in trouble? Jay was going to kill me.

"How did you . . ." I began. "How did she find you?"

"She e-mailed me!" Ken said, beaming. "Last weekend. Said you'd told her we'd be perfect for each other. And, you know, I'm starting to think there's something to that." He squeezed her shoulders.

"I finally got up the nerve to call her last night." Ken continued. "And we talked for, what—two hours?"

Haley looked at the ground. "Three."

Tinny country music filled the air: a John Denver ringtone. Ken reached into one of his many pants pockets, pulled out a cell phone, and checked the screen.

"Pamela." He and Haley wrinkled their noses. He hit a button. "Hi, Pam."

"How did you get his e-mail address?" I whispered to Haley.

She licked her lips. "The website you showed me listed the pack leader guy. So I just wrote to him and said, like, I need to talk to Ken about my cookie order. He gave me the e-mail."

My nostrils flared. "Cookies are a Girl Scout thing. Cub Scouts sell popcorn."

She rolled her eyes. "What. Ever."

"Did you tell the pack leader who you were?"

She squatted down to the dog's level and rubbed his ears. "I said I was you."

"You can't do that!"

She looked up and narrowed her blue (but not bright blue) eyes. "Why not? You say you're me all the time."

"That's different. You can't just walk around Fullerton pretending to be someone else."

She straightened. "I wasn't pretending anything. Nobody thought I was you."

"Of course they did. I live here, remember?"

"At least five people asked for my autograph. They knew who I was."

The people who know me don't ask for my autograph—but there was no point fighting about it.

Ken was deep in conversation with Pamela, a line of irritation settling between his eyebrows. I continued my interrogation. "Didn't Rodrigo think it was weird that you were on the phone for three hours Friday night? He never even mentioned it to Jay."

"Rodrigo wasn't there."

"But he told Jay that he just popped out to get you Pinkberry."

She raised her eyebrows (both at the same time since she couldn't do just one) and spoke slowly. "He lied. If he came over

at all on Friday, it's because he called the home number and I
didn't answer."

"But . . . but . . ."

"Jay thinks I can't be left alone," she said. "Which is so fucking stupid. I mean, what am I going to do?"

I resisted the temptation to offer suggestions. Drive Mulholland while drunk? Crawl down steep hillsides in the dark? Visit
men you've met on the Internet?

"Rodrigo and I have a deal," she continued. "Sometimes he
comes over—we really are good friends—but most of the time
we agree to tell Jay he's been there. Rodrigo gets paid, and I get
to be left alone. It works out for everyone."

"Jay is really worried about you," I said.

She laughed bitterly. "Jay only worries about himself and
how much money he's going to make."

Ken slipped his phone back into one of his pockets, closing
it with Velcro for added safety. He looked at Haley, at me, then
back to Haley.

"Like seeing double, right?" I asked.

He shook his head. "I don't actually think you look that
much alike."

Jay answered on the first ring. "Veronica."

"Haley's here."

"Oh, thank God." He exhaled with relief. "She's with you?"

"Well, no. But she's in Fullerton."

There was silence. "Because . . . ?"

"She met somebody. A man. And he lives here."

"Quite a coincidence." His voice was flat and accusatory. I
liked him better when he was worried.

"It's somebody I know. Obviously. And I mentioned him to Haley, and she took it upon herself to contact him."

"Somebody you know? What—you mean a boyfriend?"

"As you know, I don't have a boyfriend." And probably never will.

"That's just great," Jay said. "Now we're screwed. This guy will fuck around with her, and then she'll have another break-down, and then he'll go to the press and—"

"He's not like that," I interrupted. "He's a nice guy. Ethical. It's all been very wholesome. They talked and ate yogurt and went for a hike."

Suddenly I had a vision of Haley selling her Beverly Hills mansion and moving into Ken's little ranch house, walking the boys to school, tending a garden in the backyard. Hollywood made her miserable. Why shouldn't she just give it up? Perhaps Ken and Haley weren't such a ridiculous match, after all.

"Haley has a recording session tomorrow," Jay said. "If she misses it, we risk losing the contract."

"She'll be home in a few hours," I said. "Ken has to pick up his kids from his ex-wife at three, and he thinks it's too early to introduce them to Haley."

"He has *kids*?"

"Yes, Jay," I hissed. "Out here in the real world, people have children. They have normal jobs, responsibilities, and a sense of perspective."

"It was just a question," he muttered.

Chapter Twenty-one

When my phone rang the next Friday, I was sitting in my little living room, reading *OK!* magazine. No pictures of me—damn!

"Hello?"

"Hey, is this . . . Veronica?" It wasn't Jay. Too bad: I hadn't worked since the film premiere.

"Yes."

"Hey," he said. "How's it going?"

Was he a telemarketer? I didn't have time for this. I mean, I could be . . . cleaning my toilet. Or Googling "Haley Rush." Or finishing an in-depth article about Violet Affleck's wardrobe.

"Who is this?"

"Oh! Sorry." He laughed. "It's Brady." A week had passed without him calling; I had given up hope.

For a moment I couldn't breathe. And then I made a weird

sound, kind of like, "Oh-mu-wah," gasped a little and said, "Hi!"

"Sorry I haven't called sooner," he said. "Life's been crazy busy. But I've been thinking about you."

I said, "You have? Because I, um. The thing is, I, uh . . . okay . . ."

"Just okay?" I could hear the smile in his voice.

My brain buzzed so loudly with excitement, it was hard to think straight. "I didn't mean okay as in just-okay," I blurted. "I meant it as in, I understand. So um . . . hi!" I laughed with embarrassment.

"Hi." He laughed with something other than embarrassment. "Are you doing anything tonight?"

"Tonight?" It was Friday. I had Ben. Brady was asking me out.

"Nothing much. Why?"

"I was thinking maybe we could go out. Have some drinks. Talk."

Brady liked me—for real! I felt just like the girl in *Bling*. "That would be . . . I'd love that!" An alarm went off in the inner reaches of my brain. "But—is it okay with Jay?"

"I don't have to ask my manager permission to go on a date."

"Of course you don't. But if I'm pretending to be Haley, and he doesn't even know . . ." Oh, God. Was I talking him out of the date? What was wrong with me?

"You don't have to pretend to be Haley. Just be yourself. This isn't a photo session or a film premiere. We don't have to answer anyone's questions. And if they assume you're someone else— hey, that's their problem, not ours. I'm not asking Haley to go out with me. I'm asking you."

"In that case, I say yes." Yes, yes, yes!!!

"You want me to pick you up? Where do you live?"

Transformers, Rescue Heroes, and Legos littered the coffee table in front of me. Brady didn't even know I had a kid. I'd tell him, of course, but not now. Not on the phone.

"I live kind of far out of the way. How about I meet you at your place?"

At one o'clock, Deborah Mott was freshly dressed for the day, her hair still wet from the shower. I found her in her kitchen, standing at the island, eating what looked like cold spaghetti out of a giant Tupperware bowl.

"Hi, Deborah. I was wondering—"

"You are picking up the kids today, aren't you?" Two spots of tomato sauce clung to the corners of her mouth.

"Yes. Of course."

"Because I was just on my way to Costco, and I wouldn't be able to make it back on time." She pushed the top back onto the Tupperware and put it in the fridge.

"No problem," I assured her. "In fact—take your time at Costco. I'll keep an eye on the kids."

"Oh! As long as it doesn't put you out!" Her grin revealed a fleck of something brownish-green—parsley? basil?—stuck between her two front teeth.

"Not at all." I took a deep breath. "But, Deborah, I was just wondering. Shavonne's getting so grown-up. I mean, she's almost in junior high. So I was wondering what you'd think, how you'd feel, if she, say, babysat for Ben."

"Babysat?" She scrunched up her face.

"I'd pay her, of course. I'd have my cell phone with me the whole time, and she's got you on the other side of the yard."

"Huh." Deborah looked concerned—afraid, probably, that she'd have to do some of the work herself. "I'd have to think about it. And talk to Shavonne. When were you thinking of?"

"Um . . . tonight, actually."

"Oh! Goodness! So soon. Is it to see . . . that man?" She meant Jay.

"No," I said. "No. That's over. I mean, it was never not over—it was never on."

"That's too bad. He was really . . . yum." She licked her lips, which for some reason just really, really grossed me out.

"So—is Shavonne free?"

"You have a date with someone else?"

I was about to say no when I saw the eagerness in Deborah's eyes. If I said I was just meeting a friend, she probably wouldn't let Shavonne babysit. So I gave her what she wanted, which, oddly enough, happened to be the truth.

"Actually—yes." I smiled.

"Tell me!"

"It's just this guy I've met a couple of times. It probably won't go anywhere, but you never know. I mean, Hank's already remarried and I haven't even started dating. It's about time I put myself out there."

"You'd be a fool not to."

"But I hate Shavonne," Ben declared several hours later as I stood in front of the mirror, messing with my mounds of freshly washed-and-dried blond hair.

"That's not a very nice thing to say."

"She's mean." He sat slumped on the bed, knees up, picking at the frayed hem of his Cherokee-brand pants.

"She won't be mean tonight. She's excited about babysitting, and she wants to do a good job." (Besides, I was paying her; she had to be nice.)

I tried pulling my hair back with a clip, but that exposed my dark roots. When was Jay going to send me for a follow-up appointment to Stefano? This was getting embarrassing.

"Why can't I go to Daddy's house?" Ben asked.

"Because Daddy got to have you for the past two days. This way, I get to have dinner with you tonight and breakfast with you tomorrow." (And also, I really, really didn't want to explain to Hank why I couldn't have scheduled my date on a different weekend.)

"When will you be home?" His voice quavered.

"Oh, Benji." I joined him on the bed and put my arms around him. He didn't hug me back. "It's not that big a deal. I'm leaving at seven, and you go to bed at eight. I told Mrs. Mott I'd be home no later than eleven. It might even be earlier. When you wake up, I'll be here, and I'll make you pancakes."

I stood up and smoothed out my dress. It was royal blue, slightly off the shoulder, with a 1940s-type hourglass silhouette. Before getting the kids from school, I'd gone downtown and bought a few things at Roadkill Ranch, the boutique Nina was always telling me to visit. With the dress, I wore new black pumps and a chunky silver bracelet.

"Do you like my dress?" I asked Ben.

"No."

Brady's reaction was far more enthusiastic. "You look amazing. Just . . . beautiful. And . . . amazing."

"Thanks." I liked the way he gazed at me, as if he were trying to memorize my every curve and pore. Had Hank ever looked at me like that? I couldn't remember.

His apartment was on the second floor of an old, mint green apartment building in West Hollywood. He stood in the open doorway, leaning on the doorjamb, looking especially gorgeous in a blue-and-white-striped shirt, which he wore untucked over soft blue jeans.

See? It was possible to dress casually without looking like a slob. Jay could learn a thing or two—not that I wanted to think about Jay right now.

"You want a beer before we go?" He moved out of the doorway to let me in.

"Sure." I didn't really want a beer, but it seemed rude to refuse. Besides, I was eager to see his apartment.

It was nothing special. The main room was a big white box with a rectangular window that looked out to another tired, pastel-colored apartment complex. There was a gray velour couch, a chunky pale wood coffee table, two recliners, and an incredibly large television mounted on the wall. Shiny black boxes sat on the floor next to the television: the DVR, VCR, cable box, and video game console. There were no pictures, no candles, no vases or throw blankets.

In short, the apartment stood as material proof that there was no woman in Brady Ellis's life. As such, it made me very, very happy.

A can of lemon Pledge sat on the coffee table. I picked it up.

"Cleaning?"

"Oops." He took it from me. "Didn't want you to see the apartment in its natural state. I'm not that bad, but my roommate is a pig."

"You have a roommate?"

He nodded. "He's not here right now, but yeah. Ivan. He's a stuntman. And a little person."

"You live with a midget?"

"Don't laugh! Dude's scary. He's got tattoos all over his back and neck and arms and stuff, plus he's got a pierced ear and a pierced cheek with a chain that hangs between them." He shuddered. "Another couple seasons of *Kitty* and I should be able to buy my own place. Assuming there are a couple more seasons . . ."

I remembered what Jay had said about cutting the last season short.

"Haley does seem a little . . . undercommitted," I said.

"Haley needs to *be* committed."

When he saw my expression, he ran a hand through his thick dark hair and said, "Sorry—that was harsh. The thing is, I gave a lot of my life to her. A lot of my energy. And it was just so draining. I couldn't do it anymore—couldn't fix whatever is wrong with her. She was pulling me down with her, you know? I had to save myself."

His dark eyes grew intent. "I know it sounds selfish, but I deserve someone who will make me happy."

I nodded, fighting the urge to shout, "Let me make you happy! Me, me, me!"

He stuck his hands in his pockets. "I'm talking too much."

"No! Not at all!"

His eyes softened. "There's something about you that just makes me . . . I don't know."

"What?"

"Open up. I feel like I can relax around you. That I can be myself."

"I feel the same way," I said—and then I laughed at the

obvious absurdity of my statement. "I mean—except for when I'm being Haley."

He grinned. "You may look like her, but you don't act like her at all. You want a beer?"

"Love one."

The galley kitchen had white laminate cabinets with chrome fixtures, white countertops, white appliances, even a white tile floor. A fluorescent fixture overhead provided the only light. Aside from a faint sour smell, it reminded me of a hospital.

The refrigerator had one shelf devoted to beer and another crammed with carry-out boxes.

"Meal-delivery meals?" I asked.

"God, no. Take-out containers. I haven't gone *that* Hollywood."

He opened two beers and handed me a bottle. I liked that he didn't offer to pour it in a glass. He was just a regular guy . . . who happened to look like a Greek god.

"You want the tour?"

He took me by the hand and led me down a dark hallway. His roommate's door was open, revealing a double mattress on the floor with covers so disheveled that they exposed the striped ticking. Clothes, dishes, and magazines covered almost every bit of the carpeting.

"Scary," I said.

"Sometimes it's worse," Brady said.

Next, we passed a dark, grayish bathroom with a shower but no tub. And then we reached Brady's room. A queen-sized bed, neatly made with blue covers, took up most of the space. There was a tall black laminate dresser and a matching nightstand. There were no pictures on the walls, no photos on the surfaces—nothing. Like Haley, Brady had a guitar propped up in one corner. I felt a stab of jealousy: they had something in common.

I pointed to the guitar. "You play?"

"You want to hear?"

"Of course."

He took the guitar and settled on the bed. I sat next to him because there was no chair. And because I wanted to.

He played a soft song that I'd never heard before. His voice was smooth and mellow, full of emotion. I could have listened to it for hours.

I would have gotten lost in the music, but the little voice in my head wouldn't let me: *Ohmigod! I'm next to Brady Ellis! On a bed! Ohmigod, ohmigod, OHMIGOD—what if he makes a pass? What if he actually wants me IN this bed? Would that be wrong?*

"Did you like the song?" Brady asked.

I blinked myself back to attention. "Loved it. How long have you been playing?"

"Since high school. Music is my first love. The acting thing just kind of happened. I took the part on *Kitty* because the producers said I'd be able to play my own music, but that hasn't worked out. They've only had me sing twice, and never my own stuff and never alone."

He held my eyes. I could feel my heart beating all the way up to my throat. He put a hand on my cheek. "You're so beautiful."

My lips felt hot. He leaned forward and laid his mouth on mine, and it was like my entire body dissolved into his warmth. I put my arms around his neck and pressed myself against him.

When he drew back, it was like someone had taken my oxygen away. His breathing, still close enough to feel, was warm.

He ran a hand down my arm. It tingled. He said, "This is moving kind of fast. I don't want you to think . . . I mean, I really like you, and I don't want it to be like . . ."

"It's not," I said. "It's okay."

He grinned sheepishly. "I'd like to take you out. You know—be a gentleman."

"You don't have to be too much of a gentleman," I said, fully prepared to rip off my new blue dress.

He stood up and held out a hand. "We've got plenty of time. I want to get to know you first."

We didn't have plenty of time, but he didn't know that. If I was going to make it back to Fullerton by eleven, I'd have to leave right after we had drinks. What would Brady say if he knew I had a child? Would he still like me so much?

He dropped my hand and pulled his cell phone out of his back pocket. "I need to text a friend of mine—another actor. We've worked together on a couple of projects. He and his girlfriend are going out tonight, thought we might meet up. That okay with you?"

"Sure—of course." Did Brady like me so much that he was already prepared to bring me into his circle of friends? Or was he not ready to spend an entire evening alone with me?

This kind of overthinking was one reason why I never dated. The other reason was that Brady was the first guy to ask me out since my divorce.

He tapped out a quick text with his thumbs. Almost immediately, the phone buzzed with a response.

"They coming?" I asked.

He shrugged. "Dunno. His girlfriend wants sushi—she likes this place down in Santa Monica—so if they show, it'll be after, like, eleven.

I nodded, even though that meant I wouldn't meet his friends; I'd be home by then. It was already after eight-thirty; I hadn't bargained on spending so much time in Brady's apartment (though I was glad I had).

For the first time, I was conscious of the age difference between Brady and me. It was only three years, but we were at completely different life stages. But then, I'd skipped right over the postcollege party stage. Was it too late? Did I have to live my life in order?

The apartment building was on stilts, with a parking lot below. Brady pointed out cars. A Camaro: "Belongs to a guy used to be in *MacGyver*." A bright red Civic: "Girl was on *The Bachelor*—that one with the Italian guy. She didn't win, but she's doing some modeling and guest appearances and stuff."

Brady's car was a late-model Jeep Cherokee, gleaming on the outside, borderline-filthy within. "Should've cleaned," he said, removing a cardboard coffee cup, half full with an old brew, from the cup holder. He chucked it into a garbage can and climbed into the driver's seat as I strapped myself in.

He froze. "I forgot to open your door. I'm sorry."

"It's okay. Really." Again, Brady seemed young, but I liked it. I'd already tried the older, door-opening man route, and that hadn't worked out so well. Maybe it was time to reclaim some of my lost youth.

Bar DeLux was on Cahuenga Boulevard, a street crammed with flashy cars and trendy bars. Brady pulled up to a blocky, glass-fronted brick building. A valet opened my door, exposing me to the peering masses: girls in tiny black dresses, guys in jeans and sports jackets, photographers in bright white sneakers. Flashbulbs bathed my face before I even stepped on the pavement. Jay was going to be pissed.

Brady put his arm around me and ushered me through the crowds.

"Maybe we should go somewhere else," I whispered into his ear.

"Don't worry—inside it's dark and private. No one will bother us."

"Haley!"

"Haley—over here!"

"Haley, Brady, Haley!"

"Haley, Brady—are you back together?"

"Smile for me, Haley, Haley—smile!"

The flashing cameras had been fun on the red carpet. Now—not so much. Tonight I was Veronica Czaplicki. That's who Brady had asked out, not Haley.

At the velvet rope, the bouncer, an enormous man dressed all in black, hesitated. A line had formed to one side: people not beautiful or famous enough to get in without a wait. He looked from me to Brady and back at me, nodded once, and unhooked the rope. "Have a nice night, folks."

At last, we were in. A willowy girl with heavy eyebrows and hair too dark for her complexion waited inside the door, a velvet curtain behind her.

"Dinner?" She gave Brady a hungry-wolf grin.

Brady took my hand. "Just drinks. Can we get a couch?"

She studied a chart—not an easy task in the dim light—and shook her head. "But if you hang out by the bar, you might be able to get a table."

"You've gotta have at least one couch left," Brady said, flashing a smile.

"They're all reserved. For dinner. Really sorry."

Brady dropped my hand and took a couple of steps toward

the girl. At first, I thought he was taking her hand—I'm all in favor of getting a good table, but that was pushing it—but then I realized that he was slipping her some money. I heard him say, "Haley Rush." The next thing you knew, before I even had a chance to feel miffed at being passed off as Haley, we were past the velvet curtain.

It was like entering a different world—or, at least a different time, one of old Hollywood glamour and Art Deco sophistication. The walls were velvet, the ceiling mahogany, the couches geometric. Flames flickered inside an elaborately carved wooden fireplace. Overhead, crystal chandeliers shaped like wedding cakes cast a yellow glow. Behind the mahogany bar, a lit wall of green stained glass showed a scene from long ago: a time of blimps and Model Ts and quiet, paparazzi-free streets.

Holding hands, we followed the hostess through the small space, weaving between heavily made-up girls in stilettos and pampered guys in jeans and sport coats. At last, we reached our couch.

"It's like the Emerald City," I said, looking toward the bar. And it was, too—assuming the Emerald City was dimly lit and had a DJ playing techno pop.

Brady put his arm around me. I looked at his perfect face and thought: Is this really happening?

"You're not in Kansas, anymore, Dorothy." He touched his forehead to mine.

"I'm okay with that," I answered. Right now, Fullerton seemed as far away as Kansas.

He kissed me softly on the mouth. I didn't worry about guerilla photographers: it was too dark to get much of a shot.

We pulled apart just as a waitress appeared: yet another pretty

young woman with hair too dark and eyebrows unconvincingly
heavy.

Brady ordered a drink made with Scotch and jalapeños.
Around the room, martini glasses glowed with gumdrop colors.
The waitress suggested I try something called a Basil Berry. I
agreed, not caring what I drank, just wanting to be alone with
Brady.

"Do you come here much?" I asked.

"Not really. Couple times a month, maybe. We try to rotate."

"We?"

He smiled. "Me and my friends. You're not jealous, are you?"

"No! I—sorry. I just . . . never mind."

"I've never been here with Haley, if that's what you're wondering."

"That wasn't what I meant. Though I guess I was curious."

"We didn't go to bars much," he said. "She really couldn't
handle them. She'd get drunk and then someone would try to
take her picture, and then she'd freak out." He stopped. "Why
are we talking about Haley?"

"What do you want to talk about?" I asked, mesmerized by
his eyes.

"You."

"I'm not very interesting," I said.

"You are to me. Tell me about yourself. I want to know everything."

"I, um . . . grew up in northern California. Came down here
to go to college. I went to Cal State Fullerton and never left.
When I'm not working for Jay, I'm a substitute teacher. Elementary school. I'm hoping to get something permanent. At least I
was until . . ."

"What?"

"The Haley gig has been nice. The money, I mean. Plus, the side benefits . . ." I stroked his thigh as the words *I'm stroking Brady Ellis's thigh* shot through my brain.

"No reason you have to give that up," he said.

"I'm getting the feeling from Jay . . . I don't think it's going to last much longer."

"Jay's an asshole. You can't depend on him. Fact is, you still look like Haley. An entertainment company would hire you to be a double. You know, not to fool people into actually thinking you are her, but to be the entertainment at birthday parties, corporate events, trade shows, that sort of thing. There's a ton of Chers and Bette Midlers out there, but you'd have the Haley business pretty much to yourself."

The Basil Berry turned out to be vodka mixed with strawberries and basil. I think there was some balsamic vinegar in there, too. At first it was weird in a good way. A few sips in, it was just weird.

"How's your drink?" Brady asked. I leaned closer to hear him over the noise.

"Delicious," I lied. "Yours?"

"Hot." He licked his lips. "It's got jalapeños."

"Wow."

"Seriously."

He held my gaze for an instant and leaned in for yet another kiss. My lips burned and tingled—from passion or capsaicin, I wasn't sure.

When he pulled back, I said, "Wow" again, which he answered with another, "Seriously." We smiled in tandem. We drank in tandem. Basil and strawberry remained an unnatural combination, but I didn't care.

"I could kiss you all night," he said.

"What's stopping you?"

He kissed me lightly (and too briefly for my taste) before leaning back and surveying the room. "I saw Lindsay here once."

"Lindsay?" Was she someone from his show?

"And Paris, too. But she was on her way out."

Oh—that Lindsay. That Paris.

When he saw my expression, he laughed. "I love that you're so un-Hollywood. That you're not always looking over my shoulder to see if there's someone better to talk to."

"I already know there's no one better."

"That's sweet of you," he said. "You're a really sweet girl." He looked around the room, and his arm grew stiff. "Shit."

"What?"

He faced me, his tone urgent. "Just look at me, pretend we're deep in conversation, and maybe he won't come over."

"Who?"

It was too late.

"Yo, Brady, what the fuck's up, man? Didn't know you guys were *back together*." He made air quotes with his fingers.

I forced a smile, not expecting to recognize the face, startled when I saw the tight sandy curls, squinty eyes, too-big chin. It was Jason somebody-or-other, the guy who played Jason Katz. He wore a tight, white waffle-weave shirt—it looked like long underwear—with black jeans. Pressed against him, a tiny Asian girl with short, streaked hair sucked on a yellow martini.

He said, "Haley, you're looking like one sexy bitch, but you know that, don't you?" His face froze in mid-leer. "I thought you were . . . You look a lot like . . ."

"Jason, this is Veronica," Brady said. "Veronica, Jason."

I tried again to smile, but my face wouldn't cooperate.

"Shit," Jason said. He laughed: a dirty sound.

I'd passed for Haley in broad daylight, but that was when I wore a hat and sunglasses. Anyone who knew Haley wouldn't be fooled. In a way that made me glad: tonight it really was me and not Haley who was at Bar DeLux with Brady.

Jason put his arm around the Asian girl and propelled her toward the far end of the couch. "We were just looking for a place to crash, so if you don't mind—"

"We mind," Brady said, his tone cold.

Jason stopped. Something I couldn't read passed over his features. "Later, then."

He looked at me in a way that made me shudder, and then he and the girl left.

"Is he always that creepy?" I asked.

"Such an asshole," Brady said, his face hard.

"Do he and Haley get along?"

"God, no. She hates him. He came after her. You know— hit on her. When the show started. And even after she and I were . . . together . . . he didn't let up. It's like he thinks he has some right to her, just because he was there first."

"What do you mean—they did go out?"

"No." He shook his head. "I mean, he was on the show first." That didn't make sense. And why did every conversation always return to Haley, anyway?

When the waitress reappeared to ask us if we wanted another round, I said yes without thinking. What time was it, anyway? I reached into my purse to check my cell phone. It wasn't there: I must have left it charging in my car. Oh, crap! I'd told Deborah that I'd have it with me at all times. But, did it really matter? What if she called me? I was an hour away. Besides, Deborah dumped her horrible kids on me all the time. She and Shavonne could deal with sweet Ben for one evening.

Our geometric couch felt like an oasis in the middle of the club. The air buzzed with music and chatter. The scent of expensive cologne mingled with the aroma of Scotch and beer.

The waitress brought our drinks. The Basil Berry tasted better this time around. Brady switched to Red Bull and vodka. "I don't want to fall asleep on you." Of course, the idea of falling asleep with Brady was as appealing as it was unrealistic.

"You want to dance?" he asked me when our drinks were almost gone. A small group of people, women mostly, were swaying and stepping to the music in a clump by the fireplace.

"Sure." I would have preferred a slower song, but I welcomed any excuse to hold on to Brady.

It didn't matter that the song was fast. He pulled me to him, pressed his length against me. If not for the alcohol, I would have been nervous and self-conscious. Instead, I gave in to the moment, to the warmth and the emotion.

"I really like you," he whispered in my ear.

"I really like you, too."

Before I knew it, we were kissing, right there in front of everybody. Finally, he pulled away. "Let's get out of here."

We wove our way through the bodies back to the couch. We sat for a minute, shamelessly making out like a couple of high school kids. Finally, Brady threw a bunch of bills on the table and slid off the couch, leading me out of the bar by my hand.

I'd forgotten about the paparazzi. Their flashes started going off the moment we stepped outside.

"Haley, Haley, Haley!"

"Haley, Brady—over here!"

A valet drove up in Brady's Jeep, and a large black man with a soothing voice and wearing a pinstriped suit and fedora, guided us through the throngs and helped me inside. Even after the security guard had gently closed my door, they continued to swarm like mosquitoes. Brady couldn't pull away without hitting them, so the security guard cleared a path and waved him through.

"Is it always like this?" My hands were shaking.

"Pretty much." Streetlights lit his perfect face, like something out of a dream. He put his hand on my leg. "You okay?"

"Sure. Of course. It's just . . . I kind of understand why Haley crashed her car."

"Haley crashed her car because she mixed alcohol with about three prescription medications. She's lucky she didn't die."

We drove in silence toward the Sunset Strip, and then he turned into a parking lot. There was a donut shop (open) and a dry cleaner (closed). He pulled into a dark corner, next to an empty pickup truck, and turned off the car.

"We keep talking about Haley. It's hard not to. But I need you to know something. The way I feel about you has nothing to do with her. The very first time we met it was like I felt this instant connection. Not because you look like her, but in spite of it. I just can't get you out of my mind."

He put his hands on my face and stroked my cheekbones. "I could look at you all night," he whispered. "Or longer."

I didn't think about being in a car in the dumpy parking lot. I didn't think about the photographers or Jay or Jason or Haley. I reached out and seized the moment—which, in this instance, happened to be the same thing as seizing Brady.

Our mouths joined and roamed. He hauled himself over the center console and onto my side. Fortunately, the seat shifted back, at least a little. I straddled him (smacking my head against the ceiling in the process). When he pulled my new blue dress over my head, it caught on an earring. I winced for only an instant. Nothing mattered but me and Brady and our awkward grappling.

He caressed my breast as I undid his jeans, their buttons annoying me with their slowness. Our breathing was hard and hot, the leather of the seats was cool. He said, "God, you're beautiful," And, "God, you're hot," and a couple of other things that don't need to be repeated.

I whacked my elbow on the window and swore. I'd never done this in a car before. I closed my eyes and concentrated on the feel of his body.

When it was over, he held me in his arms, our sweat mingling, and stroked my back. "That was amazing."

"Mmm." I nuzzled his neck.

"Next time it'll be in a bed."

"I don't know. I kind of like this car thing."

"You do, huh?" He leaned back to examine my face. "Naughty girl."

All at once, it occurred to me that we were in a public place. Fortunately, our corner of the lot was still dark, the pickup truck empty. My dress lay crumpled on the floor. I slipped it over my head, careful not to snag my earrings this time. I began to giggle.

"What?"

"I can't believe we did that."

"I'm glad we did."

"Me, too."

He tried to straighten and hit his head on the ceiling. "Shit!"

I laughed. "Okay, maybe we'd be better off in a bed."

He slid back over the console, jostling me in the process, and pulled up his pants. "It just so happens that I've got one of those in my apartment."

"That sounds . . . wonderful." Oh, to be able to spend the night with Brady! "But I can't tonight."

"Why not?" He turned his key in the ignition. The clock on the dashboard read 11:52.

I gasped. "Oh, my God! How did it get so late? I've got to go!"

"Why?"

This was not the time to tell him about Ben. Obviously, I should have mentioned him sooner, but I had no idea things would move so fast.

"There's things I have to do tomorrow. I have to get up early. And if I don't get enough sleep, I'm just . . . I just need to go."

"Okay." He looked hurt.

"I really like you." It seemed crazy that I had to say that given what had just happened, but I wanted to be clear. "And I want to spend more time with you. Next weekend, maybe?"

"Can't. I'm flying to Australia this week. Tomorrow night, actually. We're shooting a Betwixt Channel movie."

"Australia? With Haley?"

He shook his head. "She isn't in this one."

Phew.

"When will you be back?"

"Shooting's supposed to take four weeks, but sometimes they run over."

"That's so long."

"Don't look so sad." He ran a hand over my messy blond hair. "It's not forever."

Chapter Twenty-two

There were four messages on my cell phone.

From Ben, at 8:13 p.m.: *When will you be home?*

From Shavonne, at 8:52 p.m.: *Ben said he won't go to bed until you're back, so my mom said to call you. Can you call him?*

From Ben again, at 10:41 p.m. (crying this time): *Mommy! I want you to come home!*

From Deborah, at 11:05 p.m. (sounding tense): *You said you would be back by eleven. Shavonne needs to go to bed.*

From Deborah again, at 11:58 (sounding pissed): *I hope you understand how much you have inconvenienced us. The night was ruined for all of us, and Ben did not behave.*

After Brady dropped me off at the minivan (I'd been afraid he'd ask why I needed such a big car, but he didn't), I tried Deborah's cell phone: no answer. I didn't dare call the house. If I woke

Shaun, I'd never hear the end of it. I might never hear the end of it, anyway.

When I got home forty minutes later, having sped the whole way, the guesthouse was empty, and the big house was dark. A piece of paper lay on the kitchen table.

Roni,

Deb called—I've got Ben.

Hank

Oh, crap! I picked up the phone to call him before I realized they'd all be asleep. Hank was an early-to-bed kind of guy, which meant he'd already been awoken once this evening, when Deborah called.

With Ben gone, I could have slept in the bed. Instead, I changed into pajamas and lay down on the couch.

"Hi, Hank. It's me. Sorry about last night."

I'd set my alarm for seven o'clock, so I could have a cup of coffee and sound reasonably alert when I called.

"Ben was really upset." His voice was soft, his tone even.

"I know. Thanks for getting him."

He cleared his throat. "It's fine that you're dating, but it shouldn't get in the way of your time with our son."

"It's *fine* that I'm dating?"

"You're free every other weekend. That should be enough time for you to do your partying."

"I wasn't partying!" I was having sex in a car.

"It's tough on Ben, this business of switching houses. We need to do everything we can to make him feel secure. When you make him feel like you're too busy to spend the evening with him—and then break your word on top of it—"

That did it.

"The only reason Ben is feeling *insecure* is because you walked out on our family! How dare you tell me when I can and can't date? If you hadn't fucked someone else while we were married, we wouldn't even be having this conversation!"

In my whole life, I don't think I had ever used the word "fucked" in a literal sense. But if not now, when?

When Hank spoke again, his voice was cold. "Ben is still sleeping. Do you want me to bring him over when he wakes up?"

"Of course not. I'm happy to get him."

My conversation with Deborah was slightly less cordial.

"I see you made it home." She stood in her kitchen doorway, arms crossed in front of her chest.

"Deborah, I am so, so sorry. Things ran late, and I should have called. I left my cell phone in my car, which was really stupid. I didn't even realize what time it was, and then when I saw it was after eleven—"

"You took advantage of my daughter. And of our friendship."

"I'm so sorry." I think I get points for not saying, *What friendship?*

"Shavonne was *extremely* upset."

"I didn't mean for it to happen."

"You know, Veronica, when I first told Paul about your situation and we talked about renting you the guesthouse at a below-market rate, he was concerned. He said, do we want to expose our own children to the effects of divorce? But in the end we decided that offering you the house was the Christian thing to do."

Silent, I stared, my hands trembling.

"But now you're running around like a teenager. Bringing one man home one night, staying out late with a different man another night."

"I never brought a man home," I said. "He was just giving me a ride."

"It makes me wonder, you know, if we made the right decision offering you this house."

The threat of homelessness renewed my humility. "I'm really very sorry, Deborah. I don't know what else to say."

She licked her lips. "You still owe Shavonne her money. You were gone for seven hours."

I was only gone for six, but I paid for the extra hour without complaint.

My cell phone rang in the early afternoon, after Ben and I had shared a mostly silent lunch of peanut butter and banana sandwiches. I'd tried, *I'm sorry*. I'd tried, *I love you more than anything*. I'd asked, *Did you have fun with Daddy?* and *What do you want to do today?* All with no luck.

It was Jay.

"I just got a call from Haley's publicist."

"Okay."

"There are some pictures of Haley and Brady. Taken last night. They're already online."

An image flashed through my mind: me straddling Brady in the front seat of his car. My entire body grew cold.

Jay said, "The pictures show Haley and Brady outside the Bar DeLux . . ."

Thank God!!!

". . . which kind of surprised me since Haley was at her house last night. With me."

"How cozy for you both."

"Excuse me?"

"Brady asked me out. I said yes. If the press thought I was someone else, that's their problem."

"You don't go to the Bar DeLux unless you want your picture taken."

"Where were we supposed to go? Chili's?"

"You can't just run around pretending to be Haley whenever you feel like it!"

"I wasn't pretending to be anybody! Brady likes me for myself. Is that so hard to believe?"

"From Brady? Yes."

Only a couple of obscure gossip sites ran the pictures of Brady and me outside Bar DeLux. I should have been relieved; instead I felt disappointed. There were plenty of pictures of Brady and Haley—at restaurants, at parties, at the beach. I wanted more shots of Brady and me, even if we were the only ones who knew my true identity.

The day would have been a complete loss if not for the final phone call, which came in just as I was putting a frozen pizza into the toaster oven.

"I'm on my way to the airport," Brady said, his voice muffled by traffic sounds. "But I needed to hear your voice before I left."

I slipped into the bedroom so Brady wouldn't hear Ben's cartoon.

"I had a great time last night," Brady said.

"Me, too." I sat on the bed and pulled a pillow onto my lap. "Jay called."

"Yeah, I talked to him. Such a tool."

I laughed. Brady could see right through Jay. That's why Jay didn't like him.

"And I talked to my publicist," Brady said. "Told her our situation. Well, not that you've been working for Jay—just that I met a girl who looks a lot like Haley and that people might get the wrong idea. She said we should wait till I get back to make any kind of comment to the press."

"Okay."

"Maybe we could even go away for a while. You know, head down to Mexico or maybe up to Santa Barbara."

My heart raced—I mean, even more than it already was. "I'd love that!"

Of course, we'd have to plan it for a weekend when I didn't have Ben—and I'd have to tell Brady I had a son. I should never have let things get this far without him knowing. As soon as there was a break in the conversation, I'd tell him. Would it change his feelings for me?

He sighed. "I miss you already."

"I miss you, too."

"And I'm not sure that my phone gets international service. So if you don't hear from me, don't think it means anything."

"Okay." I swallowed hard.

Brady said, "Oh! I also told my publicist what we talked about—you know, that you could be Haley's registered double for parties and stuff. She can totally hook you up with the right people. When I get back, I'll get the two of you together."

"Great!"

"Don't mention it to Jay, though. You know what he's like."

"A tool?"

He laughed. "Major."

Chapter Twenty-three

On Monday morning, the news was everywhere at Las Palmas Elementary: Mrs. Largent, first-grade teacher and mother of two preteens, was pregnant.

Before the bell rang, I stopped by her classroom to offer my congratulations. "You must be excited."

If I'd followed my life plan, I would have had two kids right now. Would I ever have another child?

Mrs. Largent yawned. Black circles sat underneath her weary eyes. "I will be. When the shock wears off and I start to feel better. But it's hard enough to balance work and kids as it is. My husband and I talked, and we agreed that I should take a few years off."

I missed the significance.

"So you might want to talk to Dr. Fisk," she said. "About the job."

"Oh. Right. Of course."

How ironic: there was finally an opening at Las Palmas, and I no longer wanted it.

Ken's car was parked on the same side of the street as mine, half a house away.

"Morning, Veronica!"

"Hey, Ken."

He leaned down and whispered in my ear. "Or should I call you Haley?" He chuckled: a real laugh, not his usual *Ha!*

I forced a smile. "Have you seen her lately?"

He shook his head. "Not since a week ago Sunday. But we talk every night. And Pamela's taking the boys this weekend. I was going to go camping, but I'd rather see Haley." He shook his head in amazement. "Never thought you'd hear me say that, did you? Well!" He bounced up and down on his feet. "Enjoy your day! It's a beautiful morning, isn't it?"

It was damp and gray with a heavy fog that would take hours to burn off.

"It's a morning," I said.

When I got home, there was a message waiting from Dr. Fisk: "Good morning, Veronica. I don't know if you've heard Mrs. Largent's happy news, but we have an opening for a first-grade teacher. I can't promise you anything, but I urge you to apply for the position."

I erased the message.

Jay called a few hours later, just as I was scrolling through some celebrity gossip sites, disappointed that there were no new pictures of Brady and me.

"Hi, Jay. Is this about the pictures? Because I looked online, and they're not that big a deal."

Jay hadn't hired me to be Haley for almost two weeks. Was he phasing me out, or would he fire me outright? Did it matter? The celebrity double job sounded like more fun, anyway.

"There's a video," he said.

"Really?" I clicked back to Google and did a quick video search on "Haley Rush Brady Ellis" and "Haley Bar DeLux." Nothing.

"What's the URL?" I asked.

"It hasn't been posted yet."

"Oh. Well, I know you're annoyed that I went out with Brady without telling you, but none of the gossip magazines have even picked up the photos, so I doubt—"

"You're having sex."

When I didn't say anything, he added, "In a car."

I said, "I didn't think . . . I didn't know . . ."

He exploded. "Do you understand what a sex tape will do to Haley's career? Little girls idolize her! If this comes out, we can say good-bye to all of the licensing deals—the lunch boxes and hair accessories and Halloween costumes."

"I'm really sorry."

"How could you be so fucking stupid?"

"Don't swear at me!"

"Don't swear at you? Why? Because you're so delicate? I just got done looking at a clip of you, buck naked, riding on top of that, that . . ." His voice broke.

My stomach clenched. "How much could you see of me?"

"Enough," he said. "I saw enough."

I felt nauseous. "Who showed it to you?"

"The asshole who took it sent it to Haley's publicist—who is also an asshole, and who just spent twenty minutes telling me I was a fucking moron for letting this happen. He said he was giving Haley first dibs on buying it. For a million bucks. She said no."

"Haley knows about it?"

"Not exactly. No. But she doesn't have a million bucks to spare. So now he's off to sell it to the highest bidder. It'll hit the Internet in a day or two."

"I don't know what to say."

"I thought you were different from Haley."

"I am different!"

"True. At least she can sing."

There was only one person I wanted to talk to—who I *needed* to talk to.

"Brady? It's me. Veronica. I don't know if you can even retrieve your messages from Australia, but I had to let you know what's going on. There's this tape. Of us. When we were in . . . the car. Jay's really upset—you know, about what it could do to Haley's career. And yours, too, of course. He didn't actually say that, but I'm sure he's concerned. I just thought you should know."

He called back within the hour.

"Veronica?"

"Brady! You got my message?"

"Yeah, my messages came through somehow, all in a bunch. One of the cameramen let me borrow his phone to call you back. Anyway . . . wow."

"Yeah, wow."

"I feel really bad that I put you in this position."

"Actually, I liked being in that position." I was so, so happy that he had called me back.

It was quiet for a moment, and then he laughed. "You are so awesome."

Suddenly, I was hardly even upset anymore. "Jay was pissed."

"Jay's an asshole."

"Haley doesn't even know yet. I feel bad for her—especially since it's not her fault."

"Don't." He sighed. "Haley's spent the last year doing everything she can to sink her career. I think she just wants out. Seriously. So maybe this will give her the excuse she needed."

"But she might still have feelings for you," I said.

"She doesn't. Trust me. What she really needs is a regular guy."

Once again, I envisioned Haley in Ken's little ranch house, standing over the GE range, cooking macaroni and cheese for the boys.

He said, "What really bugs me is that now people are going to think Haley and I are back together. I can't exactly say, like, this is my new girl and me on our first date. So, we're just going to have to lay low a little longer."

Brady called me his girl! *His girl!*

But he was right. If we took our romance public too soon, everyone would know it was me in that tape. I couldn't do that to Ben. I couldn't do it to myself, either. I'd never live down the embarrassment.

"Well, it's not hard to lay low when you're halfway around the world," I said. "How's the filming going?"

"It's okay," he said. "Kind of slow. Plus, it's hard to concentrate when all I can think about is you."

Oh. My. God.

"I'd better run," he said—before I could decide whether or not to admit that he was all I could think about, too. "Don't want to run up this guy's phone bill."

"I miss you," I said.

"I miss you, too."

I still hadn't told him about Ben.

Chapter Twenty-four

The Haley Rush sex tape—soon to be known as the "Haley Rush Has a Fat Ass" tape—turned up on an online muckraking site on Tuesday.

> Betwixt Channel star Haley Rush was caught in a compromising position Saturday night in the parking lot outside an all-night donut shop. Her companion is believed to be television costar Brady Elliston . . .

At least they got Brady's last name wrong. Maybe that would save him from some Google searches. Really, it wasn't so bad for him: his face was so shadowed, he was hardly even recognizable. And anyway, you couldn't really see much of him beyond his side and arms.

That's because I was blocking him. There I was, white ass bumping up against the dashboard as I climbed into position. I looked hideous: pale (I was way overdue for another spray tan), ungainly (there really hadn't been much room to maneuver), and, well, fat. In addition to what one commenter called my "bread-dough butt," the video offered glimpses of my post-childbirth tummy and my "gravity's winning" thighs. More than one person suggested that I—that is, Haley—had made a visit to the donut shop before tearing off my clothes.

The video was only a few minutes long, and it wasn't great quality, but it was clearer than I would have guessed, considering that I hadn't heard anyone drive up. The peeping Tom must have followed us from the club, parked on the street and crept around the cars. He even got a couple of shots of my face. My expression was . . . unfortunate.

By Wednesday, the trashier entertainment programs—which I was able to watch thanks to the miracle of the Internet—had it covered.

Tween idol Haley Rush has gotten herself into a bit of an awkward position! We can't show you the full tape here, but . . .

There was my facial expression again, along with a couple of black rectangles superimposed over my naughty bits.

By Thursday, it was everywhere.

A Good Role Model Is Hard to Find . . .

No word yet on how this will affect her future at the Betwixt Channel . . .

Haley appears to have put on some weight in recent days . . .

Jay didn't call me. Neither did Brady. When I saw Ken from a distance at school, I hurried the other way.

*   *   *

To add to the fun, Ben went into full mope mode.

"I'm sorry about Friday night."

Shrug.

"Are you ever going to forgive me?"

Shrug.

"I love you."

Shrug.

When I dropped him off at his classroom Wednesday morning, I tried to kiss him, but he wouldn't let me.

"Dad'll pick you up after school today," I told him. "I'll see you after dinner Sunday." When I'd been subbing, the off weekends weren't so bad because I'd see Ben at school on Thursdays and Fridays. However, I'd turned down so many assignments that the school had stopped calling me.

I ran a hand over his blond hair, which was a bit too long and therefore less spiky than usual. "I could come to school for lunch tomorrow. Or Friday. Or both?"

He shook his head.

"I could bring Jack in the Box." There was no way he could resist that.

But he did.

"Okay, then." I swallowed hard. "Have fun."

The Ben-less days that followed went something like this: Sleep late. Drink too much coffee. Eat cookies. Lie in bed and stare at ceiling. Check Internet. Mourn the injustices of the world. Shower until the water runs cold. Pinch naked flab and resolve to monitor food intake. Check dark roots in the mirror and wonder how the extensions would react to Clairol. Imagine a future with Brady. Worry about his reaction to Ben. Eat chips dipped in artificial cheese. Look at Ben's baby pictures. Cry.

Sunday night, I was on time to pick Ben up from Hank and Darcy's house. In fact, the whole next week, I was on time for everything. When Shaun and Shavonne dawdled over their Fruity Pebbles Monday morning, I announced that my van would pull out of the driveway at eight-twenty, with or without them. They made it into the car that day and Tuesday, too, but Wednesday morning I left them in the dust. Well, okay: in the bathroom. So what if Deborah kicked us out? That might be just the push I needed to get on with my life—whatever that life might be.

If only Brady would call—or even text. I could ask him more about the celebrity doubles agencies. I could get his e-mail address. Just because we couldn't talk didn't mean we couldn't write.

Was he watching our videos from Australia? It was amazing how much the press reports had focused on Haley and what this meant for her future and how little trouble they'd given Brady: just the double standard, I guessed.

Saturday morning, I made Ben's favorite pancakes (banana blueberry) and tried to engage him in conversation.

> **ME:** If you could be any animal in the world,
> what would you be?
> **BEN:** Can I watch a DVD?
> **ME:** Not now, honey. We're having a conversation.

My cell phone rang: Jay. Why was he calling? What could he possibly say, other than, *In case I wasn't clear the last time we spoke, you're a tramp and an idiot and you've ruined Haley's career.*

Instead, he said, "Haley's missing."

Of course she was. This time, however, no one could blame her.

"What did Rodrigo say?" I asked.

"I fired Rodrigo on Monday. Turns out he hadn't worked at least half the hours that he said he did."

"Oh. Yeah. Haley told me about that."

"You *knew*? And you didn't say anything?"

When I didn't respond, he said, "She has a party tonight. She can't miss it."

"Maybe she doesn't want to go."

"I don't give a shit what she wants. She isn't a guest—she's a performer. For Phil Leventhal, the COO of Mercer Media. Mercer Media owns a controlling interest in Bright Broadcasting, which controls the Betwixt Channel. Phil's paying Haley a quarter million dollars to sing ten songs at his daughter's twelfth birthday party."

When I'd absorbed that information and could adequately speak, I said, "You'd think he'd get a discounted rate."

"That is the discounted rate. At least Phil thinks it is."

"And he still wants her to perform? After, you know . . ."

"*Kitty* is Betwixt's only hit show. Without Haley, there's no *Kitty*, and without *Kitty*, there may as well be no Betwixt. All of the guests—most of whom are industry people—know that Haley's supposed to perform. If Phil cancels, he's signaling a loss of faith in her."

I swallowed hard. "I'll call Ken."

"Who's Ken?"

"Haley's, um, friend. From Fullerton. They had plans this weekend."

"Haley is ditching Phil Leventhal's party to go out with a guy in Fullerton? Fuck!"

I tried to keep my voice steady. "You should be happy for her. Ken's a nice guy. I actually think he'll be good for her. And besides, you should be glad that she's finally getting over Brady."

"There was never anything going on between Haley and Brady."

"What?"

"They were photographed together a couple of times after Brady joined the show, and rumors started. So the producers said, let's go with it. They'd already tried making it look like there was something going on between Haley and Jason Price, but he's kind of skeeve, and she wasn't comfortable with it. So they sent Haley and Brady for some dinners and on a trip to Hawaii. The producers wanted to keep it going, but Haley refused."

"They didn't go out at all?" I clarified.

"No. And it doesn't matter. All that matters is that she get her ass back here. Now."

Ken didn't answer his cell phone or his home phone. Hoping he and Haley were ignoring the rings, I dragged poor Ben out of the house. "We're going to go see Brice and Arches and—what's their brother's name?"

"Powell."

"Him, too."

"I haven't finished my pancakes."

"You can eat them in the car. Out of your hand."

He was okay with that. I did my very best to ignore the syrup dripping down his arm.

Brady and Haley were never really a couple. I was still trying to decide how I felt about that. I was hurt that he had lied to me, of course—but he had probably signed some kind of confidentiality agreement. Besides, if Brady didn't even like Haley, that meant that he liked me for myself.

Haley's big yellow truck was parked in Ken's driveway.

I let Ben push the doorbell. No one came. I knocked: still no answer. Juniper bushes ran along the front of the house. I crept through them and peeked through a living room window.

"Mommy, I don't think you're supposed to be doing that."

"It's fine, honey. The Druckers are our friends."

The living room was empty.

"Looking for Mr. Drucker?"

At the sound of the man's voice, I wheeled around to see a slightly stooped, gray-haired man in khaki shorts and a red crewneck sweater. He had a chocolate Lab on a leash.

"Oh!" he said when he saw my face. "I thought you'd gone with him."

"No, um . . ." I wiggled around the bushes. "No. I didn't." I wiped some bush sprigs from my jeans, thinking, as I always did, that juniper smells just like cat piss. "So, he's left, then?"

"Yup." He shook the leash. The dog sat down, awaiting his next commandment. "Asked me to walk Tahoe here. I was just about to take him around to the backyard."

He pointed at a cream-colored ranch house. "I live next door."

"Oh. That's nice. Did Ken have anyone with him?"

"I thought you . . ." Anxiety strained his face. That's all I needed to add to my list of sins: making an old man believe he was losing his mind.

"Ken has a woman friend who looks something like me. A lot like me."

"Okay! Now I get it." His face softened with relief. "She was with him. They left this morning, right after Ken took the boys to his ex-wife's. He said they were staying with Pamela this weekend." He rolled his eyes: not a Pamela fan.

"Do you know where they were going?"

"They had camping gear. I think he said something about Mount Whitney."

Mount Whitney is 225 miles from Fullerton. According to Mapquest (which always underestimates how long it takes to cross the Los Angeles basin), it would take approximately four hours to drive there. Even if I left a message for Haley at all of the Whitney base camps (assuming such a thing was possible, which it probably wasn't) and even if she agreed to come home (which she probably wouldn't) there was no way she could make it back in time for tonight's performance.

I considered just telling Jay that I had been unable to track her down, but my conscience got the better of me. The situation was at least partly my fault. Without me, Haley would never have met Ken. And without me, Haley wouldn't have been attacked for the sex tape. In my defense, Haley was an irresponsible nut job before I got involved, and if she hadn't taken off with Ken, she might have taken off alone or with someone else, or she might have stayed in her velour sweats and locked herself in her room.

"Jay? I've tracked down Haley." I was in the bedroom. Ben was in the main room watching yet another DVD.

"Oh, thank God," Jay said. "Where is she?"

"On her way to Mount Whitney."

Outside my window, Shaun Mott was shooting Nerf arrows across the pool. Oops—one went in the water.

"Where?" Jay asked.

"Mount Whitney. It's a mountain."

"Yes, thank you. I got that. The *Mount* tipped me off."

"It's the highest mountain in the continental United States," I said, as if describing a really cool field trip. "She went with my friend . . . her friend . . . Ken. He's an experienced climber. So, she'll be completely safe—you don't have to worry. But there's no way she's going to make it back by tonight."

"She has to! Where is this mountain? How far away is it?"

"It's like five hours from L.A. There's just no way . . ."

The line was so quiet that I thought he'd hung up. No such luck.

"Fuck! Fuck, fuck, fuck, fuck!"

Reflexively, I looked at the closed door, afraid that Ben could somehow hear the distant profanities.

I did my best to keep my voice steady. "You'll just have to say she got sick. Laryngitis, maybe. Or a sinus infection. You ever have one of those? They really knock you out."

"They'll know."

"No, they won't."

"Haley never leaves the house. How could she get sick?"

"She does leave the house! She comes to Fullerton."

He moaned. "If she doesn't show tonight, her career is over. Not only will she piss off Phil Leventhal—a no-show will confirm what everyone suspects: that she's unreliable. Nobody will ever sign her again."

"Well, Haley's not going to show," I said.

"Yes, she is."

"Jay, you've got to be realistic."

"Haley's going to show because you're going to be Haley."

I froze. "I don't think this is a good—"

"It's our only shot."

"Jay, I can't sing. And when Haley's friends see me up close, they'll know I'm not her. There's just no way that—"

"You'll lip-sync. Nobody there knows her well enough to see the difference. And only the kids will really be paying attention, anyway—the adults will be too busy drinking and schmoozing."

Ben opened the door. "There's nothing good to eat."

I covered the phone with my hand. "Give me a minute, Benji. Just let me finish my phone conversation and—"

"I'm hungry." A whine was quickly working its way into his voice.

"One minute."

He kicked the door.

"Benji!"

"I haven't even had breakfast, and I want something to eat!"

"You have had breakfast! I made you pancakes! Jay? I need to call you back."

In the yard, Shaun Mott retrieved the Nerf arrow, reloaded his plastic crossbow, and aimed for my front door.

"I'm sorry, Jay, but I can't do it."

Fifteen minutes had gone by. I had told Ben he needed to show better self-control, I had made him a cheese sandwich, and I had told him that he had lost all DVD privileges for the weekend and possibly for the rest of his life.

Clearly, he hated me, though he was smart enough not to tell me so. He took his cheese sandwich and went outside to brave Shaun Mott.

"Come on, Veronica. You owe me this," Jay pleaded.

"I have my son this weekend."

Outside my window, Ben sat on the front stoop. Shaun sauntered over to retrieve his arrow from the bushes.

"So get a sitter."

"I don't have a sitter."

"So call an agency."

"I don't live in your world, Jay. I don't call agencies. And I'm not going to leave my son with a complete stranger." Of course, at this point, he'd probably prefer a stranger to me.

"So bring him to Haley's house. The party's not far, and you'll only be gone for a couple hours, maybe not even that long. He can hang out with you while you get dressed and he'll see you as soon as you come back."

"And who's going to stay with him? You?"

"I can't. I've got to take you to the party. Esperanza can probably do it."

"I can't stand that woman! There is no way I'm leaving my—"

"I'll call one of the security guys, then. Elliott likes kids. At least, I think he does."

"You're kidding, right?"

He sighed. "Fine. I'll stay with him. We'll watch movies."

I pictured Jay and Ben in Haley's theater room, eating popcorn, and watching an animated film—something brand-new that he hadn't seen before. And then I imagined telling Ben that I was leaving him. Again.

I sighed. "I can't."

"I'll pay you ten thousand dollars."

It took me a moment to speak. "Are you serious?"

"I'm desperate. So, yes—I'm serious."

Shaun Mott stood over Ben, burying him in his shadow as he threatened to shoot the arrow.

"Fifty thousand," I blurted.

Immediately, I regretted my greed, afraid Jay would refuse to pay me anything at all.

"Be here in an hour," he said.

Chapter Twenty-five

Target carried *Kitty and the Katz: Season One Soundtrack*; *Kitty and the Katz: Season Two Soundtrack*; and *Kitty and the Katz: Greatest Hits*. I went with the greatest hits.

"So you know how people say I look like Haley Rush?" I said to Ben as we pulled onto the freeway. In the interest of time, Jay decided it was best if I simply drove to Haley's house, even it meant risking curious stares. Right now, that was the least of our worries.

"Who?"

"Kitty from *Kitty and the Katz*."

"Oh. Yeah."

"Well, the funny thing is, her manager thinks I look like her, too."

"Who?"

"Her . . . this guy. Anyway, since Haley's so famous, people are always asking her to go places. Only, she's so busy that she can't always go. So her manager has asked me to dress up and pretend to be Haley."

"You mean, like Halloween?"

"Kind of. Except I'm the only one dressed up. And, I have to memorize some songs," I told him. "Maybe you can help me."

We sang all the way to Beverly Hills. The benefit of Haley/Kitty's simplistic songs was that they were easy to learn. They were catchy, too, I had to admit. My favorite went like this:

I LIKE ME (JUST THE WAY I AM)

You tell me to change my clothes—
My hair, my eyebrows, laugh, and nose.
You say I'm not good enough right now.

But I like me just the way I am—
My crooked grin and my too-big hands.
I like facing another day as meeeeee . . .
Because I'm not you, you see.

When Jay answered the door, in his red high-tops, faded jeans, and white T-shirt, he didn't even look at me. Instead, he fell to one knee and spoke to Ben.

"You must be Veronica's manager."

Ben shook his head.

"Agent?"

He shook his head again.

"Not even a *secret* agent?"

Ben started to giggle.

"I know! You're her bodyguard!"

Ben thought that was hysterical. If Jay could keep this routine up while I was gone, everything might be okay.

Finally, he stood up and sort of smiled.

"No paparazzi?" I asked. I hadn't realized how uncomfortable I'd feel, knowing that Jay had seen my ass on YouTube.

He ran a hand through his hair. "I called security an hour ago, and they shooed them away. They've been swarming ever since . . . that thing."

Blood ran to my face. I looked at the ground.

Jay cleared this throat. "So, anyway—this is how it's going to go. Elliott will be here in three hours to drive you. Phil Leventhal's assistant, Caitlin, will meet you at the side entrance and take you to your dressing room—a guest bedroom, probably. I'm going to give you an iPod. Keep it in your ears the whole time—that way, Caitlin won't try to chat.

"The sound guys are over there now, so everything will be ready to go. I'll text them the final playlist as soon as we figure it out."

"Won't they think it's weird that I'm lip-syncing?"

He snorted. "Haley always lip-syncs her performances. The sound guys would think it was weird if she actually sang."

I spent the next three hours in the Frontier Land living room, watching Haley's music videos on the giant television and doing my best to imitate her. She was big on stepping from side to side, punching her fist in the air, and tossing her blond mane.

Jay assigned Ben to play backup air band, though he didn't quite get the message that "air" equals "silent."

"Freeze and smile at the end of each song," Jay instructed as I finished a number.

I froze. I smiled.

"No," he said. "Watch the video."

"Boo-ya!" Ben shouted.

I collapsed on the soft leather couch and watched. As with every song, when Haley hit her final note, she held her position as long as she could while breathing hard from the exertion, and she beamed. Eyes wide, she blinked at the lights, as if she couldn't quite believe that she, a little country girl from Montana, had wound up on stage. Her smile was toothy, enormous, and genuinely joyful. She wasn't a good enough actress to fake it.

I got up and did it again. Ben switched from air guitar to air drum.

Finally, it was time to get dressed. I put on the midnight blue minidress that Simone had brought over weeks earlier. I wore my hair down to provide maximum facial coverage.

"No Simone today?" I asked when I came out to model.

"She quit. Because of the recent photos."

Simone saw my butt. Crap.

When Jay saw my expression, he said, "Not those. The ones from the film premiere. The cowboy stuff. Which she's trying to blame on Haley even though she put the outfit together herself."

"Hey, Mom? Can I take drum lessons?" Ben asked.

"We don't have room for a drum set," I said. "But ask Daddy. I bet Darcy would love to listen to you practice."

Jay checked his expensive watch. "We've got about fifteen minutes before Elliott gets here. You want to run through a couple of the numbers one last time?"

"Sure." I didn't need to write the lyrics on my arm, after all. My head buzzed with Haley's songs. I tossed my mane, pumped the air, and dove into the music, finishing the set with a masterpiece of irony.

JUST LIKE ME, ONLY BETTER

When I was a little girl
I dreamed of who I'd be.
Now I look in the mirror,
And she's looking back at me.

She's just like me, only better!
She's cool, she's smart—a true go-getter!
I can't believe I'm seeing what I see—
That better girl is me.

I froze. I smiled.

Ben said, "Bud-da boom bah!" and hit an imaginary drum. Jay applauded.

I brushed a blond clump out of my eyes and bowed.

Jay's phone rang: just a normal tone today. He checked the display and rolled his eyes. "Hey, Brady."

Ohmigod, ohmigod, ohmigod!

"I haven't heard anything," Jay said. "I'll call Monday."

He wandered across the room, but I still caught everything he said. "I *did* call yesterday, but nobody called me back. Last I heard, the project hasn't even been green-lighted yet, so it's a little early to—" He stopped walking. "I don't know. Fifty-fifty? Sixty-forty? . . . Monday. Right."

He turned off his phone and slipped it back in his pocket. He held my gaze and waited for me to say something. When I didn't, he said, "That was your friend."

"Yeah. I got that." If Brady was able to borrow someone else's phone, why wasn't he calling me? My phone was in my purse, in the other room. Maybe he was leaving me a message right now.

"Do you know when he's coming back from Australia?" I asked.

Jay squinted. "Huh?"

"I haven't talked to him in a couple of weeks, but he said the shoot was going longer than expected so he wasn't sure—"

"Brady told you he was in Australia?"

Dread pricked my skin. "Isn't he?"

Jay didn't say anything.

"Where is he?" I asked, my voice suddenly hoarse.

"At the moment? Culver City."

Chapter Twenty-six

When I woke up on the January day that Hank left me, I only had one concern. How was I going to get Ben's dinosaur diorama to kindergarten?

We had spent two weeks building the scene in a Stride Rite box. Ben and I (but mostly I) had built papier mâché hills and painted them green. We had fashioned little trees from sticks and dinosaurs from clay. A winged pterodactyl dangled from a bit of thread. Ben was terribly worried the thread would break.

And now it was raining.

"Maybe you could drop Ben and me off at school today?" I suggested to Hank. A plastic garbage bag would keep the diorama dry, but the less distance it traveled from car to classroom, the better shape it would be in.

Hank looked up from his paper. "What?"

"His diorama is due today. And it's just a long way to walk if I have to park on the street."

Hank glanced up at the wall clock. "Sure. If we leave soon."

"I'm working in the classroom today." I had volunteered to cut out circles and stars for a solar-system mural. "So I'd need you to pick us up at twelve-thirty."

That changed everything.

"I can't do that," Hank said quickly. "I've got a big job today—new construction. The windows are all custom, and they want fabric shades, so I've got to measure."

"Is that from that real estate lady?" Over the past few months, Hank had been getting all kinds of referrals from a local Realtor.

"Yeah."

"Well, you'll need to take a lunch break, so—"

He cut me off. "There just isn't time."

"Fine," I said. "I'll deal with it."

The thread broke. The pterodactyl's head shattered. In the classroom, I blinked away tears, Ben rubbed my back and said, "It's okay, Mommy. We can glue it."

It wasn't the damage that upset me so much as Hank's reaction. He'd barely even looked at the diorama. He didn't understand what it meant to Ben and me. But that was typical. Lately, he smiled politely whenever I talked—about Ben's interest in Cub Scouts, or about a new recipe I'd tried, or about our gopher problem in the backyard—but he'd never respond, which made me wonder if he was even paying attention.

He was still sweet to me. He kissed me hello and good-bye

and complimented my dinners. He'd given me a ridiculous number of presents for Christmas: jewelry and perfume, kitchen gadgets and gardening tools.

But still. I sensed we were drifting apart. Maybe I'd ask around, see if anyone had a babysitter. Maybe all we needed was some time alone, without Ben.

When he came in through the garage door at three o'clock, I was mixing batter for Morning Glory muffins. The muffins had carrot, pineapple, oatmeal, cinnamon, walnuts, and raisins. Ben loved them.

Hank stood in the middle of the kitchen, looking slightly ill and clutching his keys, which he normally tossed on the counter as soon as he walked in the house.

"I've fallen in love." His voice was husky.

Call it denial, call it delusion: I thought he meant with me.

"That's sweet. I love you, too." I smiled and wiped my hands on a kitchen towel so that when I hugged him, I wouldn't get flour on his royal blue Discount Blinds polo shirt.

"I mean, with someone else." His face twisted, and tears slid down his cheeks.

I clutched the kitchen towel. Surely he didn't just say . . .

I need to find a babysitter so Hank and I can spend some time alone. So we can reconnect.

"I'm so sorry," he croaked. "I didn't mean, I didn't mean . . ."

Ben was in the next room. Ben couldn't hear this.

"Not now," I said, with more than a little desperation. Nausea washed over me, as if I'd been attacked by a quick and terrible flu. This couldn't be happening.

"Yes, now. I've waited too long already. Oh, Roni, I've tried. All these years. When you—When Ben happened, I thought I was doing the right thing, I thought everything would work out okay. But I can't go on living like this."

A ray of sun streamed through the window; the rain had cleared, leaving the sky an uncommonly crisp blue. In the kitchen, the muffin batter waited in a glass bowl on the counter. Ben's painting of "my famlee" drooped from two refrigerator magnets.

"Living like . . . what?" *Who is she?*

"Like I'm dead. Every day, it's the same thing. I got up, go hang blinds, come home, eat dinner, ask you and Ben about your day. I watch television and then go to sleep. Every. Single. God-damn. Day."

"You don't like your job, so you go out and have an affair?" *Wasn't that what he'd said?* Or did he say that being married to me was like being dead? The queasiness increased. I leaned against the counter.

"Roni." He wiped his red face with his large, callused hands. "I didn't wait so long to have a family because I hadn't found the right person. I waited because I wasn't sure I wanted a family. The responsibility. The routine. It's like I'm drowning. You're so young. It's not your fault . . ."

"Who is she?" *Not my fault?*

"Darcy."

That threw me. "Who?"

"Darcy DeCosta. The Realtor. You know, the one who's been giving me all the referrals."

I had Darcy DeCosta scratch pads all over my house. A Darcy DeCosta magnet was one of the two holding up Ben's family picture.

Darcy DeCosta was hard. She was old. She didn't stand a

chance. I wasn't sure if I could ever forgive Hank, but we could get through this. We had to. We had Ben.

"We'll work things out," I said.

He closed his eyes. "I don't want to work things out."

While I finished the muffins and started dinner, he went into the bedroom to pack. He stayed for my cornflake-crusted chicken with green beans and apple sauce. I was on autopilot, reminding Ben to put his napkin on his lap, cutting his chicken, answering Hank's awkward questions about the dinosaur diorama. It was so strange and unreal. It hadn't even occurred to me to cry yet: that would come later.

After dinner, still dazed, I did the dishes while he read a story to Ben. That gave me hope. He'd never read much to Ben; that had always been my job. Hank's job was to watch television with Ben. Maybe this meant that Hank was rethinking his plan.

I heard the suitcase wheels before I saw him. I stayed over the sink, water running, scrubbing brush in my hand.

He put a hand on my shoulder. Finally, the tears came.

"I told Ben I'd be back tomorrow night. To read to him."

I nodded, salt water cascading down my cheeks and into the sink.

"I want you to be happy," he said.

I was too crushed to get angry, to tell him that was the stupidest thing anyone had ever said. I squeezed my eyes shut. When I opened them again, he was gone.

Chapter Twenty-seven

So I can't say that Brady's betrayal was the worst I'd ever experienced: not even close. But the familiar dizziness and nausea drenched me. When anger bubbled up, it was directed at myself. After all I'd been through, how could I be so stupid?

Jay shook his head in disgust. "Such an asshole."

"But why me?" I said. "If he and Haley were never even a couple—I mean, he could have anyone."

"And he does," Jay said. "Makeup girls, caterers, personal assistants . . ."

"But I've looked him up on the Internet." Repeatedly. Obsessively. "Aside from Haley and one other girl, there was nothing."

"Brady's not famous enough for anyone to care who he—" Just in time, he remembered Ben, who was studying a horse painting nearby. "Dates. Besides, he's buddy-buddy with the paps. He doesn't want his picture taken, they don't take it. In return, he tells them where to find him and Haley."

"Like the Bar DeLux." The night I'd gone out with Brady, he'd texted someone: a friend, he'd said. He'd told them where we'd be.

"Yeah," Jay said. "Or a parking lot."

Of course. Brady could have seduced me anywhere: a hotel, his apartment. Why would he choose a parking lot unless he wanted to be caught?

The intercom buzzed; the closed circuit TV showed a black Escalade at the gate.

"Elliott's here," Jay said.

"What?" I blinked at him, my concentration shot.

He saw my expression. "Oh, God. I never should have told you. Shit." His eyes shot to Ben. "Sorry. Language. And sorry—about Brady. I should have warned you, I just thought . . ."

"That I was smarter than that." Oh, crap. I was going to cry. Was this mascara waterproof?

"I just hoped you'd have better taste." He retrieved a tissue box from a side table and held it out. I took one.

"Your mom's going," Jay told Ben.

"Huh?" Ben looked away from the horses. "Oh. Okay."

I kissed the top of his spiky head. "Love you, Benji. Love you, love you."

"Okay," he said.

So maybe it wasn't so surprising that I forgot the words to Haley's songs. And I'm not talking a few flubs here and there. The lyrics were gone, all of them, as if I'd never even heard them before.

The party was outdoors, around an enormous rock pool with

a swinging bridge and three separate waterfalls. Several kids splashed in the water, ignoring the cold gusts from a threatening storm. Adults clustered around tall propane heaters, sipping alcohol, forcing laughs, and checking their cell phones. Impossibly beautiful servers in white shirts and black pants passed trays filled with champagne, punch, and miniature kid foods: cheeseburgers, hot dogs, tacos.

The sound guy set me up on a platform—it wasn't big enough to call a stage or lofty enough to call a pedestal—with nothing but a microphone, some lights, and two enormous speakers for company. The lights changed colors, switching my glow from pink to green to yellow.

Jay was right. The adults ignored me, at least at first. But the children—there must have been fifty of them, hair glossy, clothes trendy, expressions alternately jaded or enraptured—caught my every move and expression. They saw me freeze, panic on my face, and then try to cover it up with a laugh and a mouthed "Baby, baby" (while the background track played something else entirely). Some laughed. Others pointed. A few looked like they were going to cry.

When the first song ended, the sound guy hopped on stage and asked, "You want me to rearrange the playlist?"

There was no point: I had complete amnesia of all of Haley's songs. I shook my head, unable to even speak.

He shrugged and turned the music back on. What did he care? He'd get paid no matter how much I bombed.

I held the microphone in front of my mouth, blocking it as much as possible. Only seven more songs and I was out of here. I swayed in time to the music and made this kind of "mah mah mah" sound. My mouth was opening and closing. Maybe that would be enough.

It wasn't. The red-faced birthday girl, whose name was Star (of course it was), did this air-slap, foot-stamp thing before pushing her way through the child mob. By the time I began the third song ("Just Like Me, Only Better"), about half the children had drifted away, leaving a pack of horrified-looking adults in their place.

Just a child . . . chin aimed high . . . something about a mirror . . . Damn it, I should know this one!

A silver-haired man—potbellied, squinty-eyed, big nose, silk luau shirt—held up one finger, and the sound guy cut the music. The crowd parted like the sea at the Universal Studios lot.

Phil Leventhal stood at the base of the platform. When he spoke, his voice was quiet, raspy, and filled with disgust.

"Go home."

Jay and Ben had been playing checkers. When Jay opened the front door, Ben, kneeling on the floor, hunched over the coffee table, glanced up, mumbled, "Hi, Mom," and went back to studying the board.

"Haley has board games?"

That was easier to say than: "Thanks to me, the head of Mercer Media thinks Haley doesn't know the words to her own songs."

"I brought the checkers," Jay said, closing the door behind me.

"I'm impressed. I was sure you'd be glued to a movie." I followed him across the room. I'd wait till they finished the game to break the news.

"Ben told me he wasn't allowed to watch TV." He sat back

down on the soft leather couch and rested his chin on his hand. "Oh, man! You trapped me!"

Ben beamed. Jay moved a red checker into an open spot, quite obviously setting himself up for a slaughter. Ben triple-jumped him, hopped up from the floor, and did a victory dance.

The air smelled like tomato sauce. "You ordered a pizza?"

Jay shook his head. "We used one of those Boboli things. You want a piece?"

"No, thanks. I'm not really hungry." Failure and humiliation will do that to you.

I took a deep breath. "Things didn't go so well tonight."

"I know."

For the first time, I realized that Jay hadn't met my eyes since I'd come in the house. I waited for him to continue.

Instead, he plucked the red and black circles off the table and placed them in the cardboard box. He folded the board and put it on top of the pieces and finally closed the box.

"Good game, Ben."

"Can we play again?"

"No can do. It's late. You and your mom have to hit the road."

When Jay spoke again, he kept his voice steady and his eyes on the checker box.

"Phil Leventhal called. He said that the woman I'd sent over was obviously not Haley. And that if the publicity wouldn't be so bad, he'd sue me for everything I'm worth. So, instead, he'll just make sure that Mercer Media never hires Haley or any of my other clients ever again."

He looked up and finally met my eyes.

"Game over."

Chapter Twenty-eight

My life couldn't get any worse. Except, it did.

Sunday afternoon, Paul Mott knocked on my door. Paul was a pale, thin engineer with thin, reddish-blond hair and a general air of unease. Every time I talked to him, I had the sense he couldn't wait to get back to his computer games.

"Good morning, Veronica."

"Hi, Paul."

"Though I guess it's afternoon." He cleared his throat.

I laughed politely. "I'll let it slide."

"So." He cleared his throat again. "Deborah and I were talking." He put his hands in his pockets and looked at his feet. "You've been a great tenant and all, but the thing is, uh—" He cleared his throat yet again. I resisted the urge to suggest a sinus rinse. Finally, he said it.

"We kind of miss having a place to put out-of-town guests.

We have some people—my cousins, they live in Seattle—who are thinking about coming to Disneyland this summer, and, you know, hotels are kind of expensive, and, uh . . ."

He waited for me to help him out. I didn't. He cleared his throat again, louder and longer this time—*uh-mm-MM!*—and delivered the final blow. "Do you think you'd be able to find another place to live?"

Wimp. What would he do if I said no?

"Do I have a choice?" I asked.

"Not really." He looked up for a brief instant before turning his attention to a tree.

Monday I stopped in the school office after dropping Ben at his classroom. I'd planned to ask—okay, beg—Dr. Fisk to consider me as a replacement for Mrs. Largent. Dr. Fisk wasn't there.

Instead, I talked to scary Margery at the front desk. "I'm not working that L.A. job anymore. So I'm available for any subbing assignments."

"Thanks," she said. "But the list is pretty full."

On the way out I saw Nina and Terri, heads close together. I hurried past them and managed to catch Mrs. Largent before she went into her classroom.

"Do you know if they've hired anyone to replace you?"

"Have a little sympathy, Veronica. My body's not even cold yet."

"You're not dying—you're just pregnant."

"Easy for you to say, you skinny you-know-what. Anyway, I'm kind of out of the loop, but I heard they're giving the job to another teacher from within district."

*   *   *

Tuesday I ran into the former Pamela Drucker as I was walking across the blacktop. She was wearing pale pink capri pants, silver sandals, and a white sweater. A pink Coach bag swung from her shoulder. Her blond hair was highlighted so perfectly it made my Haley extensions—and Veronica roots—look especially trashy in comparison.

She stopped in her Joan & David tracks and stared at me.

"Hi, Pamela." I kept walking. Wasn't Ken back from Mount Whitney yet? Had she really spent four days with her children?

"I thought you'd gone away with Ken," she said.

Oh, of course. I shook my head. "There's this woman who looks a little like me."

"He was supposed to be back today," she said. "But last night he left me a message saying he'd be gone until the weekend. It's a long drive up here from Newport Beach," she added, as if Ken's absence were my fault, even if we weren't dating. But of course—it kind of was my fault.

"I bet," I said, with a lame approximation of empathy.

"This shared custody thing isn't easy, is it?" She shot me a conspiratorial smile.

"No, it's not." I hurried away before I could say anything I might regret.

And then I went home and bleached my roots.

Thursday morning Hank called to ask me to lunch "so we can talk." We met at the Cheesecake Factory, where we had to wait fifteen minutes to be seated. Hank clutched the buzzer and gazed up at the faux Italian murals on the high ceilings while I feigned interest in the cheesecake display.

When we finally got a table—about three inches from a family of four (harassed and overweight mother, detached and tattooed father, two small, squabbling children)—I spent a long time studying the selections even though I already knew what I wanted. Finally, I closed the fat menu and put it on the table.

"Fish tacos?" Hank said.

"Always."

In spite of everything, this old familiarity sparked pleasure inside me. Who else could name my favorite thing at the Cheesecake Factory?

"And you'll be getting the fish and chips," I said.

He stacked his menu on top of mine. "Actually, the orange chicken. Darcy turned me on to it."

So much for the spark.

He tapped his thick fingers on the table. "Ben tells me that you went into L.A. on Saturday night. With him."

"It was actually Beverly Hills, but—yeah."

He fiddled with his fork. "He said you got all dressed up. And that there was a man. Some kind of manager. And then he said . . ." He abandoned the fork and reached for his water glass. He took a long, long drink.

Finally, he continued. "He said a car came for you. Something fancy. And he stayed alone with this man, this *manager*, for about an hour until you came back."

"They made pizza," I said. "And played checkers. It was all very wholesome."

"There is nothing wholesome about what's going on here."

Oh, great. Ben told him I was impersonating Haley.

"I'm just trying to make ends meet," I said. "And build a better life for Ben." I considered making a crack about his sugar mama but decided against it.

"You have an education—you can get a regular job. And to bring Ben along, to involve him in this disgusting . . ." He was so angry, he was actually shaking.

"Oh, for God's sake. Ben spent an hour in a very nice house in Beverly Hills. He had a wonderful time."

"Wonderful. Right. While you're out selling yourself." His face was bright red.

The waitress chose that time to show up to take our order. When she saw our faces, she said, "I'll come back later."

I was all set to blow up and play the infidelity card when I realized what he was saying.

"Oh, my God. You think I'm a *prostitute*?"

The cranky parents at the next table stopped yelling at their children and turned to stare. Hank looked like he was going to cry.

I burst out laughing and kept going until my stomach hurt and tears ran down my face. Finally, I calmed down and patted my face with a nonabsorbent polyester napkin.

"Are you . . . a dancer?" he asked.

That set me off again.

Finally, leaning over the table and keeping my voice low, I told him the whole story. Well, okay—I left out the episode at Bar DeLux. Actually, I left out everything to do with Brady.

"But why didn't you just tell me that from the beginning?" he said.

"I signed a contract saying I wouldn't tell anyone. But now the secret's out, so I don't think it matters."

The waitress, looking a little nervous, came back and took

our orders. For an instant, I thought Hank would order the fish and chips, but he stuck with Darcy's favorite orange chicken.

The waitress was about to leave when she hesitated. "Can I have your autograph?" she asked me. "I have a little sister, and . . ."

"Sure." I took her pen and pad and wrote *Veronica Czaplicki.*

When she left (looking really confused), Hank asked, "Were you tempted to write Haley's name?"

"Not really. I can do her signature, though. Wanna see?" I pulled a pen and scrap of paper from my purse and scrawled a perfect signature with a fat heart. "Keep it," I told Hank. "It might be worth something some day. Though I doubt it."

He left the paper sitting on the table. "I'm glad—really glad— that your job isn't . . . you know. But I'm still concerned about Ben. He's just not himself. Crying a lot, kind of clingy. Doesn't want to have friends over. I've never seen him like this."

"Well, I have. That's exactly how he acted when you left."

Hank gnawed on his bottom lip and didn't say anything. As usual, my moral victory felt empty.

"It's over, anyway," I said. "I just took the job so I could make enough money to move."

"I thought you liked it at the Motts'. They've got the yard and the pool, and that cute little house. . . ."

"We have to ask permission to use the yard, we almost never get to use the pool, the house is too small for two people, and Deborah is a bitch. And her kids are awful. They're kicking us out, anyway, so it's a moot point."

The lunch had been much more fun when Hank thought I was a hooker.

"I wish you'd said something sooner. Darcy can help you find something."

I nodded, feeling grateful and defeated in equal measures.

We were quiet for a long while, sipping our water and staring at nothing. The waitress brought our meals. Reflexively, I pushed half to one side of the plate: I'd take it home and eat it for dinner.

"You were never happy," Hank blurted.

I blinked at him.

"I'd come home from work and ask how your day went, and you'd tell me how many times Ben had cried and how much laundry you'd done and what you didn't like about the house."

"I was just making conversation." Conversation with Hank had never been easy. How was your day? Do you think it's going to rain? I hear they're building a new Target. Do you think we should try planting tomatoes?

"I felt like I should be able to fix everything," he said. "Your mood, the leaky faucet, the weather."

"I never expected you to fix the weather," I said, attempting levity.

"The thing is, the more you expected from me, the less capable I felt. And the cheerier I pushed you to be, the more depressed you got."

"I was never depressed until you walked out." My throat swelled.

"You weren't happy. And when I . . . walked out . . ." He paused, having spoken words he generally avoided. "I'm not going to say I did it for you, because obviously I didn't. Darcy . . . I hate to say she *completes* me—" He paused to laugh at the lame movie reference. When I didn't respond, he continued. "But we bring out the best in each other in a way that you and I never did."

"Um, Hank? I was feeling crappy before I got here, and, frankly, this isn't helping."

"I'm sorry. I didn't mean to . . ." He took a deep breath. "You're young. You'll find someone."

I hate it when people say that.

"You deserve the kind of love that Darcy and I have. And I want you to know that Darcy and I will support you. If you need to switch weekends or have us take Ben for an evening, we're happy to do it."

I nodded.

"Is there anyone in your life right now?" he asked.

"What—you mean a man? Nobody."

"Really? That's too bad. Because people keep saying you and Ken Drucker are going out, and I always thought you'd be good together."

Back at the little house, my answering machine blinked. Stefano had called.

"Veronica, my sweet, my darling, my pussycat—I haven't seen you in a lifetime. But I've seen some pictures of you, and oh! My! God!"

He saw the sex tape. Oh, crap.

"You cannot walk around with our roots showing like that! Cannot, cannot!"

I called him back. "I'd love to have you do my hair, but to be perfectly honest, I can't afford it."

"Oh, don't be silly. I'll do it for free. Monday work for you?"

"Really?" I was touched.

"Well, free-ish. I expect some good gossip in exchange."

I laughed. "I'm rolling in that."

Late Friday morning, I capped off my week with a visit to the principal's office. I wore my brown turtleneck dress because it was the most professional looking thing I owned. Bad choice: it was already over eighty degrees outside. The heat sweat paired with my anxiety sweat. I'd need another shower after this.

Gayle Fisk was on the phone when I peeked in, but she motioned me to take a seat in one of the hard guest chairs. Her walls were covered with school awards and student art: trees and flowers fashioned from ripped construction paper.

"You've come about the job," she said when she got off the phone.

"Yes."

She smiled sadly. "I'm sorry, but it's too late. I called you, but . . ."

"I know. It's my fault."

"There are other openings in the district. I'd be happy to put in a good word." She had said this before. Usually I said no: I had to stay with Ben. Things had to be perfect.

"I'd really appreciate that." It was time to make a new life for myself and Ben—a life I chose and made, not just one I fell into.

Afterwards, I lingered in front of the school, waiting for the lunch bell. When it finally rang, I strolled over to the lunch tables, which were outside under an enormous roofed structure. When Ben sat down by himself, my stomach began to hurt, but it wasn't long before he was joined by Carson, Tyler, and several other kids I didn't know.

"Hey, Benji. Hey, guys."

In the past year, I'd spent so much time subbing that Ben wasn't surprised to see me.

"Dad make you that lunch?" I was trying to see what was in his Ninja Turtles lunch box without looking like I was trying to see.

He shrugged. "Darcy did."

"Oh. How nice. What did she make you?"

He peered inside and rattled off the contents. "Cookies . . . Cheez Whiz crackers . . . Goldfish . . . gummy bears . . . and Diet Coke."

"But what's the main course?"

"The Cheez Whiz crackers."

"Can I have one of your chocolate chip cookies?" Carson asked.

Ben handed him a plastic bag. "You can have them all. I don't really like them."

I was still steaming when I ran into Nina, coming out of a classroom.

"I was helping out with math lab in Mrs. Bayati's class," she said, as if I had accused her of something.

"Darcy made Ben's lunch today. Cheez Whiz and Diet Coke. That's the healthy part."

She smiled but still looked guarded.

"Anyway," I said. "Hank's got Ben this weekend, but we'd love to have Carson over next week. I'm not working in L.A. anymore, so I've got plenty of time."

"About that L.A. job . . ."

I flushed. My armpits were soaked.

She said, "I got my hair done earlier this week."

"It looks nice."

"Oh. Thanks." She rolled her eyes up at her head. "A little shorter than I like, but it'll grow. Anyway, while I was under the dryers I read some magazines—all the trashy ones, you know, about Brad and Jen and Brad and Angelina, and whatever. And there was this, um, section. About fashion. Like, it showed celebrities wearing really fugly outfits and then it said, 'What was she thinking?' or 'Bad idea,' or something like that."

I knew where this was going.

"There was this picture of Haley Rush. She was going to a film premiere and wearing this really stupid cowboy outfit."

She stopped. I met her eyes.

"Those were your knees," she said.

"My *knees*?" I had to laugh.

"Yeah. They're kind of square." She reached down and pulled my brown hem up a couple of inches to reveal my, yes, square knees.

"Thanks," I said. "That's sweet."

"So afterwards I went home and did a search of Haley Rush's photos. Her knees are round. And so finally I checked YouTube, and there was this really blurry tape outside a nightclub. The way the girl tilted her head, the way she walked . . . it was you."

I nodded.

Her eyes bore into me. "I just need to know one thing."

A pair of little girls skipped past us, waterproof lunch boxes swinging from their hands.

"Yes?" I said.

Nina grabbed my arms and squeezed so tight it hurt. Her eyes bugged out and her voice pitched with excitement. "Did you really bag Brady Ellis?"

Chapter Twenty-nine

On the way home from the school (I'd stayed for another forty-five minutes to fill Nina in on some of the highlights of my life-as-Haley), I took a detour.

Haley's yellow truck still sat in Ken's driveway, only now it had company: Ken's Ford Explorer. I may have ruined Haley's career (of course, she'd messed it up pretty well even without me), but I had helped her find love. She'd been thrust into the limelight at far too young an age, but it wasn't too late for her to build a normal life.

When Ken opened the door, my first thought was: he looks wonderful! Funny how being in love can make you more attractive.

But then I realized that his beauty came from the outside at least as much (maybe more) than it did from the inside: new haircut, smooth complexion, a sage T-shirt, designer jeans, and leather flip-flops from someplace other than REI.

"Veronica—hey! Haley, Veronica's here!"

Behind him, the room was dark, the blinds drawn, the only light coming from the flickering television set. Haley was not planting tomatoes, making pancakes, or otherwise embracing normal domestic life. Instead, she was sprawled on the plaid couch in one of her velour track suits (brown today—Ken liked earth colors, after all). She held up a hand (not the whole arm, just the hand) to greet me before returning to her familiar fugue state.

"I just wanted to make sure you got back from Whitney safely."

"Oh, Whitney." Ken laughed. ("Ha. Ha.") "We didn't go."

"But . . ."

"We started up there, but after about an hour on the road, Hay said that what we really needed was pampering, so we went to a spa instead. You ever been to the Bacara?"

"Uh, no."

"Just north of Santa Barbara. Goleta I think. Nice setting, lousy service. But Hay was right: it was exactly what we needed. Wasn't it, babe?"

"Mmm. Hmm." Haley ("Hay," "Babe") managed to answer without moving her mouth.

He rubbed his perfectly smooth cheek. (Facial? Acid peel? Dermabrasion?) "It was great to get away. For both of us. The distance allowed us to see things more clearly and to envision the kind of future we want to live."

Across the room, Haley moved! She shifted her weight and reached for the remote and hit a button and . . . that was it.

"We're moving to the Santa Ynez Valley," Ken announced. "You're the first person we've told."

"Oh," I said. "My God, you're . . . wow."

"We went up there to go wine tasting one day—Fess Parker, you been there?—and fell in love with the area. So the next day we went back and had a Realtor show us around. Found a piece of property—forty acres of gentle hills, mature trees. There's a two-bedroom house on there now, along with a barn. We can live in the house while we build."

"But what about the boys?"

"They'll come with us, of course. Hay loves kids. Don't you, babe?"

"Are there any more of those pastry things?" she replied.

"Oh! Of course!"

I followed him into the kitchen. The bright light hurt my eyes after the darkness of the living room. The ceramic tile counters gleamed, empty except for a pink cardboard box. A clean frying pan sat drying in the dish rack. Ken pulled a white Corelle plate from the cabinet and plucked a shiny Danish from the pink box. "You want one?"

I shook my head.

"Haley loves them." He pulled a few brown vitamin bottles from another cabinet, twisted open the caps, and lined the pills up next to the Danish.

"Haley's eating habits are not the best. Ha, ha. So I've started her on supplements."

"Does this mean you're selling your house?" I asked.

"Yup. Realtor's coming by this afternoon. I'm using Darcy—hope you don't mind." He replaced the caps and put the bottles away. "And I've got a couple calls in to Beverly Hills Realtors. Our ranch purchase is contingent on the sale of Hay's house, so the quicker we get it on the market, the better."

I leaned against the counter. "Ken, I don't mean to intrude."

I'd done an awful lot of intruding lately. "But isn't this kind of quick? It's great you two get along so well, but to be selling your house and moving the kids. And for Haley to give up her career . . ."

"Haley's not giving up her career."

"She's not?"

"Of course not. With her talent? We're giving up the kiddie stuff, though, and moving in a new direction."

"We?"

"I'm Haley's new manager." He beamed.

"Oh, my God. I mean—but what about Jay Sharpie?"

"Haley texted him earlier. He's history. We're going to build a recording studio at the ranch. So she doesn't need to leave if she doesn't want to. And she's going to record the kind of music she loves rather than that teenybopper stuff."

"You mean soul and R&B?"

He shook his head. "John Denver. Would you believe she'd never even heard of him? We listened to his songs all week."

"John Denver," I said, still not believing it.

"We're hoping to start with a cover album—get this: I'm thinking we call it 'Rocky Mountain Higher.' I've got a call in to John's estate; need to get the permission issues sorted out. After that, Hay will write the kind of songs John would have written had his life not been cut so tragically short."

He picked up the plate and strode back into the darkness. "Here's your pastry, Hay-Babe."

Chapter Thirty

Stefano had a new 'do: still black, but short on the sides with a long, curly lock in the front. He'd filled his studio with jasmine sprigs. The scent almost managed to overpower the smell of dyes and relaxers. There was even a big bouquet of flowers in the fireplace; it was much too warm to burn anything.

"Girlfriend. OMG." He grabbed a lock of my hair—I think it was mine. "You're like a cross between Boy George and Britney Spears."

"You said I didn't look like Britney."

"Well, today you do. In a bad way."

"It was worse before I bleached the roots."

"You colored your own hair?" He bit his knuckle. "Well, let's not waste another minute. Go change out of those Kohl's clothes and put on a kimono."

I was wearing straight-cut jeans and a green V-neck T-shirt.

"How did you know this stuff came from Kohl's?" I'd gone shopping over the weekend, figuring a splurge would make me feel better. It didn't.

He giggled. "Did it really? I was just joking."

I handed him a foil-covered paper plate. "I made you blondies— they're like chocolate chip cookie bars."

He took the plate and inhaled deeply, his eyes wide with wonder.

"They're a little dry around the edges," I admitted. "I made them in my toaster oven."

"I've missed you, Veronica Zap."

"It's actually Czaplicki, but I've missed you, too."

When I finally got settled in Stefano's comfy chair, he said, "So tell me the look you're going for. Spoiled heiress? Hollywood royalty? Film executive wife?"

"How about Orange County schoolteacher?"

He looked appalled for just an instant before he said, "I've never done that one. Might be kind of fun."

Three hours later, I left with the best haircut of my life: just above the shoulders, lightly layered and swingy. The extensions were gone (getting them out was easier—though somewhat more painful—than putting them in) and the color was close to my natural medium brown, now with a warm touch of copper.

In return, I left Stefano with the story of Ken and Haley as well as the details of my seduction by Brady. I didn't tell him that Brady and Haley had never been connected for anything other than professional reasons. It felt like a betrayal of Jay—and I'd messed up his life enough already.

Stefano had heard about the Leventhal party from a woman

who'd been there—only she couldn't remember Haley's name, just called her "that not-that-talented blond girl from that TV show that all the kids seem to like for some reason that I'll never understand." She hadn't realized that the blond woman on stage wasn't Haley, just that, "She acted like she'd never heard those songs before." Stefano guessed it was me.

"I'm just not cut out for Hollywood," I said as he brushed some sprinkles of cut hair from my neck.

"That's not necessarily a bad thing." He held out two pieces of hair, one from either side of my face, to make sure they matched. "Though I couldn't bear to live anyplace else. I'd die of boredom."

I was kind of hoping he'd offer to cut my hair for free again. Instead, he recommended that I have someone take my picture as soon as I got home so I'd have something to show future stylists. "And then tonight you should go dancing—or at least out to dinner. You look too gorgeous to stay home."

"Oh, I've got plans." My plans involved heating a frozen pizza and watching a Disney DVD with Ben, but he didn't need to know that.

I'd never written down Jay's address, but after a few false turns around Melrose, I found his fairy-tale house with the Mini Cooper parked in the driveway. I hadn't planned on stopping by, but getting the extensions out had been quicker than expected, and things with Jay felt unfinished. He might not want to see me, but I needed to tell him I was sorry: about Haley, about Brady, about everything.

At some level, I expected to find him unclean, unshaven, and depressed. But if anything, he looked tidier than usual—not that

that's saying much—in dark blue jeans and a worn black polo shirt.

He gaped at me for a minute and then said, "Wow. I mean, hi."

"You're probably surprised to see me here." I'd been rehearsing this speech for the last ten minutes in traffic.

"You look amazing," he said.

That threw me. As I'd rehearsed the speech in my head, I'd expected animosity.

"Thanks." I blushed. "Stefano took pity on me and gave me a freebie."

"Nothing is free in this town. How much did you have to tell him?"

"Not everything." My speech, my speech . . . what the heck was supposed to come next?

"You want to come in?" he asked.

The house was just as I remembered: gleaming hardwood floors, arched windows, comfy leather furniture. It smelled of lemon polish and Windex. Soft rock played over the speakers.

"I was afraid I'd find you watching TV in your underwear, surrounded by dirty dishes," I admitted.

He smiled. "When I get tense I clean."

"You must clean a lot."

"You have no idea. Want something to drink? Coffee? Tea?"

"Tea would be great, thanks."

In the small, gleaming kitchen, he filled a stainless steel kettle from a Brita pitcher and set it on the stove.

"I doubt you're very happy to see me," I blurted.

He squinted in puzzlement. "Am I acting like I'm not happy to see you?"

"No. Actually, you're—it's just . . . you see, on the way over I figured out what I wanted to say to you, and things aren't going quite the way I expected. I kind of thought we'd have this whole conversation on your doorstep and then you'd slam the door in my face."

"We can go back downstairs if you'd feel more comfortable. Though I'm not planning on slamming anything."

I shook my head. "No, I like it up here." I blushed again. And then I felt ridiculous for blushing.

I took a deep breath. "I'm sorry I ruined your life."

He raised his eyebrows. "Is that what you came here to say?"

"Not exactly. I was actually going to lay a lot of it on you. Say you shouldn't have thrust me into such an uncomfortable position and that you should have told me the truth about Brady from the beginning. But the fact is, I'm a grown-up, and nobody forced me to do anything."

He opened a cupboard. "You want something to eat? Crackers? Some shortbread? My mother keeps sending me shortbread. I must have liked it when I was a kid or something."

"No, thank you."

He closed that cupboard, opened another, and pulled out two white mugs and a box of teabags. "How do you take your tea?"

"Milk and sugar. Thanks."

He bustled around, making the tea, acting as if we weren't going to talk about what had happened. It wasn't until we were in the living room, settled on opposite ends of a couch, when he said, "You didn't ruin my life."

"If I hadn't introduced Haley to Ken, she would have been around for the Leventhal party, and everything would be fine. Did you know that she's planning to move to a ranch in the Santa Ynez Valley and record John Denver songs?"

He laughed softly. "I knew she was selling her house, but not the rest. John Denver. Wow." He sipped his tea.

"You must be a little mad at me," I said.

"I was upset about the car thing." He didn't even want to mention Brady's name. "But I never should have let you meet him in the first place. I guess I just thought that you . . ."

"What?"

"Nothing."

We drank tea without talking for a few moments, which wasn't as awkward as it sounds. Finally, Jay put his mug on the big coffee table and said, "Rodrigo is writing a book. A tell-all about Haley. He signed the contract last week. It's got everything—her drug and alcohol use, the bulimia, the agoraphobia, the bipolar stuff. The girl's a walking psych textbook."

"But the nondisclosure contract . . ."

"He signed it under Rodrigo Gonzo. But it turns out his real name is Rodrigo Gonzalez: that's what's on his license, his credit cards, his apartment lease—everything. So the contract wasn't valid."

"So all that time he spent with Haley, pretending to be her friend . . ."

"Research. Nice, huh? So you see—what happened at the Leventhals' didn't matter. Haley was going down, and I was going with her. For what it's worth, your encounter with Brady—you know, in the car—"

"Yeah, I know."

"It actually hurts Rodrigo's credibility. Because he goes on and on about how Haley and Brady faked their relationship, and there's that video of them obviously not faking anything."

"There may have been a little faking involved," I quipped before I could stop myself.

He burst out laughing.

Eager to change the subject, I said, "But won't Rodrigo just say it's me?" Oh, crap: now everyone would know. There goes my teaching career.

"Rodrigo has no reason to think you and Brady were ever even involved. Brady's thrilled about the publicity, and you can bet he will tell anyone who will listen that he and Haley were in love and that Rodrigo is a compulsive liar who's made it all up."

"So Brady knows about the book?"

"Yup. I told him about it when I called to quit as his manager."

"But doesn't that leave you with . . ."

"A stand-up comic, a performance artist, and a handful of D-list actors who will be lucky to be cast in commercials. And, oh—a documentary filmmaker. Remember Kim Rueben, who we met at the film premiere?"

"But you said there's no money in documentaries."

"There isn't. And there isn't a lot of money in comedy or commercials, either." He looked around the beautiful, expensive room. "Financially, I did pretty well as Haley's manager. So it's not like I'm starting from nothing. From now on, I'm only going to take on people who know what they want and are willing to work for it."

"And who aren't crazy?"

He looked at me and grinned. "That would leave me with nothing."

"Was Haley always this way?" I asked.

He shook his head. "When I first met Haley, I was a production assistant on that sitcom, *The Crazy Life of Riley Poole*. It ran for three seasons, which I never understood since it didn't seem like anyone watched it. It just got lucky on the time slot.

But Haley always looked so thrilled to be on set. She stood out, too. Not because she was such a great actress, but because she just oozed innocence and enthusiasm.

"One evening I gave her a ride home. We hardly knew each other, but it was late and she couldn't get ahold of her mother—which was pretty typical. Their neighborhood was crappy, so I walked her to the door. And then asked if I could have a drink of water." He paused to sip his tea before continuing.

"The apartment was disgusting: clothes, filth, dirty dishes, papers. There wasn't even a clean glass. I asked Haley if she was going to order a pizza or something for her dinner—there was no way anyone could cook in this place—and she said no because she didn't have any money."

His voice grew angry. "This kid had been working since she was nine years old, and her mother didn't give her a dime. Supposedly it was all in a trust, but that was total bullshit. So, for the next few years, I helped Haley out—drove her places, got her dinner. I even bought her a new pair of sneakers once. And you've got to understand, I hardly made enough money to buy my own food and clothes.

"We made a deal: when she turned eighteen, she'd fire her mother, and I'd become her manager. I'm not going to lie. It wasn't completely—or even mostly—altruistic. I knew this kid was going places, and I wanted to be along for the ride. But I really thought that once Haley got away from her mother, once she got some financial security, she'd be okay."

He shook his head and finished his tea, still lost in his memories of a freckle-faced teenager who loved to perform.

"I never thought things would get this out of control," he said.

I put my empty mug on the table. "I'd better go. Ben gets out of school at three."

We stood up at the same time and carried our mugs to the kitchen, setting them side by side in the sink.

"How is my pal Ben?" he asked.

"Good," I said. "Better now that I'm not pretending to be Haley."

"Tell him I said hi."

"I will."

"I'm sorry, too."

"For what?"

He ran a hand through his hair, which still needed a trim. "For sucking you into this whole mess. You're just—you're too nice. Too trusting. You see the best in people, even when there's not a lot of good to see."

"You mean Brady."

"Actually, I meant me."

We were standing very close, next to the sink. Outside the window, birds jumped among the tree branches. The afternoon sun brought out the gold in his eyes.

He said, "My comic is doing the opening monologue at the Brea Improv this weekend. So if you're free Saturday—or Friday or whatever works—"

"I'd love to," I said.

"Great."

And then I remembered. "But I can't. It's my weekend with Ben." Nothing kills a romantic mood like the mention of a child, but Ben had to come first.

"Maybe I could come out early then. Take the two of you out to dinner?"

"He'd love that. I'd love that." Mischief bubbled up inside of me. "How about Red Lobster? They've got one at the Brea Mall."

Jay paled. On impulse, I leaned forward and kissed him.
"Gotcha."

He hesitated for only a moment before taking me in his arms.
When we broke apart I was almost afraid to look at his face. Was
he thinking about Haley?

He smiled. "That was nice."

"Not like kissing Haley?"

He looked horrified. "I never kissed Haley. And I never
wanted to. What I meant that time you were here, what I should
have said earlier—" He sighed in exasperation.

"What?"

"From the day we had lunch and you walked in looking all
sweet and school teacher-y, I just, I just—"

"What?"

"That was it. I was done for. The only thing that put me
off was how much you looked like her. But the more I got to
know you, the less I even saw the resemblance. And then when
you were here, out on the deck . . . It felt so right. And then the
kiss . . ."

"Yeah. The kiss."

"It was all so perfect, and then I opened my eyes, and there
you were with Haley's hair and makeup and dress and it was
just—*aargh*!"

"You mean, you didn't kiss me because I looked like
Haley?"

"God, no! I *stopped* kissing you because you looked like
Haley."

"I wish you'd said that at the time."

"Me, too." He smoothed my hair. He gave me one more
kiss and then said, "You'd better go. Don't want to keep Ben
waiting."

*   *   *

I got to Las Palmas Elementary School five minutes early. The moms and dads were waiting, perched on benches or pacing the blacktop, ready to feed their children sliced apples and peanut butter crackers, to ferry them to Little League, piano lessons, tutors, or ballet. There were no cameras on hand to record the moment, no stylists or screaming fans.

Finally, the bell rang, and the doors swung open. The children streamed out, as their parents called:

"Noah!"

"Kelly!"

"Nathan—over here!"

The children looked up and smiled, basking in the glow.

Acknowledgments

I was maybe a hundred pages into telling this story before I realized that I didn't know nearly as much about the entertainment industry—or even Los Angeles—as I thought I did. And so: a bazillion thanks to my good friend Rafael Suarez, who gave me guided tours through West Hollywood, Los Angeles, and Beverly Hills; answered multiple phone queries; and reviewed my final manuscript. Any inaccuracies in this book are entirely Rafael's fault, so please direct all complaints to him.

I am indebted to the people who posted YouTube videos of themselves getting hair extensions and spray tans. They were very helpful. Bonnie Largent was nice enough to answer my questions about substitute teaching, which is why I named a character after her. The real Mrs. Largent is not pregnant. At least, not that I know of.

Thank you to Cindy Hwang, Leis Pederson, and all the wonderful people at Berkley for turning my manuscript into a real-live book; to the art department for designing yet another clever cover; and the sales department for getting the final pretty product into stores.

I am, as always, grateful to Stephanie Kip Rostan for being such a brilliant agent, sounding board, and friend, as well as Monika Verma, Miek Coccia, Elizabeth Bishop, and everyone else at the Levine Greenberg Literary Agency for their smarts, professionalism, and overall niceness.

Finally, thanks and love to my parents, Tom and Peggy Snow, for giving me a normal childhood, and to my husband, Andrew Todhunter, for cheering me on, making me pizzas, and reminding me that I always panic halfway through my books—and yet they always turn out just fine. At least, I think they do.